"While you were sleeping, Mike called. Someone was messing around in your backyard again."

"Someone?"

He shrugged and gave her a pointed look. "Most likely the same Peeping Tom."

"What did he do this time?"

"Scratched your fence. Tried to set your dock on fire with a Molotov cocktail."

Her eyes bugged. "What?"

"It didn't work. Mike will take the jar to his field office to check for evidence. We don't want to run it through the local forensics lab in case something bigger is going on. This might help us prove it."

"Do I need to worry?" She nodded at their waiter and waited for him to set their meal on the table before continuing. "I mean, more than I already am?"

"Whatever's going on, it's in North Carolina. Getting away for a bit is a good thing."

"I've got enough to worry about right now with the production, so until you tell me to panic, I'll stay calm."

Mine by Design

by

Becky Moore

This is a work of fiction. Names, characters, places, and incidents are either the product of the author's imagination or are used fictitiously, and any resemblance to actual persons living or dead, business establishments, events, or locales, is entirely coincidental.

Mine by Design

Contact Information: info@thewildrosepress.com

Cover Art by *Diana Carlile*

The Wild Rose Press, Inc.
PO Box 708
Adams Basin, NY 14410-0708
Visit us at www.thewildrosepress.com

Publishing History
First Edition, 2021
Trade Paperback ISBN 978-1-5092-3340-3
Digital ISBN 978-1-5092-3341-0

Published in the United States of America

Dedication

For Matt: I'm certain my heart beats for you.
You make life better than fiction.

Chapter One

After weeks of false alarms in the middle of the night and exhausted from looking over her shoulder at every turn, paranoia finally squeezed out the last vestiges of Abby Markham's peace of mind.

Most days, jogging over the back-country roads of her small, rural North Carolina town relaxed her. Not today. Not when one of the few stoplights in town separated her from the safety of home.

"Come on. *Turn*. Come on, come on," she chanted through heavy, measured breaths. Her muscles, like her mind, may be running on fumes but she was determined not to be held hostage by fear. Plus, she was equally determined to set a new personal record on her weekly long run. "Oh, come on."

No amount of pleading worked; the light turned red as she approached the edge of the highway. She pulled one of the small water cartridges from her belt and drank quickly, ignoring the trickle of water running down her chin and the nasty stitch in her side. She checked her pulse, swiped at loose tendrils of hair plastered across her forehead, and visualized sprinting the half-mile home from the opposite side of the road.

Anything to avoid wondering if someone watched from the shadows.

A lone car zoomed past, leaving in its wake a deafening silence that made her shudder. Giving in to the demons that had haunted her for weeks, she finally looked around, willing the boogeyman to show himself from the thick copse of trees and kudzu lining the roadside.

Abby huffed out a breath and rolled her shoulders, working through the feeling of uneasiness. "Jesus, just stop it!"

Shifting her weight from side to side, she pressed two fingers against her carotid artery and checked her watch on the other wrist. Good pulse rate. Another deep breath. If the light turned right *now,* she'd beat her regular ten-mile time by three whole minutes. *Three minutes!* She took another couple of breaths and shook out her arms, grinning. Hello, second wind. Fuck you, boogeyman.

The light turned green and she took off in a dead sprint. Even thought she'd been forced to wait for the light to turn, she was about to set a new personal record with a couple minutes to spare.

As she came up on the big bridge for Lake Jordan, she noticed a black sedan parked cock-eyed on the shoulder across from a gravel road that led to the wild bird rehabilitation center. Strange that the driver had cut a path through a thick stand of weeds rather than pulling onto the path.

Angry shouts carried through the woods, drawing her attention to two men fighting.

"Oh, shit!" she gasped, and pushed harder, trying to get out of their lines of sight.

A loud *pop!* echoed through the woods followed by a loud grunt. She stumbled over loose rocks on the pavement and went down hard on both knees.

A gun! Ohmigod! Oh, shit!

She scrambled into an overgrown hedge of azaleas and wax myrtles lining a well-worn path. Blood seeped down her shins in lazy trickles to mix with dirt and gravel. The scrapes stung like a bitch, but she ignored them and inched around the hedge. After a couple of long, agonizing minutes, crawling on hands and knees, she worked her way back to the highway. Her neighbors, the Crenshaws, lived about a quarter of a mile around the next bend; she could call the police from there.

She was almost clear of the underbrush when another series of *pops* peppered the air. One long scream of agony made her heart stutter. The dead silence that followed made it race. She scurried back to the hedge, crouched as low as possible, and burrowed under the bottom branches. Hiding. Waiting.

Then nothing. No sound. *Shit.*

In its own way, the silence was as damning as the screams and pops. Out here, in the middle of nowhere. Alone, with two men beating the hell out of each other—and at least one of them had a gun. Oh, God.

For once, she prayed for traffic, wishing she was anywhere but on the isolated country road in Pittsboro, North Carolina. As it appeared no one but runners, cyclists, and yard-sellers were out at seven o'clock on a Saturday morning, she was on her own. With a couple crazy-assed men playing out their own personal fight club. Good lord.

Worst of all, this stretch of her run was known for crappy cell coverage, a fact she'd learned the sad way a couple weeks ago after she came up on a baby deer that had been hit by a car. The poor thing was mangled, but alive. With no cell service, she'd not been able to call animal control, so she did the next best thing and carried it down to the rehab center. As soon as she walked into the building, the call went through to the Sheriff's Office.

Now, hoping against hope for service, Abby pulled her phone from the zipped pocket in her shorts and dialed 911. She inched down the path, silent as a mouse. On the other end, a muted voice answered—just as someone ran right at her.

Curling into a tight ball under a bush, she prayed the runner wouldn't see her. Panic and hysteria became a debilitating one-two punch to her solar plexus. But giving in to either would mean discovery. Knowing silence would be the key to survival, she pressed a hand over her mouth and closed her eyes.

Once the footsteps faded, she peeked through the dense shrubbery and caught sight of a man clad in a black nylon running suit standing at the end of the path, arguing with himself. Without warning, his head jerked up and around. He seemed to be glaring straight at her hiding spot.

Wishing for invisibility, she held her breath, then let it out when he turned and sprinted across the road and disappeared from sight. Moments later, she saw the sedan skid onto the highway, heading toward Durham, and tossing a wide arc of gravel and dust in its wake.

Abby wiped at her cheeks, yelping when the tears scalded her raw palms. A few yards ahead she saw a man struggling to sit up. With one fortifying breath she ran to help him. The low, erratic murmur of his voice greeted her when she reached the clearing.

But it was the spreading pool of blood beneath his torso that dropped her to her knees.

“Sir,” she called out nervously. He stilled; she cleared her throat and said, “I’m here—just hold on.”

He looked terrible. Swelling had kicked in from the earlier fight; his bloated face was covered with bruises. One eye was completely shut; the other one tracked her motions with slow, agonizing effort. “I’m going to move closer so you can see me better, okay?” As she went to touch him, she saw the badge pinned to his chest, the utility belt circling his waist.

Oh, Lord. A uniformed police officer—covered in blood—and struggling.

She tried to still his frantic, uncoordinated motions. He’d managed to wedge one hand under his hip, making it possible to sit up. The other pressed over a gaping wound in the center of his chest about an inch above the edge of his bulletproof vest. Crimson rivulets of blood dribbled down his chest, soaking into the dusty boot prints covering his torso. Another wound, high on his left thigh gushed rhythmically as did the one from his chest.

Horrible gurgling sounds ripped from his throat. Violent tremors wracked his body. It was terrifying but she couldn’t leave him.

He reached out to grab her by the back of her neck and pulled her face close. “S—saw y’ run by,” he said weakly. “Chief,” he whispered. His head tipped back.

Groaning under the strain of his weight hanging on her neck, she hooked both arms around his torso and lowered him to the ground. She pulled free of his hold to shrug out of her fleece vest, and put it under his sweaty, battered head. Her long-sleeve T-shirt was drenched with sweat, from her run, from her fear, from…everything. God, if he’d seen her while getting the living hell beaten out of him, surely the fleeing shooter noticed her, too.

She couldn't think about that right now, though. Instead, she ripped her shirt off and tied it above the bullet hole on his thigh, pulling it as hard as she could. His weak scream broke her heart, but she forced herself to focus on reducing the blood flow with the makeshift tourniquet.

"Shhh, it's okay," she crooned. "I'm going to help you, officer."

Now was not the time to panic about her safety. She touched the side of his face gently and then pressed both of her hands over his to help stem the flow of blood. "I'm Abby," she said, trying to calm him down enough to check him out. She looked at the name tag on his uniform shirt. Lawson.

"Officer Lawson, please try and calm down so I can help you. I haven't done CPR since I learned it as a teenager."

Silent tears ran down her face and her stomach clenched tightly as she fought against retching. He looked horrible. Officer Lawson quieted a little but then began to tremble again. He pressed his lips together and stretched his left hand toward his hip. It was awkward and his motion was uncoordinated. Tears ran down both cheeks as painful, agonized animal sounds tore from his throat. His pain was palpable.

"You want the phone?" He let out a huge sigh, nodding. "No, don't try to reach it," she said. "I'll get it for you. Who are we calling?"

"Home," he whispered.

She pulled the phone from his belt and held it close enough for his fingerprint to unlock it, and then with slow, jerky motions he opened the phone app and pressed the "home" preset. With a deep exhale, he laid his head back on her vest and closed his eyes.

"Hello," said a soft, feminine voice after a couple of rings.

His breathing grew more erratic, and his good eye opened with a wild, panicky gleam. "Sally," he muttered with a lot of gurgle.

The tone of the cheerful voice echoed beyond the phone speaker; Abby smiled at him, like maybe if her smile matched "Sally's" tone, Lawson would draw some comfort. "Hey, honey," she said. "What's up?"

"Love you…so much," he whispered. The birds from the sanctuary around the next corner made such a racket it washed out his voice.

"What, honey?" Suspicion filtered through Sally's voice. "Can you repeat that?"

He covered the wound on his chest with one hand, and the other wrapped around Abby's wrist. He tried to say more, but that awful gurgling sound came from his throat and both of his hands dropped to the gravel beneath them. He was out.

"Oh, God," Sally yelled. "What's going on? Where are you?"

His head rolled toward his right shoulder, knocking Abby back and pinning her torso beneath his weight. In the distance, loud sirens pierced the silent air. Relief came with the knowledge that if emergency teams were close enough for the sirens to be audible, the shooter would stay away.

Abby took the phone from Lawson's hand as she eased herself out from under him. "Ma'am?"

The slight movement jarred him, and he turned his

face toward Abby's voice. They watched each other for a silent moment, the weight of the situation heavier than the burden of Atlas. He looked tired; the tears had stopped falling from his eyes and his breathing was so brutally shallow. He latched back onto her wrist with his good hand.

After a minute of struggling he whispered, "Left pocket," and then let out a huff of breath and closed his eyes. "For the chief." A tiny trickle of blood dripped out of the corner of his mouth, and what little skin on his face that wasn't bruised and bloody had turned gray.

Since she couldn't get her wrist free from his grasp, she used the other hand to fish around in his pocket. The only thing in there was a small red flash drive, about an inch and a half long, so she held it in front of his face. "This? This is what you want me to give to your chief?"

He gave a weak nod. "Only him."

"Who is this?" Sally, who'd been quiet for a moment, broke into the conversation. "Where's Jason?"

Abby wiped the sweat and tears from her cheeks with her forearm and worried about how much the man struggled in order to breathe. She'd been sitting with him almost ten minutes and the blood still flowed just as freely from the bullet hole in his chest as when she'd found him. Hopelessness overwhelmed her, and she prayed that he wouldn't bleed to death.

Once Lawson was settled, she spoke into the phone. "Mrs. Lawson—my name is Abby Markham. Your husband was shot. I came up on him while I was running this morning."

"What! Oh my God! Where are you?"

Abby spoke over her. "Look, I'm going to lay the

phone next to him so he can hear you. Help's on the way…I can hear the sirens getting louder." She couldn't tell the whole truth, that she *knew* he would be dead before the ambulance arrived. So, she stretched out next to Lawson and held the phone against his ear. His large hand still wrapped around her wrist.

"Sally," he whispered.

"Oh, honey. I love you so much. I don't know what to say. Um…the pink peonies you put in last year opened for me this morning. They look so pretty in the sunshine." Sally reeled off facts like she was playing a trivia game, her voice soothing her beloved.

"Love you." His voice drifted off. A smile curved his lips one moment; in the next it flattened, and his hand dropped heavily onto the gravel.

Abby slumped next to Jason, flat on her back and half pinned, and let the phone fall to the ground next to his ear. She covered her face with her free hand and sobbed. After a moment, she noticed Sally's babbling had turned to sorrow.

Eventually someone walked over, spoke a few quiet words into the phone, then ended the call. After rolling Jason away, they helped her stand and used a handkerchief to wipe away some of the blood from her face and chest before helping get her settled in the back of an ambulance.

Even though the sun was high, and the day had heated up enough that the chill was gone, she stared at the sky in a daze, huddled with a blanket around her shoulders. It was like watching through a warped pane of glass while everything happened around her. The dried blood on her body itched; each time a tear ran down her cheek to plop onto her chest, the scent of blood almost overwhelmed her.

One of the EMTs took her pulse and used a penlight to check her pupils. “I’m Kevin Benson, ma’am. How are you feeling?”

“Okay, I guess.” She looked down at the new bandages on her knees and wondered how they got there. A spot of blood darkened the left one. She rotated her sore wrists and shook her head, glancing down at the gauze wraps that padded the heels of both hands. She was starting to look like a mummy—and didn’t remember any of it.

A tall man in uniform walked up, nodded at Kevin, then turned to her. “I’m Chief Randolph, ma’am.” His deep voice was quiet and kind. “Hell of a thing you came across today. How are you holding up?” He tilted his head toward Jason Lawson’s sheet covered body. A uniformed officer stood guard.

Kevin made some notes on his tablet and sat it on the bench next to her. “Here you go, ma’am,” he said, helping her stand and then smiled in a knowing manner at her wince.

“She’s a little shocky,” he told the chief, “but there are no injuries other than her knees and hands which took the brunt of her fall. I’ve washed and bandaged them. She’ll be sore for a couple of days.” He looked at her straight on. “I told her I think she should get checked out at the hospital, but she declined further treatment.”

Randolph leaned over to look her in the eyes. “You got anybody at home who might be able to keep an eye on you for a bit?”

She nodded. Because she did *not* want to go to the hospital, she’d figure out what to do after she got home.

When she could take a shower and cry her eyes out without everybody looking at her.

Kevin made one last note on his tablet before tucking it into a sleeve next to the ECG monitor, then shook Randolph's hand. "Sorry about Lawson, Chief. Everybody liked him a lot. He didn't deserve this."

Abby's knees gave out and before she could drop to the ground, the chief grabbed her by the shoulders and drew her against his chest. "Thank you, son," he said. Grief etched his face as he observed the EMTs and his officers work the scene. "He was a good man."

Twisting fistfuls of his blazer into her hands, Abby took a deep, rattling breath and tried to control her breathing so she wouldn't hyperventilate. Parts of what she'd just witnessed flashed across her brain. Before she could stop it, a huge sob broke from her chest. Choppy breaths sawed in and out of her lungs.

The weight of the world seemed to have crumbled down around them.

Chapter Two

After a couple days of R&R, Ben Owens was on his way home from the mountains. He hadn't taken vacation in over a year and felt so wrung out, he couldn't focus. But Asheville's crisp air and beautiful rolling hills helped settle his mind—enough to get him back to the grindstone of working for the Apex Police Department. His father always told him he needed to be a patrolman, working a beat for a few years before he upped the ante to detective.

Get to know the people you're gonna be working for, son. The people out in the community.

Too bad Ben decided to take the road less traveled from the Army, then to Quantico, before he figured out detective work at home was just as important—and a lot less dangerous.

But getting to know the folks he served sometimes proved to be a real pain in the ass. If Mrs. Tally called him before six o'clock in the morning again, asking him to get her champion Boxer in out of the rain, he'd shoot the damn dog. Because, really, do other detectives make house calls for dog walks and mowing the grass?

No. They do not.

Bottom line: he had to move out of his grandmother's house. Didn't matter that it was in the middle of downtown a fast block away from the station, freshly renovated and fully paid off. He should have let his numbnuts brother have the house after the funeral, but that would have been another in a long string of bad decisions. After Gran died, Ben never expected to resume his high school handyman duties for the community. Did "former FBI agent" hold any mystery for the people of Apex? Garner any admiration?

No, it did not.

Coming back home may not have been the best choice—he was just looking for a little break. Didn't they realize at thirty-five, he had a real job now? Maybe he should've just stayed in DC after his accident—or transferred to a local precinct *other* than the hometown where his family had lived for three generations. Now he and his younger brother Jamie were all that were left. Since Jamie was living the high life, literally, as a wilderness guide in Denver, Ben was on his own.

Shortly after noon, Dispatch broke the silence and roused him out of his mental meanderings. "Ben? Benji, you out there?"

"Yeah, Rose. I'm here. What do you need?"

Ben's father, the former chief for the Apex PD, called him Benji his whole life. Even after the old man made a career advancement by leaving to head up the major crimes task force for the North Carolina branch of the feds, his colleagues continued to use his dad's nickname for him.

Once, he'd loved the name. Now it made him sad. Chuck Owens had been in his mid-forties when Ben was born, and his death from pneumonia complications two years ago still brought tears to his eyes. The Owens men had been a tight unit, even though they'd been spread out across the country. He sighed, resigned enough to realize these older officers who grew up babying him would never get past his daddy's influence. Or the fact that he, too, had been a G-man. The familiarity was just too much for people to overlook. Detective work in tiny Apex, North Carolina, may be less grueling—in terms of the intensity of the cases—but he still had to adjust to the more familiar way people treated him. He was, after all, one of the least chummy people he knew.

"Chief Randolph said he figured you were close enough to home by now. I know you're off until Monday, but he needs you to swing by the old Sykes place." She rattled off the address to an old farmhouse near Lake Jordan. "House belongs to Abigail Markham. Looks like she's been having trouble with her silent alarm system for a couple weeks now. The chief wants her to talk to a detective. Patrol's never found anything to explain the alarms going off. You know that type of thing works their nerves, but she's a real nice gal."

He sighed. Technically, the Chatham County Sheriff's Office would catch most cases around Lake Jordan since it was more in the rural, unincorporated part of the county than the nearby town of Apex, but it was a Saturday and man power was stretched real thin while many of his colleagues squeezed in one last vacation before school started. As the only detective on the APD with any real experience outside their small community, Chief Randolph lent his services out regularly.

"Text me the address so I can pull it up on my phone."

"Sure thing, Benji. See you soon."

In under a minute his phone dinged, which made him chuckle. Rose may be in her fifties and their office might be small, but she was sharp as a tack and had taken to the evolution in technology like a boss. She maintained the servers for the Apex PD and texted faster than a moody teenager. Christ, in the minute since he'd hung up, she'd written an entire paragraph. He ignored what was most likely further ramblings on ways to keep the aphids away from her tomatoes, which was last week's instructional conversation, and clicked on the address so it would update his map.

Since he'd been directed to a house having problems with silent alarms, he figured he would go in silently and try to avoid escalating whatever situation might be happening and not scare the crap out of a probably already twitchy female. He pulled his classic, beat-to-shit jeep under a bank of weeping willows, cut the engine—and caught his first glimpse of the house.

"Wow."

A green slate roof topped the old, white clapboard house. The home looked huge, framed by a wrap-around porch filled with rocking chairs and a porch swing painted a pale lavender. Growing up, he'd been as enamored with this old place as the rest of the community. Decades ago, it belonged to the Sykes family, but after Quincy Sykes became a US senator and moved to DC, he'd abandoned the house. His dad had despised Quincy, and it wasn't just because the senator was part of the other political party. No, Quincy had gotten the lion's share of his support from farmers across the state who were allowed to keep most of their land rights after the state began its shift away from its mostly agrarian nature in the early eighties. Plus, his unwavering support for the expansion of the four major military bases in North Carolina didn't hurt. Civilian employment skyrocketed. So did Quincy's popularity.

If Ben closed his eyes, he still heard with great clarity his father's Sunday morning diatribes over coffee and the newspaper, cursing Senator Quincy Sykes for the roadblocks he erected in terms of keeping businesses, therefore progress, out of the state.

He leaned back against the headrest and closed his eyes, taking a moment to ground himself. If memory served, it had been a near hovel while the Sykes family still lived there. Though still large and majestic on the surface, it was run down and badly in need of renovations which never did occur.

"The fire" was big news in the seventies, and everybody who grew up in the area was well-versed in the sad drama. The Sykes family had owned that property since the Civil War, or some crazy statistic like that, but the family and property had fallen on hard times during the Vietnam War after the only son, Quincy, shipped out.

He came home a war hero, married his high school sweetheart, and started a family. They seemed to be getting their feet beneath them when a lightning strike devastated the structure. As a kid, Ben recalled the ladies auxiliary at his mother's church did some fundraising to restore the property, but he'd stopped paying attention to that bit of business after he discovered breasts.

Things were sure different now. He took another, longer look. *Nice digs.*

The new owner had turned the grounds into something lush and beautiful with meticulously landscaped gardens his mother would have given her right arm for had she still been alive. A large red barn stood behind the house and looked to be connected to the main house by a walkway. A tall fence wrapped around the right side of the house from the back yard. Rose's text indicated the homestead sat on somewhere near five acres of land, but that was hard to tell since thick woods surrounded three sides of the house where it butted up to the Lake Jordan watershed preserves.

Skirting through the gardens, he bounded up the veranda stairs to a beautiful stained-glass front door and jiggled the handle. It was locked, so he cupped his hands and squinted through the glass. Everything in the wide foyer looked normal—no bodies on the floor or splashes of blood and gore. He spied an alarm security panel through the glass door, and it was lit up like Christmas.

It would be a shame to shatter the front door masterpiece, so he walked farther down the porch to check one of the corner windows. A small yellow cat jumped from the banister to the floor and paced anxiously from the door to the window where he stood. Was there someone in the house with her? It was so quiet and still to his human ears, but the cat was twitchy like the alarm was making it crazy. He pulled his gun and tried to jimmy the window open with his free hand. It didn't budge.

He was on his way around to the other side of the porch when the phone buzzed in his back pocket. Pulling it out to read the screen one-handed, he made his way back to the front door, distracted by the text conversation.

—you at markham's yet?—

—yeah. just about to knock. what's up—?

—figured you didn't see my note before, so

randolph wanted me to make sure you read it first. didn't want you going in blind. scroll up and read it now, r—

"What the hell?" he muttered, scrolling back up to find Rose's note. He'd forgotten about the earlier message but scanned it quickly. His heart stuttered painfully in his chest.

—jason lawson murdered this morning. abigail markham on scene—has something for you. randolph wants you to take her statement and keep watch until further notice. keeping her name off the books for now. no announcement made yet.—

"Oh, God." He pressed his fingers against his mouth and, closing his eyes, let out a low moan. He'd grown up with Jason; he was a good guy. Had a great wife, great kids.

The quiet snick of an opening door caught his attention. He looked up and had to blink. More than once. Goddamn, the woman standing in the doorway was beautiful. Like, so beautiful she made him stupid. He just stared, mesmerized, with his mouth open. She wore running shorts and a tank top; a messy ponytail topped her head.

It was the pale thigh-high stockings and mismatched stiletto sandals that tripped him up.

Her eyes showed the puffiness of substantial crying, but even with that, she was just so, so pretty. All professionalism vanished; common courtesy receded. And his brain, between the shock of Rose's text and the unexpected woman greeting him, put his body on reboot. She said something, and he blinked again.

"Officer!" she said sharply, as a bright blush raced across the skin of her collar bones and neck.

The noise startled him, and the gun he'd pulled on autopilot dropped from his numb fingers with a clang. It all happened in slow-motion, like a bad horror movie… it bounced, and the grip knocked against the sidelight next to the stunning front door with a little pixie-like *tink* before it came to rest on its side. Ben huffed out a breath, relieved that his stupidity hadn't destroyed the vintage-looking door.

And then the glass shattered.

She yelped, then jumped back, awkward on a pair of funny looking shoes. He surged forward and caught her by the wrist to keep her from going down, praying this wasn't the Abby Markham he was here to see.

Oh, God. How mortifying. He grabbed the gun, checked the safety, and re-holstered it before he killed them both. Broken glass peppered the front porch and just inside the entryway, and when the breeze swept along the porch, the last of the shards dropped from the pane like tinkling raindrops. If he could disappear into a hole in the universe he would.

"Well, damn." He forced his brain to reengage as vivid heat of embarrassment spread from his neck up to his hairline, like oil spreading over a hot cast iron skillet. But he had a job to do; one that didn't include fantasizing about beautiful women. His voice was a little strangled when he confirmed her identity. "Miss Markham, right?"

She grinned, like, with her whole body, then burst into laughter. "Yes. You broke the window."

Shit, he couldn't believe he dropped his gun. "I'm a little surprised you opened the door to a strange man holding a gun."

She snorted, clearly not afraid of him. "Chief

Randolph said to expect Detective Ben Owens, and I figure that must be you…plus you've got a badge on your waistband." She pointed to his belt.

He glanced to where she pointed and blinked. It took a minute to figure out what she indicated because his thoughts oozed through his brain slow as molasses. Right, his badge. *Sigh*. Her eyes sparkled with mischief, and in light of the terrible circumstances that brought him to the door, he was relieved to lighten her mood for a moment. "I'll fix your window, ma'am. I'm so sorry."

Abby shrugged. "I know." She stepped aside and opened the door wider, sweeping her arm to the side. "You gonna fire that thing or are you gonna come in? I mean, you're here for something, right? I figure you might as well get something done besides standing there gaping at me."

Feeling like a fool, his shoulders dropped before he fell into step behind her. "Do you have a broom?"

****

Abby couldn't help smiling. She'd had a bad fucking day and was on edge waiting for the other shoe to drop. The nightmarish loop she'd replayed in her head over the last few hours was working on her last nerve. She'd already tried tweaking her gown for next week's gala, and that hadn't helped. Going out for another run was out of the question because there was no telling where the gunman was. Perhaps recounting the events of the day would help her regain focus and begin to process the awful experience of watching the officer die.

While she waited for Owens to get it together, she checked him out. She couldn't help it, he was just, so, handsome. He was tall—maybe a couple inches over six feet—with broad shoulders, a lean stomach and hips, and long, long legs. The muscles in his thighs flexed against the fabric of his faded low-rise jeans as he shifted his weight from hip to hip. Thank God for whoever made jeans cup a body lovingly and thank God for heavy badges that weighed down the waist.

There were interesting bulges in other places, too, but she glanced away because now wasn't the time to flirt. Thick eyelashes and cool, black-rimmed glasses framed his pale green eyes. His hair, so dark it looked almost blue, curled on the ends around his forehead and his ears. She checked him out from head to toe and back again, and realized she was busted. A huge grin split his face, and those lush red lips were bracketed with dimples, and *shazam*! That was all she wrote.

"Crap," he muttered softly and swiped the edge of his blazer aside to tuck his gun in its holster at the back of his waist. It took him two tries. He was flustered for some reason, which made it all the more charming as he wrestled with his clothes. He was irresistible, really. He cleared his throat. "Are you ready to give your statement?"

She blinked to focus harder on the situation at hand. "Um…" He'd been talking to her while he exchanged the phone for a small notebook and pen. "Come again?"

It made her self-conscious when he dropped his gaze to check out her legs, with her crazy mismatched shoes. The one on her right foot was closed over the toe, but the left sandal let her toes peek through, with their happy apple green polish. She didn't have to look down to know her legs looked pretty silly, too, with her high-sided running shorts, bandaged knees, and old-fashioned stockings.

But bless his heart, he was trying to be professional. He cleared his throat and asked, “I know it’s already been a long day, Miss Markham, but there’s a lot of stuff we need to get through. Are you ready to give your statement?”

“Yeah, come on, let’s head to the kitchen. I was getting ready to have some coffee. Would you like some, too?”

“Sure.” He was distracted, looking behind him at the broken glass. “How about I clean up that glass before we get started?”

She waved a hand over her shoulder and kept walking. “Nah. We’ll get it in a few minutes.”

Eventually he followed her through the open living room. The old house had high ceilings and arched doorways as it led into a large and modern kitchen, and she never got tired of its lovely architecture. Little knickknacks from her travels around the world peppered the built-in bookshelves and little side tables, along with the artwork her eccentric father had given her through the years. It was a lot for a new person to take in.

“I guess,” he hedged, stopping in the middle of the room. “I need to talk to you about this morning, but your security panel is lit up like Christmas. Are you in here alone?”

Sucking in a breath, she whipped her head around to look at the lights. Fighting a bubble of panic, she made her way to the panel. Crap, she hadn’t even noticed the alarm system. “Uh, no, it’s just me,” she said as she keyed in a code that made everything stop blinking. “I’ve been calling about these stupid silent alarms for a couple weeks, but each time an officer came out to check, nothing was discovered. They thought I was crazy."

"What do you mean?"

"I mean, they never took me seriously."

"Well, why not?" He poked a finger around the security panel, like maybe it had a loose wire or something.

"Last week when I called, I talked to the officer from the porch. He didn't even come up to the door. Just rolled his eyes and headed off around the house. When I ran through the living room to watch him through the back windows, he was on his phone, wandering through the flower garden. He didn't check any windows—he never even came close enough to touch the house."

That got his attention. His eyes narrowed. "You're kidding, right?"

She smirked, oddly satisfied that he seemed as insulted as she. "Nope. Why don't you sit down while I get coffee ready?"

Chapter Three

Ben remained quiet while she putzed around the kitchen, assembling a tray with coffee service. She skirted around the bolts of fabric leaning against the cabinets with the agility and grace of a running back in stilettos and worked around a large cutting mat stacked on one end of the table. Eventually curiosity got the better of him.

"Tools of the trade?" He swept his arm in a wide arc around the kitchen and looked pointedly at the mismatched shoes on her feet.

She smiled and ran a hand through her ponytail. It wasn't the first time he'd noticed the shy gesture. "Sort of. I'm a costume designer by trade, but this is for a gown I'm wearing to a gala next week. I'm having a hard time deciding which shoes to wear." The events of the day were obviously distracting her, but she shrugged and wiggled her toes.

He eyed her legs. "Other than the most comfortable, I'd say go with the open toes. Then you won't have to wear stockings." The heat rising in his cheeks made the nerve endings in the scruff on his jaw tingle.

She nodded. Her beautiful mouth tipped up in a smile, probably knowing he was sweating bullets beneath his blazer. "No stockings, huh?"

He cleared his throat and shifted in the chair, trying

to make everything in his pants more comfortable. "My mother said stockings were invented by the devil."

"Ha! That's the truth."

He waited to see if she would break eye contact or make other nervous gestures, but she stayed calm. He sensed nothing sneaky or any covert attempt to hide something. "If nobody's in here with you, what do you think set off the alarm *today*?"

He propped his hands on the table and poised the pen, ready to take notes. He needed to steer the conversation back to Lawson's murder, but the whole interaction with Abby and the security panel had distracted him. And if he was being honest, he was okay delaying the inevitable.

"I don't know." She unbuckled her shoes and shook them off. "This is about the fourth or fifth time it's been triggered, but I'm not usually home when it happens. Mrs. Dixon left early to run some errands, and I didn't get any packages today. Although, I guess the delivery guy could've come while I was in the studio out back—did you see anyone outside when you arrived?"

She paused in rolling down the stockings and glanced at him. The motions of her slim fingers working the delicate fabric down those endless legs mesmerized him. When she slipped the right one all the way off, Ben realized he was staring, so made himself look down at the table. The last thing he wanted was to make her uncomfortable. But, oh, baby. . ..

He cleared his throat and scribbled something on the pad. "Uh, no. There weren't any packages out front. Who's Mrs. Dixon?"

"My assistant." Finished with her task, she sat back

and crossed her legs in the chair, yoga-style. "Look, detective, the anxiety is killing me. I just can't talk about those stupid alarms anymore. I need to tell you about this morning." Her pulse hammered visibly against the delicate skin of her throat. "That's why you're here, right?"

"It's Ben," he said, wiping his hands down the sides of his face and nodding. Now that they were down to business, the weight of Rose's news felt like a crushing weight on his soul. "You can call me Ben."

"Okay, then. I hope you'll call me Abby. I want you to know I'm so sorry about Officer Lawson. Did you work together?"

"Thank you," he choked out, looking over her shoulder and letting his eyes lose focus somewhere in the mid-distance. "Jason and I didn't work together, but we've been friends a long time. I was away most of the week on R&R. Actually, our dispatcher, Rose, caught me about half an hour outside of town and asked me to swing by to take a statement from you."

He had to stop and clear his throat because it was closing up. "She texted me the details, but I didn't read anything until I was walking up on your porch." And he'd gotten distracted with the fumbling gun-breaking glass deal.

She laid her hand over his, rubbing her thumb back and forth across the backs of his fingers. "Chief Randolph said I'm not supposed to talk about it with anyone but you." She spoke quietly, like projecting with any volume was painful.

He stayed quiet, waiting. After a dozen years in the military, then federal law enforcement, he was an expert at discerning when to scare the hell out of a suspect and when to let a witness speak uninhibited. If Abby Markham was like most civilians, she'd get caught up in the retelling of the ordeal and feel compelled to fill in the silence.

"Tell me about this morning."

She closed her eyes for a moment, as if grounding herself. "I'll never forget it."

Quietly, she recounted what she witnessed, pausing when she became overwhelmed by wracking sobs. Her mourning so profound, Ben felt compelled to scoot his chair next to hers and take her into his arms. One hand cupped her head to his neck while the other rubbed the long line of her slim back.

In the station, he would never offer comfort like this, but just the two of them? His mama didn't raise him to ignore the suffering of another if he could ease it with kindness. "I've never seen anybody…*die*." Her voice was so small. So broken.

Inwardly, he seethed at the violence. "Jas—" He had to clear his throat and start again. "Jason was my friend. His wife and I grew up together. I was at their wedding. He was a great guy. A good cop."

When his breath hitched, she rested her hand over his heart, returning the comfort to him. Her long, wet eyelashes brushed against the sensitive side of his neck, sending goosebumps racing down his arms and, to his shame, bolts of desire straight to his groin.

As the air began to crackle with awareness, Abby sat upright in her chair to take a sip of coffee. "His wife was on the phone with us when he died. I tried to help him, but there was so much blood. I couldn't…" She trailed off and looked down at her hands. She rubbed them in a rhythmic motion, like she was trying to get the blood off. “I didn’t want her to hear it.”

“Hear what?”

“Him. *Dying*.”

Ben made a choking sound.

Her choppy breaths came quicker and quicker, until she was nearly panting. Fearing she would rub her skin raw, he took her hands again, stilling them against his. “Abby, stop,” he said in a low tone, but with a snap. “Did anyone see you?”

“I don’t think so.” She took a deep breath and blew it out in a slow stream. “I jumped behind the bushes before the guy ran past, but he looked back to my spot in the woods before he drove off.”

He made a mental note of that, so they could come back to it. “How about from the department? Were there many officers on the scene?”

That faraway look re-entered her eyes. “The EMTs are who I remember the most, until Chief Randolph got there. I think there were a couple of other officers, too.”

He nodded, running scenarios through his mind. It was one thing for him and the chief to know about her being a witness to murder—but a whole crime scene team? Shit, that was a lot of people to monitor.

“I need to call the chief, so I’ll step outside.” Whether or not she saw through his ruse, he needed a moment alone and was relieved she didn’t argue.

“I’m going to run upstairs and wash my face. Why don’t you go out back to the garden to make your call? There’s good shade and right now, it’s not as warm as the porch.”

Ben was finishing up the call with Chief Randolph when she came back downstairs. Her face was still splotchy from crying, but she looked steadier than before. "All good?" Hope filled her question.

No, he gave her the side eye while figuring out how to tell her the back yard was covered in footprints. Like, music festival amounts of footprints.

Instead he asked, "You live here alone, right?"

"Yes, why?"

"We'll come back to that later."

Tension took up residence in his shoulders an hour ago, and no amount of shoulder rolling helped. The whole day had been like falling through the looking glass, but it was important for him to keep the focus on Jason Lawson for a bit longer.

"I gave Chief Randolph a thousand-foot view of your statement." He took a deep breath and pressed his fingertips against his temple. "Jesus, I can't believe you were there."

"But I didn't *see* anything." Frustration laced her tone. "I *heard* them fighting. The shooter ran at me. But I didn't actually *see* him shoot Officer Lawson."

"But what you saw is enough to hold the suspect until we can do further investigation. We've just got to *find* him."

She sighed. "I know. I mean, all I have is an impression of a man rushing at me, but I'll help if I can. Do I need to look at pictures, or some sort of lineup, or something like that?"

That made him smile. "Yeah, photos will be good once we get a suspect in custody. I want to work up a description before I leave, but before we work on that, we need a plan. Chief Randolph will put a gag order on the on-scene officers to keep your presence out of any formal reports. Three EMTs and six officers know you were with Jason when he died, but none of them know you were present for the fight. We'll keep that between us for now."

"But I didn't see—"

"I know. You didn't see the shooter. But you have awareness of his body. You know how he was dressed. You know he's bigger than you. Hell, you know it was a man and not a woman. That's something."

She stopped fidgeting. "I guess."

The conversation fizzled; the jig was up. His cheeks puffed with air before he let it out in a whoosh. "Abby, look, I found footprints around the back side of your fence, along the side that faces the woods."

She shrugged. "They're probably from when I had the fence built."

"How long ago was that?"

"About two months."

"Well, damn."

Chapter Four

"I don't want to scare you, but the footprints were fresh," he said in a quiet, reassuring tone. "We've had too much rain for these to be left from the construction done two months ago. In light of today's events, I have to wonder if the alarms going off have any correlation to Lawson's murder."

"What?" She shot up out of the chair to pace in nervous circles. "Shit. It never occurred to me that someone violent enough to kill a police officer would try to get into my house."

She grabbed a bottle of bourbon and a highball glass from the cabinet above the sink. Refusing to give into panic, she glanced at Ben over her shoulder. "I need something stronger than coffee. You?" She poured two fingers, knocked it back, then took a healthy swig straight from the bottle.

When she offered him the bottle, he considered but ultimately shook his head no. "Ask me another time."

She blinked and tried to pick apart what he was trying to say. His face was so serious, but his eyes were full of emotion. "After all these months of officers coming out here to check on things and finding nothing wrong, I started to believe them. Like maybe it was tree branches scraping against the house or squirrels gnawing on the wiring that set things off. It got so I didn't pay attention to it. Now, I just don't know."

Ben chewed on his bottom lip. She could see he wanted to say something, so she waited him out.

"Okay," he admitted with a heavy sigh. "I'll admit that my guys *might* consider you're looking for attention—or something."

This guy was too much of a gentleman to suggest that she might just be a bit crazy, but he squirmed in his seat and stared for several moments before continuing. "I'm not just a beat cop, annoyed at being called way out here to the middle of nowhere. It's entirely possible someone *has* targeted you. You mentioned your studio—can you get to it through the house or do you have to walk outside?"

"That old barn was beautiful, so when I renovated last year, I had the architect add a connecting hallway through the kitchen. I spent a fortune shoring it up and converting it to my studio, but it's my favorite space in the house."

His eyes lit with interest. "I love old architecture. How big is it?"

"The main house is about three thousand square feet, and the studio doubles it."

Ben's phone dinged. "Oh, wow—uh, excuse me." He glanced down at the screen, then took a quick second to reply. "Chief Randolph just confirmed what I've been thinking: there's too many coincidences between your alarms going off and the proximity of the murder. Since we're trying to keep a lid on your involvement, I'm going to take a few preliminary photos of the footprint patterns and document them. Wait here, okay?"

She nodded and waved him out, taking a big, calming breath as he walked away. There was no need to borrow trouble, and until Ben gave her the high sign, she wasn't going to panic.

He walked down to the marshy bank of the lake, near the small dock where an upside-down kayak leaned against a locked fence gate and turned back to look at the house. Even from a distance, she watched him taking in details. His lips moved, like he was talking to himself, and after a moment he snapped on a pair of gloves and made his way back to the house in a serpentine motion. He stopped several times between the lush bed of ruby loropetalum and the gate, bending down and taking photos of the ground with his phone before stepping through to the back yard.

She brought out two glasses of water and sat down at the table on the back deck, watching as he worked. He measured footprints, took photos with his phone, jotted down notes and occasionally scooped up surrounding soil. When he did a double take at something he saw on the ground, then jerked sharply toward the side door of her studio, fine hairs went up on the back of her neck. He walked swiftly, eyes glued to the ground like a bloodhound, and stopped at her studio door. "Well, fuck."

Abby jumped at the passionate reaction. "What's wrong?"

Frustration etched every line of his body. It was obvious he was trying to get himself under control. "My guys really dropped the ball on this one. Stay here for a minute; I've got one more thing to look at."

It was hard watching him take one more trip around the back yard, this time sticking close to the fence, then veering off to take more photos of the ground. The longer he took, the quieter he stayed, the more she worried. Each time someone from the Apex department came out, they'd insisted nothing was wrong. Ben's reaction was much different than the department's *laissez faire* attitude. It became torturous waiting for him to finish.

After a few more minutes, he headed back to the deck where she sat on the edge of her chair, twisting her hands together and tapping her foot.

"Someone's been casing your house," he said without preamble.

Just a deep breath and solemn expression and *bam!* Abby sucked in a breath and he kept going. "I found three distinct and methodical trails between the dock and your house. I repeat, none of them could be left over from when you had the fence built. Too much time has passed. Too much rain has fallen."

She exhaled with a big *whoosh* and slunk down in the chair. She was insured through the wazoo for her art collection, something her father had insisted upon. Any costuming or restoration work she did was individually insured through the customer's respective companies—so other than *her*, there was nothing of interest to anyone here. Except . . .

"What do you mean when you say 'casing'?"

Rolling his head on his broad shoulders, Ben shrugged. "Casing. Looking around for…something. This doesn't look like some random person out on the lake for the day and rolling up on your lawn for a picnic. This is deliberate. I can't leave you alone out here, Abby."

She just blinked. "What? Why?"

Ben picked up a glass of water and downed the whole thing in a single gulp, then plopped it back on the table with a loud bang. “Goddamnit, there goes the rest of my weekend.”

“I don’t understand. Your guys said—”

“Abby, my guys are a bunch of lazy idiots.” He visibly choked back his feelings. “I can’t leave you out here all by yourself. Not after someone killed a cop less than a mile from here—and especially after I’ve got evidence of someone staking out your house.”

Her heart stopped beating for a tick and then slammed so hard against her ribs it hurt. “Is it time to panic?”

“Yeah. It is.”

Chapter Five

"Okay, Martha, let's go through this again," Senator Quincy Sykes said, irritated and losing the shiny veneer he was known for.

"Again?"

"Yes, *again*. Three weeks ago, out of the blue, a woman named Abby Markham walked into the home office in Apex and said, 'Here, I found this box while I was digging in the garden. I thought the senator might like to have it.' Is that what you're saying?"

He hit mute on the live videoconference feed with his hometown staffers and pointed to the screen of his computer before he launched out of his chair. Live and in color, the box in question sat safely ensconced on a bookshelf in the quaint little office he maintained in Apex, hundreds of miles away to the south. "It's right there," he sneered, giving the screen a tap. "Look for yourself."

Martha Scott, his executive assistant, paused in the small bathroom attached to his senate office in Washington, out of sight from the prying eyes of the hometown office staff, and tucked the tails of her silk blouse into her slim-fitting pencil skirt. She'd started working in his office twelve years ago while she was in college and had proven her worth time and again by navigating the treacherous waters of Washington politics, seeing to it that nothing ever caught him off guard. *Nothing.*

Except for the damn box.

"What's in it, Quincy?" She glanced at him as he moved toward her but made no attempt to see what was on the screen.

As the chairman of one of the Senate's most powerful weapons committees, not much fazed Quincy Sykes these days, but he smirked at her swollen reddened lips, the only evidence of their latest fast and furious fuck. After ten minutes of banging her head against the wall, there wasn't a single hair out of place, yet that mouth gave her away. Every time. And though she knew where all his political skeletons had been buried over the last dozen years—she'd been party to most of them—she remained ignorant about *the box.*

He waited for her to rinse her mouth with mouthwash, then touch up her lips with her signature peony pink lipstick. And as she stepped away from the sink, he wrapped his fingers around the base of her neck. Her racing pulse beneath his fingertips made the brute in him grunt in satisfaction. *Still got it.*

"Oh, it's nothing for you to concern yourself with, dear," he said, making his voice silky smooth and deceptively gentle. He stood behind her, watching her in the mirror's reflection, at her parted lips and cheeks, still flushed with excitement.

He possessed a mean streak that few ever witnessed first-hand. But in all things involving Martha, she was the only person he allowed to see the ruthlessness beneath the surface. And she liked it. He enjoyed the way she tried not to wince or show any sign that his fingers digging into the tender flesh of her neck and collar bone hurt. His fingertips pressed against the tendons of her neck until she sucked in a breath. She'd always been a sucker for the aggressive, dominant side of him and craved the bite of pain as much as the oblivion of pleasure.

"Just a time capsule Margaret and I buried after Steven was born. I'm looking forward to picking it up next week."

Irritated, Martha sniffed. He was well aware she didn't like to hear about Margaret the Saint, the love of his life and main reason why he'd never marry again. For a dead woman to hold such power over a man like Quincy made her crazy. He guessed she was also pissy because he hadn't told her what was inside the box.

"All right, Quincy," she said. "The box is there in Apex. It's still locked, isn't it?"

"Yes."

"Then what would you like me to say? Or do about it? This Abby Markham dropped it off, said she found it in her garden. What is your problem?"

Mask of indifference in place, she brushed past him to grab her phone from his desk and scroll through a string of text messages. "You've got a meeting with the Prime Minister of Turkey tomorrow afternoon; your chief of staff wants to go through the salient points prior to the meeting. You'll have about ninety minutes for lunch at the barbecue lodge."

Quincy nodded and shrugged into his jacket. "Grab the bottle of Tums, would you? You know how I loathe southern cooking."

Chapter Six

"Mrs. Dixon was right. Damn it." Abby huffed out an irritated breath. "She said it was probably some kids, maybe hunters."

"Who's Mrs. Dixon again?" Ben asked. "You mentioned her before."

She handed him a glass of water, then walked ahead of him into the house. She didn't stop until she was back in the kitchen and heard him following along behind. "My assistant. She and my mother were friends when they were young."

"It must've been nice to connect with acquaintances when you moved back here."

"She retired from Duke about five years ago—she taught French history—and was bored. She's a huge help with research."

His phone buzzed, and he touched her lightly on the shoulder. "Hold on a sec."

With a nod, Abby leaned against the counter, eavesdropping with abandon. After a few moments he said, "Okay, we'll be ready." He looked down at his phone for a moment. "Dispatch is sending over Officer Sykes, who responded to the first alarm. Remember him?"

"Sort of. This was his family's land before the lake came in, right? He was *really* irritated about the 'false' alarm." She rolled her eyes.

"The footprints I just found mean we need to change the way the department proceeds. Mrs. Dixon is most likely right, but now we've got a reason to take a closer look. If we can get some of the soil in the print analyzed, we'll know if it's a match to the rest of the soil in your yard. And that might help us figure out where the person is coming from. And why they're walking all over your back yard."

"Yeah, that makes sense."

He nodded, looking a bit distracted. "And, you should know Lawson was Sykes' partner. I'm not sure why he's still out on patrol—maybe the chief hasn't told him yet."

"Doesn't the department make an announcement when officers were killed on duty?"

"Normally, yes. But in this case, an officer was gunned down in broad daylight. Since Sykes wasn't on the scene before or after you got there, it means Jason was down an old dirt road, doing something by himself. Maybe it was something sketchy, maybe it wasn't. Maybe Sykes had today off; I don't know. But the one thing I'm certain about is that he has no idea you saw anything with regard to Jason's death, and he definitely won't know the real reason why I'm here. Rose, our dispatcher, wouldn't have put him in rotation if that were the case. He'll have the same information as the rest of the department—I took the call because I was driving by on my way back into town."

She opened her mouth to say something, but he raised one hand. "No, don't worry. I spent a couple days at a buddy's cabin, hiking and kayaking. I've been pulling double shifts for the last month. I'm not due at work until Monday, but I'm going to stay here with you. With Sykes…we're erring on the side of caution. Since he's the on-call man right now, you'll answer questions about the alarms. Can you do that?"

"Won't it be weird to have a detective here for a simple alarm going off?"

"The chief wants me to stick with you for a couple days while we investigate Lawson's death—just to be sure there's no connection between Jason's murder and someone casing your home." Wrinkling his nose, he gave her an aw, shucks grin, "And since I'm both single and not blind, it makes sense that I'm sticking around because I'm interested in *you*. Is that okay?"

As she was both single and not stupid, maybe this could work in her favor. "I guess. I mean, I've never dated anyone in law enforcement before." She shrugged. "But how long do you think this will take?"

He winked at her before heading toward the front porch. "Some people have trouble with the long hours and dangerous situations cops face, but our area isn't plagued by crime like my old post in Los Angeles. Why don't you have a seat while I clean this up." He gestured toward one of the rocking chairs while he swept up the glass from the broken window.

It was a pleasure to watch him work. His large body took up most of the space between the railing and her chair, but he was agile and efficient. The muscles in his forearms rippled as he wielded the broom. His broad shoulders stretched the cotton material of his shirt near to bursting.

"Hopefully we can get it wrapped up this week," he said. "The longer it takes, the colder the trail gets. Sorry about the broken window, by the way."

"Not to worry," she said quickly. "There's some

heavy-duty plastic in my shop we can use to cover the void until it can be replaced."

"While Sykes is here, I'll run up to the home improvement store around the corner. You won't be alone, and then we won't have to worry about an easy point of access."

"Let me grab my credit card—hold on."

Ben snorted. "No way. I broke it, I'm fixing it." He sat back on his heels and looked up at her. She sensed something was bothering him because the smooth skin between his eyebrows and hairline wrinkled.

The old porch was one of her favorite spots on the property; a big willow tree provided enough shade that, even in the heat of the day, it was pleasant. A light breeze ruffled his hair, and the sweet scent of tea olives made her feel content. Like the events of the morning could wait a few more minutes before assailing her memories and make her stop looking over her shoulder. Like maybe this strong man kneeling at her feet might slay any dragon coming in her direction.

He smiled and touched her hand where it curled loosely over the arm of the rocking chair. She startled and realized he'd asked her something. "I'm sorry, can you repeat that?"

"I asked if you would consider dating a cop."

But she knew what he really meant: would she date him if it weren't a ruse. She was certain there was more to him that what she could see on the surface. Sure, he was handsome and big and sexy, but he'd proven to be kind and protective and dedicated to his profession. Before she could respond, a police cruiser pulled into the driveway. The driver remained in the car, watching her through the windshield. It had to be Sykes. Tension outlined what she could see of his body. If this was a cartoon, he'd have a dark raincloud hovering over his head.

Oh yeah, he looked pissed, probably because he'd been summoned back here by some hot shot who'd been taken in by a sob story spun by a whack job. Deciding this was not going to be a pleasant experience, Abby girded her loins, rose from the rocker, and went to the edge of the veranda to greet him.

The officer finally got out of the car and nodded to Ben. As he reached the porch steps, he offered his hand, with visible reluctance. "Miss Markham, I don't know if you remember me, but I'm Officer Sykes. I've been out here before."

Whoa, she thought, *he looks bad.*

One of the things that stood out from when he responded to the alarm call a couple weeks ago was that his good looks were wasted on his dickish attitude. Today his hair looked unwashed and oily, almost plastered to his scalp. Deep circles surrounded both eyes; his entire body looked like it might snap in half from the least amount of stress. If this man were to meet her on a dark street, she'd immediately run toward the criminals on the other side.

"I remember you, Officer Sykes." She smiled but didn't go down the steps to shake his hand. Because, well, fuck him. He'd treated her like an annoying drama queen. Something she'd never ever been.

Ben went down to the sidewalk, shaking the man's hand in greeting. "Steve, I've found a couple interesting footprints on the back side of the fence. I'd like for you to check them out. And I'd appreciate if you'd also grab some soil samples."

From her place on the veranda, Abby heard Sykes sigh, heavy enough to blow down the hundred-year oak in the side yard. "As I told Miss Markham the last time, the footprints are likely from the fence installers." He looked up and gave her the side-eye. She fought the urge to flip him off.

Ben's counter to Sykes' opinion made her smile as the men made their way up the steps onto the porch. "I'm sure that was the case a couple weeks ago. But we've had several inches of rain since then, and these footprints are too new and fresh to be left over from the installation."

He pointed at her feet. "It's pretty obvious those little feet didn't make these big imprints. Plus, someone's been standing outside several of the windows, which is not cool. While you're working here, I'm going to town to grab a new window. Don't leave until I get back, okay?"

Sykes just glared and gave a what the hell type shrug. Abby tried to be extra patient because he clearly had no idea anything unusual was going on. Plus, when the time came for the department to tell him about his partner, Officer Sykes' whole world would come crashing down.

She tried to remember empathy, even for a man who didn't know how to give it. "I think I've got a Peeping Tom, officer," she blurted out nervously.

Ben groaned and rolled his eyes, but she couldn't help it. Short of slapping Officer Sykes just to relieve the tension, she had to say something to wipe that smirk off his face.

Sykes reared back and shifted his eyes between the two of them, squinting as he worked out something in his head, and then finally said, "Okay. Yeah, I wouldn't want anyone peeking in through my windows and watching my wife."

"Thanks, man," Ben said. "I won't be long." He bounced down the steps to his car. Before backing out, he rolled down the window and called out, "Abby, I don't think we'll need to change dinner reservations, either. See you in a few minutes."

She noticed the flush on Sykes' cheeks after Ben pulled out of the driveway. Oh yeah, he wasn't happy, but he was doing his job. "Should I wait here?"

"It's your house, ma'am. Whatever's comfortable for you is fine with me."

Abby shrugged and walked with him around the side of the house, grabbing an old black plastic pot from beneath a lush stand of hellebores. While he took measurements and notes, and she kept her eye on his actions, she'd to do a little weeding.

Focusing on work seemed to settle him, and in no time, they established a comfortable stop-and-go rhythm. When he spoke from farther down the fence line, she followed along so they could talk.

"I understand you took a time capsule into my dad's office."

Happy for a change in topic, she smiled. "I did, though I don't know if it was a time capsule or not. It looked like the old metal ammunition boxes they used during World War II, like you'd see at an Army surplus store. If I'd known there was a Sykes in the police department, I would have contacted you through your office."

"It's fine." He took another photo or two of the ground around the fence, then stopped and looked down at her feet. "Uh, would you mind stepping this way a bit?" He positioned her next to a footprint that made her foot, in its dime store flip-flops, look like a child's.

"Those aren't work boots," she said, wiggling her painted toes.

Sykes just shrugged. "Did you open it? The box, I mean."

"Of course not, it's not mine. It had the number one written in something waxy, like a crayon. And your last name scratched in, like with a knife or something. It seemed important, and since your family maintains ties to the area, I figured dropping it off at his local office was my best bet."

He pinned her with a glare. "Only one you said? Why didn't you take in the rest?"

The question and tone were so menacing, as was his body language, she took a step back. "I, uh, only found one box, officer, and I didn't look inside. I don't know how many boxes there are in total. It seemed like the senator would be excited to see it."

She turned slowly and walked with careful steps, as if she'd been retreating from one of the red wolves inhabiting the area. Ben hadn't gotten back yet and the anger radiating off Sykes set off all her alarm bells. "I need to grab my gardening gloves. I'll be right back."

She heard him following her to the front side of the house. As soon as she put some distance between them, she sped up and went to sit on the far side of the porch. "Holy *shit*."

Clearly furious, Sykes stomped along the garden path like an angry, frustrated child. Or maybe a psychopath. Ben pulled into the driveway just as Sykes cleared the side of the house and instead of stopping to talk, he stormed over to his cruiser and climbed in. "I'll get this logged into evidence before my shift ends." He slammed the door and drove away, his tires spraying pieces of gravel in the car's wake.

Ben hauled a bag of hardware stuff out of the back of his car. "What's up with him?"

"I don't know." She cleared off a corner of the old sideboard against the railing so Ben could use it as a work surface. "He asked me about a time capsule I took over to his dad's office, then got angry when I told him there was a number one written on top. He acted like a dick when he came out a couple weeks ago, and he was a dick again today."

He looked off in the direction of Sykes' cruiser, and frowned. "I'm sorry you were uncomfortable with someone from the department. I'll have a talk with his supervisor next week."

"Good lord, don't do that. Of you need to send someone else to look at stuff here, can you ask for another officer? Sykes makes me nervous."

He took out a crowbar-looking tool and worked to loosen the broken sidelight's frame, working at a steady, careful pace. In quick order, he pulled out the old frame and glass remnants, and put them in the black trash bag he'd set out on the porch. Between the din of the cicadas and the intermittent sounds of drilling and hammering, she was mesmerized.

The setting sun cast flame-colored shadows over his hands, holding her enthralled by the competent way he used the tools. His long fingers and broad palms were sexy. As she rocked in the old porch chair, the events of the day passed through her mind in slow motion. Jason Lawson's hands, broad like Ben's, slid something from his… "Oh shit!"

With a sharp whack, and equally sharp curse, he lurched back, holding his thumb to his lips. "Geez, Abby. Give a man some warning before you—"

"I'm sorry," she said quickly. "I just remembered something!"

He sucked on his thumb. "It's fine—hey! Where are you going?"

She ran through the kitchen back to the laundry room and rifled through the pile of clothes she'd dumped in the washing machine. Thank God she hadn't started the cycle yet. The hidden key pocket in the back waistband of her running shorts was tiny to begin with but stuffed with a thumb drive and fighting her nervous fingers turned it into negative space. *Ha! Got it!*

Ben was sweeping up the last of the broken glass and wood shavings beneath a rocking chair when she ran out. "I still need to paint it for you, but it closes in the space. I'm sorry it's modern glass. We can paint it tomorrow, if that's okay."

She grabbed his right forearm to get his attention and thrust the flash drive into his hand. "Jason gave it to me this morning and said I had to give it to Chief Randolph, but the chief said to give it to you."

His face drained of color, and he grabbed her clenched fist. Tears welled in her eyes, but she laid it in his palm. "I'm sorry it slipped my mind earlier."

Chapter Seven

Steven Sykes paced in the garage, listening to the quiet murmurs of his wife and Sally Lawson as they planned Jason's funeral. He couldn't sit on the couch and choose scripture or pall bearers or debate an open casket versus a closed one any longer. While both sets of kids played quietly in the living room, he took advantage of their sympathy and escaped. The women assumed it was just too much for him to bear, and they were right.

Sweat poured down his back and his head pounded so hard he heard the blood rushing through his ears, behind his eyes. The migraine came on over the last hour; the nausea in the last ten minutes. Talking to his dad gave him anxiety on any day; today was going to be a bitch. Grabbing a bottle of water out of the fridge, he knocked half of it back before dialing the mean, old bastard.

The phone rang twice before the senator answered, snapping with his characteristic lack of patience for his only son. "What is it?"

Sykes swallowed convulsively. Nausea would win if he let it. "Dad. Uh, sir," he stuttered, and cleared his throat. "I'm sorry to interrupt dinner, but I have a question."

The senator made an impatient sound. "I'm not at dinner. I'm waiting in line for a glass of champagne—

I'm at a fundraiser for the children's home down the street."

Steve took another long swallow of water. "Are you still coming into town on Monday to get the time capsule?"

"Why?" The old man's voice, filled with suspicion, sounded distracted—no big surprise given all the noise in the background. "Hold on a minute." Quincy then spoke to someone else, "I'm in a conversation with my son, dear…I'll be right there."

The senator was as much a bastard behind the closed doors of his youth as he was on the senate floor, though Steven doubted Quincy's constituents would rally behind an emotionally abusive father like they did behind the "iron horse senator." The only reason he mentioned "my son" was because it would make him look fatherly. Trustworthy. Asshole.

"The woman who found the box—Abby Markham—she's the one who lives out at the old homestead."

"Oh, of course. I'm happy that old place is somebody else's headache to keep up now. Come on, Steven. Get to the point."

"She's made some complaints over the last couple weeks about a Peeping Tom, but we've never found anything to support her claims. Mostly they seem to be false alarms. Only—"

"Hold on—ah, yes, Madam Secretary. It's so nice to see you, too…I am, I am. I love the ballet, and *The Sleeping Beauty* was Margaret's favorite. I look forward to seeing you there, too. Ah, Steven—I've got a second. What were you going to say? She only *what*?"

"I was called out there again this afternoon—for *real* footprints this time. And they didn't come from work boots."

Silence.

"There was a detective talking with her," he added, just for good measure.

"So?" Quincy barked. "Detectives talk to people every day. And footprints don't prove jack shit."

"Ben Owens isn't just any detective, sir. He was a former FBI agent and rejoined the APD last year. He's, like, too much of a big deal to be talking to someone about footprints on their property. Plus, he was fixing a broken window on the front porch."

Steven knew by the change in the old man's breathing patterns he finally had the senator's attention. "And I don't think she brought everything to your office, either, sir."

"Why do you say that?"

The voice, dripping with malice, made the hair on the back of his neck stand on end. "Because she said it had the number *one* written on it. Like, how many did you and Mom bury?"

The senator swore under his breath and was quiet for another moment. "Can you meet me at the campaign office on Monday morning?"

Dread filled his already queasy stomach. "Yes sir."

"Good. I'll see you at seven o'clock."

After his father hung up, Steve let out his breath in a *whoosh*. Talking to the senator was always the worst thing that could happen on any given day. He leaned his forehead against the garage wall, rolling it back and forth to relieve some of the tension radiating out like the horn on a rotten unicorn. Acid burned in his gut that no amount of drugstore antacids relieved. Between his fucking old man and Jason's death, he was close to breaking.

But he'd rather take a beating—literal or figurative—from the old man than go back inside to help Sally Lawson plan the memorial. He was Jason's best friend and partner, which meant he had to be Sally's rock.

Right now he felt about as stable as an Alpine rockslide.

Fuck.

Chapter Eight

By three-thirty Sunday morning, Ben was on his fourth cup of coffee. Exhaustion made his brain feel like it was full of cotton balls; his hands shook like a leaf in a gale; and his gut sent out warnings in protest of the cup of precinct sludge in his hand.

He pressed a fist into the space just below his sternum where stomach acid currently tried to eat its way through his gut. Maybe if he'd taken Abby up on the offer of whiskey, there would've at least been a numbing buffer between his stomach lining and the coffee. He listened to the chief and their tech expert, Cindy McGee, argue about their next steps in the investigation.

McGee was on the ball. She'd already made two copies of the flash drive—one copy was locked up in Randolph's desk, waiting for Art Zothner from their local FBI office to pick up at eight o'clock. The other was plugged into an air-gapped laptop McGee used for looking at secure data. The original had been logged into evidence and sealed.

Chief Randolph stood, then rolled his neck from side to side and clapped her on the shoulder. "Good work, McGee. So far, we're the only people who know what's on this drive. Until we talk to the FBI in a couple hours, I don't want this information shared."

Wincing, Ben stood and tossed the cup in the trash.

He wasn't used to sitting still for long periods of time, but when the first picture from Jason's flash drive came up on the screen showing a tall man poking around Abby's fence, Ben rooted his ass to the chair.

Somehow, Lawson had stumbled across Senator Quincy Sykes, in the flesh, peering over the back corner of Abby's fence. And he appeared to be searching for something. It wasn't far-fetched to assume the senator was the one who'd been setting off the alarms, but what was he looking for? What could have been so important that he would have chanced being caught snooping around when he could have just walked up to the door and asked about it?

Abby Markham lived on what everybody in town referred to as "the old Sykes place." The senator sold the land to the Army Corps of Engineers back in the seventies so that part of it could be flooded and turned into Lake Jordan.

Granted, folks might occasionally stop by their former homesteads for old times' sake but watching an esteemed US senator casing the joint he once owned felt seriously wonky.

"You need to wake up Miss Markham," Randolph said. "See if she has any idea why Sykes might be nosing around her place."

Ben nodded. "Yes, sir. I'll go get her."

Last night, after he'd hustled Abby into his jeep, they drove straight to the precinct downtown, about ten minutes from her house. She was currently curled into a tight ball on the old leather couch in his office, huddled beneath the cardigan McGee always kept hanging on the back of her chair.

"It's cold in here," she'd complained after he

escorted her into the office. Himself, he was glad for the AC because his body always ran hot.

Her sleep had been troubled and restless, and each time he'd come in to check on her he'd had to drape the sweater back across her arms. She must have sensed him looming overhead and jerked in her sleep. He gritted his teeth and sat on the arm at the other end of the couch, tapping her ankle.

"Abby," he said softly. He didn't want to scare her, but they had work to do.

When she unfolded a bit, her calf grazed his fingertips, and that passing glance made his heart feel like it would beat through his chest. She woke in increments, shifting on the couch and drawing his attention to her shapely legs. Her life as a professional dancer and avid runner showed clearly in her limbs. Looking at her body made him feel lecherous, so he cleared his throat and spoke with purpose. "Abby, you need to wake up."

Her eyes popped open, and she sucked in a breath, looking a little wild-eyed as she surged forward. McGee's sweater drifted to the floor next to his feet.

"It's okay—it's me. It's Ben." He held onto her forearm while she got her bearings, making sure she didn't topple onto the floor. As soon as she focused on his face, her breathing leveled out, and she nodded.

He walked over and turned on the overhead lights. "Sorry about that, but Chief Randolph has some questions. You ready?"

"Yeah." She rubbed the sleep from her eyes and grabbed her backpack, digging around for a comb. "Do you mind if I go to the restroom first? I need to freshen up a bit."

"Of course."

"Oh, my God, it's almost four o'clock." She looked at her watch, then at him. And her stomach rumbled loudly. "I'm starving."

"I know. I'm sorry to pull you out of your normal routine. I don't think we'll be much longer."

She pulled out two peanut butter granola bars from her pack and handed him one as she walked through his door. "You didn't have dinner either."

"Nope. I'm so hungry I could eat a sandwich sitting on a dead horse, so thanks for sharing. The bathroom is around the corner. I'm going to wait for you, and then we'll talk with Chief Randolph. Okay?" He made a mental note to buy a box of granola bars to keep in his desk.

She took a big bite and hurried to the door. "Can we stop for breakfast when we leave?"

He nodded, but she was already in the hallway. Yeah, breakfast sounded pretty good. Way better than the bar of dried whatever he practically inhaled due to his near starvation status, but it was something. "You owe me a meal for feeling me up while I was sleeping."

The mouthful of granola sliding down his windpipe nearly choked him to death. He guessed he deserved it for looking at her with anything other than his cop goggles. In no time, Abby came out looking a little more alert than before and ready to face whatever questions awaited her. She pulled out two bottles of water from her backpack and handed him one.

"That bag of yours is magic," he said, gesturing for her to lead the way.

The chief met them at the door. Abby smiled at him and Cindy McGee. "Thanks for the cardigan."

"You're welcome. We spoke briefly last night," McGee said, "but most folks just call me McGee."

"Ah, well thanks for the cardigan. I didn't know we'd be so long. I would've worn something warmer."

"Miss Markham," Randolph said as he held the back of the chair for her. "Why don't you sit next to McGee while we walk you through the images."

The photos were already queued up to make the process quicker. Abby touched the screen and looked at McGee. "Who's the dude at my fence? The fence crew wore work clothes…this guy's wearing a suit."

"Exactly," said Randolph, glancing at Ben. "Most footprints from the crew have been washed away, but Ben noticed a few intact ones under the trees, and beneath the fence line." He pointed to a spot low on the screen. "And here, it looks like some of the trails were made by a wingtip, not a work boot." He gestured for McGee to click ahead and tapped the screen after another couple images went by.

"There—stop!" Abby said. "Zoom in on the shoes, please."

Collectively, they leaned forward. "Those shoes are known as bespoke brogues," she said. "I know the style because my dad wears them. He gets them at a haberdashery in Paris."

McGee tilted her head and squinted, looking closer at the shoes. "Say that again."

"Handmade wingtips," Abby said. "Expensive, but worth it. Well, according to my father anyway."

The chief asked, "He isn't in town, is he?"

"No, he and Bob only come back to the States in the fall. They usually stay with me from Thanksgiving to Christmas."

McGee raised her eyebrows but clicked on to the next image. Ben grabbed his notepad. "Can you give me their whole names, Abby?"

"My father is Joseph Markham, but he goes by Jack. And his partner for the last twenty-five years is Robert Pissarro. He goes by Bob."

He opened his mouth, but closed it, working around the familiar sounding name. He tilted his head to the side. "Why is that familiar—Pissarro?"

Abby patted him on the flank, and he snapped to attention. Everywhere. *Shit*! He quickly shifted his gaze to see if anyone had noticed.

"Bob's great-grandfather was a famous French Impressionist," Abby explained. "I have several of his paintings at the house."

"You've got an original impressionist painting at your house?" McGee sounded dumbfounded. Like she couldn't wrap her head around something so foreign.

Abby grinned. "Actually, I've got four."

Chief Randolph murmured, "Okay, so you've got *some* priceless artwork at home. Could that be what he's looking for?"

She shrugged and gestured for McGee to go back through the photos and tapped the screen when they got to the picture of the man looking over the fence. In the next one, he was farther away from the fence, walking toward the back-tree line and closer to the water. Ben held his breath, waiting to see if she'd recognize Sykes.

She watched the screen, distracted from the conversation by the images. "Yes…my father is more of a modern art fan than I, but we meet in the middle—taste wise—with Expressionism. Dad tends to give me something from his collection to celebrate the big moments in life, like when I graduated from college, or after I costumed my first opera. I'll inherit everything when he dies, but he said he wants me to enjoy them now while he's alive to share them. They're insured through the teeth, but I don't really have them on display. In fact, most private owners don't broadcast their collections."

McGee's eyes widened, but she kept them glued to the screen. Nobody could figure out what to say to that. Abby wasn't bragging or trying to discuss her awesome art collection. She seemed unaffected by it. The chief shook his head.

"What do you do with them?" McGee asked, and grunted when Ben smacked the back of her shoulder. "What? I'm just curious."

Clearly not insulted, Abby snorted. "I hang them and enjoy looking at them." At McGee's laugh, she said, "Seriously, I rotate them depending on the assignment I'm currently working on. If I have something dark and moody, I move those into the studio. When the task is happy and light, I swap it out for something brighter." She gave a blithe shrug. "A large panel of water lilies currently resides in the downstairs bath."

Chief Randolph wore a "who the fuck has priceless paintings in their john?" look, but asked, "Why do you think he's walking back into the woods?"

"There's a small drop-off just beyond the fence line, which is kind of nice because it keeps everything dry during a big rain," Abby said. "I was worried about flooding when I bought the place, but the property is well above the hundred-year-flood-line. Well, if the lake had been there a hundred years. I think it's only been there about thirty years, or something."

She leaned forward, watching the images as McGee continued clicking through them. It was kind of like watching an old black and white movie, had there been big gaps between the cells. "Whatever the timing, it's high enough that I don't really worry. Wait!"

She sucked in a breath and shot up out of her seat. "That's Senator Quincy Sykes! What's he doing at my fence? I already dropped off the time capsule."

"What time capsule?" Randolph and McGee asked in unison.

Chapter Nine

"Uh, the time capsule the fence builders found a couple weeks ago. I can't believe you didn't see it on the news. Good grief, you'd think I found the lost ark, or something. Every news station in town called me for a sound bite."

Ben spun her chair around and leaned close. "What was in it?"

She shrugged, then stretched her neck from side to side. "Don't know. Don't care."

"So why the media hype?" Randolph asked. "Far as I know, Senator Sykes only comes home during campaign season."

"I talked to three different reporters, who basically opened with some spiel about me living in the old Sykes place. I told them all the same thing—I didn't grow up in this area, so I don't have much connection to the house beyond loving the setting and appreciating the workshop possibilities. They sort of left me alone after that."

Ben snickered. "I'm sure Quincy Sykes wouldn't be happy to be unrecognized."

McGee who'd been clicking wildly on the keyboard, made an excited sound in the back of her throat as she read from the screen: "Senator Quincy Sykes will be in town on Monday, October 9, to discuss the defense authorization act, and its effect on North

Carolina's three military bases, as part of North Carolina State University's Office of Emerging Issues Military Impact series. He plans to stop by his home office in Apex beforehand to open the time capsule recently uncovered on his family's historic property."

Abby pointed to the screen. "I did my part for history. Is there anything else you need from me right now, Chief? I'm starving."

Randolph shook his head. "No, ma'am. Not right now. I know I don't need to say this, but you should keep all this private for the time being. Between Lawson's murder and now the senator lurking around your property—and your proximity to both events—it's clear something's going on." Visibly exhausted, he rubbed his eyes and rolled his shoulders. "It's going to be a long week while we work Lawson's case. I know Sally's going to want to get it wrapped up soon so she can bury him."

Without warning, McGee's breath hitched. Ben grasped her hand.

"Look," said Randolph, "we know you had nothing to do with either situation, but I've got to ask that you not leave town while we continue to investigate. Two *unusual* things have happened, and you're connected to both. We want to keep an eye on you, too."

"No way!" Abby squared her shoulders as three sets of eyes bore into her. "I mean, no, sir. Mrs. Dixon and I are headed to DC this week to get ready for a performance of *The Sleeping Beauty* at the Capital Ballet Company. I've spent the last three and a half months costuming it. We need to be there to focus on final fittings and any other last-minute issues."

Shaking his head, Ben moved from McGee when

the chief spoke. “That’s not going to be possible—”

“Oh, yes, it is,” Abby said with a fair amount of heat and frustration at being told what she could and could not do. “I didn’t kill Officer Lawson, and I did my good neighbor part when I took that damned box to Senator Sykes’ office. Plus, *the President of the United States* is going to be there on opening night.” She stood and started pacing, anxiety screaming from every pore. Then she pointed at Ben. “You can’t keep me here against my will. I won’t stand for it. Got me?”

He held up both hands in a gesture of peace. “Whoa there. When are you supposed to leave?”

“I’m driving up on Monday. Mrs. Dixon’s coming on Wednesday night. We’ll work through technical rehearsals and be ready for the final dress on Thursday. The production opens to the public the next day, on Friday. That’s when POTUS will be there. I’ll be a guest of honor, and you bet your ass I plan to be sitting right beside him.”

“When were you planning on coming back?” Ben asked.

“Not until Sunday night.”

He counted on his fingers. “That’s eight days, sir. Her getting out of town to go to Washington is cheaper than putting her into protective custody. I can’t speak to the fence situation, but hopefully we’ll have Jason Lawson’s murder wrapped up by then.” His expression didn’t reflect the hopeful sentiment of his words. “We wouldn’t have to worry about keeping extra eyes on Abby while we investigate.”

Abby was happy to jump on Ben’s bandwagon. “Out of sight, out of mind. I can even stay in DC longer if you need me to. I love the city.”

Randolph tapped his pen against the desk, checked his watch, then looked at Ben. "She's right. There's something weird about the senator slinking around her place like that. I need you to clean up and grab a little shut-eye, and be at Sykes' office in the morning before his entourage rolls in. The element of surprise will be our best bet for now."

Then Randolph dropped his final bomb. "We'll see how the day goes tomorrow before I make a final decision on whether Ms. Markham can leave town."

Crossing her arms over her chest, Abby glared at the three officers—a visual reminder that *no one* was on her side. "With all due respect, you're going to have to arrest me to keep me here. I've worked my ass off to get where I am. And with the President attending? Nope. *Not going to* Washington is off the table." She grabbed her bag and started toward the door.

Ben huffed out a frustrated breath. "Sir—I'd rather use the day to inves—"

"I know, son," Randolph snapped, before closing his eyes and taking a deep breath. "I'll be working in the field to help the investigation along. You're the best person to work the Sykes angle—between your work with the FBI and now as a detective. You're my ace in the hole. I cannot stress enough the importance of keeping this effort between the four of us right now. Until we know what's going on, we can't risk Steven Sykes catching on, then alerting his father to anything. Who knows what kind of shitstorm we'll incur if *anyone* finds out we're investigating a United States senator? Use today to research everything you can about Senator Sykes. You can keep an eye on Ms. Markham to make sure nobody comes snooping around from Lawson's murder. Meet me here on Monday around noon—you'll have looked the senator in the eye, and we should have a better idea of what's what."

Abby waved her arm to the room at large. "You need to check out that time capsule. There's got to be something he wants in there. I mean, there's no way I should even *be* on his radar. My house was abandoned when I bought it, so it's not like I bought it out from under them."

Ben couldn't believe the unexpected shift. Babysitting duty was bullshit on any day, regardless of any connection between the two events. Even though Abby needed help, it irked the ever-living shit out of him to *not* be involved in the homicide investigation.

She touched his elbow. "I can grab a car, Ben. You don't need to go with me right now—this is where you need to be."

"Actually, he does," said the chief. "I don't believe in coincidence, but I do believe in being prepared. Ben is sticking with you through the rest of the weekend."

"Yes, sir," he muttered petulantly.

"And Ben," Randolph said, "when I said I'd decide tomorrow if *she* could go to DC, that meant *you*, too. Get close to her and stay close. We're missing something."

Abby blanched. Even McGee shrugged. Arguing was futile. "Well, damn."

The corner of Ben's mouth kicked up as humor cracked his somber expression. She pointed at him. "You owe me a big stack of pancakes."

Chapter Ten

There were two things Quincy Sykes appreciated about middle-of-the-night road trips: no traffic jams, and the presence of congressional license plates assured *no* delays due to speed traps. He'd made the trip to Apex in a little over three and a half hours. Had he waited to drive down in the afternoon with Martha, it would have taken nearly twice that time. Though she was royally pissed at being left behind, she was happier to not have to spend her Sunday with Steven's family.

"You're welcome to come with me, dear, but we'll be going to the family church for service," he'd told her in his smooth, bedroom voice. "Margaret's people will most likely be there, though…I'm sure they would welcome you, too."

To reinforce appearances, he planned to have Sunday dinner with Steven's family, followed by an invigorating hike around Lake Jordan. The hike he genuinely enjoyed; the rest was smoke and mirrors. He'd left Martha with a pile of paperwork to sift through, knowing she'd have the latest statistics to pad his presentation Monday morning—and that she'd hand-deliver it at his North Carolina headquarters.

He'd parked under a copse of trees just down the street from the Markham house—*his* old homestead—for about half an hour, making sure the car was hidden from passersby and watching for any movement inside.

A car sat in the driveway, so he'd assumed she was home. Unfortunately, he'd learned the hard way that she had a motion-detector on her security alarm.

Since he had no intention of setting it off tonight, he was content to watch the house and visualize her sleeping peacefully. The little bitch was hiding something—like the fact she must've also found the second box. The one he should have burned on that fateful night so long ago.

He'd nearly had a stroke when Steven called last night. The boy had confirmed every paranoid fear he'd had for the last few weeks: Abby Markham had to be aware of the second time capsule. Why else would a burned-out Feeb turned Apex PD detective be sniffing around?

His thoughts drifted back to the chaotic weeks following the fire, the night that changed the trajectory of his life. What a nightmare it had been. He'd buried one old ammunition box in the wee hours of the morning after the bodies had been carted away and the firefighters and sheriff had left the property. The second capsule had been buried sometime later by his brother-in-law, Terrence.

When government engineers came a couple years later to survey the land for flooding, one of them had remarked on the beauty of the repaired farmhouse, despite the scars left over from the fire. And even though Quincy despised the house due to the memories invoked by the tragedy, he'd agreed to have it moved to higher ground.

Between the relocated house and the now-sprawling Lake Jordan, he couldn't remember where either box had been buried. It wasn't like he'd made a map with an X marking the spot. His system had been more of a "ten steps to the left and twenty off the north corner of the house" scenario. Now, more than three decades later, his sentimental gesture came back to bite him in the ass.

He needed to stop sneaking down to North Carolina to count off steps and orient himself to the box's location, but he couldn't rightly ask Steven to help him search. He was going to have to hire it out. He was the chairman of the Senate Armed Services Committee, for crying out loud. He'd just finished writing the parameters of the defense authorization act. There was a reason his professional opinion and personal mantra was "keep it off the books."

He knew people. And Abby Markham was nobody.

Another hour passed, and his mood blackened even further. Patience wasn't a virtue he was known for, and during his time in the military he'd been known to have a hair trigger. Nowadays it was called PTSD. In the Vietnam era, the pros termed it "anxiety." He would never admit to the PTSD today, but the anxiety definitely struck when he was stressed. And he was so stressed right now his eyeballs throbbed in time with his racing heartbeat. Bright flashes of fury sparkled in his periphery, and before he knew it, violent ruminations swirled through his mind.

Abby Markham had unearthed the one thing that could take him down, and he was a fighter. Who the fuck was she to take his private property out for the world to see? To drop it off publicly, knowing the media would jump on it like the juiciest of scandals. To threaten his job and livelihood...to threaten his life! That bitch had to die.

He flipped through his mental black-ops rolodex, brainstorming who could most easily take her out with a minimal of fuss when a later model jeep slowed in front of her house. The door slammed and jerked him out of his head, where he'd been stuck for God knew how long.

"Fuck!" He slid farther down in the seat as it pulled into the driveway. Fuck Abby Markham for sending him into an anxiety attack.

He snapped the elastic band that was always on his wrist, hidden by his watch band, three times. Hard. Each sting of the band brought clarity, helping him focus on the here and now. He refused to snap it a fourth time, like his therapist encouraged, because he was bigger than his outrageous imagination. He tilted his head from side to side, stretching the tendons in his neck that were so taut he could barely move his head, and grabbed the binoculars. The driver walked around the back of the vehicle and opened the passenger door. Abby Markham got out and leaned into the man, wrapping her arms around his waist and laying her head on his chest.

"God damn it!"

He slammed his hand against the dashboard. She hadn't even been home, and he'd been having a heart attack and envisioning her painful demise. Fury bubbled up his throat so quickly he nearly choked. He wrenched open the glove box and pawed past the bullshit stack of papers to his pistol and the burner phone he'd purchased for cash during a stop for gas and the toilet. Though he was an unapologetic card-carrying member of the national gun lobbyists, it was vulgar to brandish a hip holster on the Senate floor. He grabbed the phone and powered it up, then keyed in a number from memory.

After a moment, his connection picked up. "Go, Forth."

Quincy smirked. Jim Forthmann was as lethal an assassin as he'd ever run across, but he possessed a warped sense of humor. Most likely it was the younger man's coping mechanism for the brutal lifestyle he led, but it was irritating as shit. "How long will it take you to pick up a package in central North Carolina?"

The man in question was silent for a moment, then responded, "Five days—I'm out of country, wrapping up a project."

"I'm texting coordinates. Call when you get to town."

Quincy didn't wait for confirmation before hanging up. The countdown had begun.

Chapter Eleven

When the keys rattled against the front door at nine fifteen the next morning, Ben went on instant alert. He pushed the kitchen chair back so fast it tipped over and banged against the floor, but he managed to scramble into the foyer quick enough to shove the business end of his pistol in the face of a wild-looking old woman.

"Stop!" he yelled in his meanest, most authoritative voice. "Hands up!"

Her head reared back at the snap in his voice, but otherwise she didn't flinch. Of course, she didn't put her hands up either, or drop any of the things she was holding. Instead she shifted her gaze over his shoulder toward the stairs and yelled, "Abby!"

"Lady, I said to put your hands up. I suggest you do it right now before I shoot you." He tipped his head in her direction and gave her the crazy eye. Again, she looked unaffected. Which was pretty badass on her part. On the other hand, it might get her a fast trip downtown in the back of a squad car wearing his fancy bracelets.

He opened his mouth to give a final warning when Abby came tearing down the stairs. He shifted his stance to open his feet and threw his left hand out in time to grab her around the waist, pulling her in tight. It was like trying to catch a squirming eel. Though her momentum just about toppled them, he'd been ready.

"Let me go!" she said heatedly, squirming against

the arm locked around her, trying to climb up and over his side like a monkey.

He shifted and pushed her behind his hip, then grabbed a handful of…skin. He glanced down for a moment and was struck dumb again. All she had on was a little pair of bikini panties and a tank top. Christ, she was going to make him go blind. Or send him into terminal priapism.

He shook his head. "What the hell are you doing down here?"

He set her on the floor and whipped his arm around the other way, so he was pressing her against his back, still held securely by his arm. Lord, her breasts were smashed against his back. Between trying to hold Abby back, control his cock, and focus on the fearless old woman, he was sweating bullets. Abby popped up on her toes to look over his shoulder. Jesus, the woman had no sense of self-preservation.

"That's Mrs. Dixon! Get your gun out of her face."

When she tried to worm her way around the other side of his body, he let her go. He recognized that name, so he lowered the barrel to the level of the old lady's knees. And not being stupid, he kept the safety off in case he needed to use it.

"It's Sunday—what are you doing here?"

Mrs. Dixon closed her eyes to half-mast and glared at him, nodding toward Abby, who fluttered around, checking for broken bones or something. He fought the urge to snort, because that wouldn't help anything.

"Young man, I haven't done anything wrong. But since you are clearly protecting my Abby, I've decided to let your behavior go."

Mrs. Dixon lifted her arms and nodded to her

bundle of bolts of material and sequins. "There's a lot more in the car. I would appreciate if you would grab the rest of it. Everything in the trunk and back seat must come in."

She shouldered her way past him and headed toward the kitchen table, a smirking Abby following behind like a little duck. She set her bundles on the table and heaved a huge sigh of relief, then let Abby squeeze her in a tight hug. "Now, please. You're burning daylight."

He muttered something under his breath about bossy women and headed for the door, catching Abby's brilliant smile before he slammed it shut behind him. He jumped from the side of the porch closest to Mrs. Dixon's car and lifted a dozen or more shiny to the point of eye-popping costumes from the back seat. Some were soft and flimsy, while others had stiff pieces with sharp edges that dug into his forearms. With nowhere to go but back into the house, he sucked it up. Doing shit for old ladies in town seemed to be his new lot in life.

Mrs. Dixon closed the door behind him and pointed toward the back of the large sunroom, to the long hallway on the backside of the kitchen. "Let's save a trip and go ahead and get these to the studio."

"Yes, ma'am."

She was like a little drill sergeant, leading him through the house and *tsking* when his arms lowered enough to let leotards and fabric touch the ground. She toggled a couple of light switches and bright overhead lights filled the open barn-style studio. He blinked to get his bearings and followed her over to a corner on the right side where empty clothing racks waited.

"Just hang them all along here…that's good. Now, if you'll make sure you've gotten everything from the car before you lock it up for me, *and* bring everything from the kitchen table, we'll call it even."

He was struck dumb by her lavender-tinted hair, leopard print cats-eyeglasses, and blood red lipstick. When she finally stopped moving and winked at him, it broke the spell. Nodding, he took in the larger picture and noticed her tailored suit. It was the color of the Mediterranean Sea in the summertime and, rather than clashing with her wild hair, looked lovely. Her purple running shoes made him smile. This was turning into one weird day.

By the time he brought in the final load, Abby had changed into black yoga pants and a long-sleeved black T-shirt and stood next to the older woman. Since they were lost in conversation, he took in the beauty who'd deftly turned him into a stuttering packhorse. Her comfortable outfit made her look reed-thin and about seven feet tall, but it was the flashy purple running shoes like Mrs. Dixon's that made him shake his head.

"Ladies," he said in a quiet voice so he wouldn't startle Abby. When they remained deep in their conversation, he cleared his throat. This time she turned and smiled. Like a blow to the solar plexus, it took his breath away.

"Oh! Hang the rest of those costumes on this rack here—" She grabbed his elbow and pulled him along to another clothing rack a couple feet farther down the wall. "And you can put the loose stuff over here."

She waited for him to follow her to the middle of the room, where a large, square, waist-high table with tons of shelves sat beneath four pendant lights. Four sewing machines lined a long table against the farthest wall, where another couple of pendant lights shone straight down. The ceiling looked to be twenty feet high, but it was an optical illusion. Tall mirrors lined one of the walls, and a ballet bar was installed on the front wall. Abby could do some serious work in this space.

He pressed his fists into his lower back and stretched, looking around. He turned to her and realized she'd been watching him, so he said, "Wow." Which made her snicker before flashing that paralyzing smile at him again. Mrs. Dixon cleared her throat and stepped up next to Abby, putting a motherly arm around her shoulders.

She held out her hand and said, "I'd like us to start over, Agent Owens. Abby filled me in on the Peeping Tom and poor Officer Lawson while you were outside. I didn't mean to startle you."

He scowled at Abby.

"I'm Gladys Dixon, Abby's assistant," she said, offering her hand. As wild as her getup was, she was a very lovely woman. Maybe it was age that had tipped her over from "crazy" to "artsy." As an afterthought, she added, "My son Michael is an FBI agent, like you."

He paused for a moment, recognizing the name and trying to visualize Michael Dixon, then grinned. "Nice to meet you, too. I left the FBI last summer, so it's just Detective Owens now." He gave her hand a gentle shake. "And regardless of who your son is, Abby is not supposed to discuss the details of her situation with anyone." He gave them both a stern glare. "*Anyone*."

Mrs. Dixon took Abby's hand. "Young man, I love Abby like my own child. My husband, Stewart, was the chief of police before Ward Randolph took office, and Abby knows Mike. Of course she's going to discuss her situation with me."

Abby did have the grace to look guilty and a little sorry. "Plus, she wanted to know who my new boyfriend was."

Gladys narrowed her eyes in thought, and Ben could practically see the gears of her mind working. "You're Chuck Dixon's boy, aren't you? I should've seen it right away," she said. "The last time I saw you, you were a toddler."

"Yes, ma'am," he said with caution. He could feel the blush rising up his neck but refused to give in to the urge of retreating to the kitchen.

"When your daddy left law enforcement, Stewart was promoted to chief. Chuck was such a funny guy. I'm sorry to hear of his passing."

"Thank you, Mrs. Dixon. I appreciate your kind words. But we've got to set some ground rules, okay ladies?" Once they nodded, he continued. "First of all, I went through the academy with Mike. He's a good guy. His detail kept him in DC, but I was assigned to the LA field office. That said, we don't discuss *anything* about this investigation with *anybody*. Not your husband, not your son, not your bridge club, not your preacher. Understand me?"

Mrs. Dixon narrowed her eyes. "Yes, okay. I haven't spent the last four decades connected to law enforcement to share any pillow talk I may or may not have overheard."

He looked at Abby with one brow raised.

"Okay, I get it! But she knows about the alarms, Ben. I didn't want her to find out through the grapevine that I was the one who came across Officer Lawson yesterday. Plus, she was going to have Mike stop by to do a little looking around when he gets here Wednesday night. I didn't want him to interfere."

"I appreciate your thoughtfulness," he said, sarcasm lacing his tone. But he caught her undertone and tilted his head in acknowledgment. "It's good you put a hold on Mike checking it out, but from now on, it's just you and me. There are a lot of moving parts to this situation, right?"

She nodded, broadcasting with her eyes that she'd said nothing about the senator or her experience during Lawson's murder. Her poker face wasn't worth shit.

"Mike's coming on Tuesday so he can take his dad to a doctor's appointment on Wednesday. When they're done, Mrs. Dixon will ride back with him. She'll be with me for the rest of the week for technical rehearsals."

"How's she getting home?"

Mrs. Dixon gave him jazz hands. "Don't you worry about me, young man. I've got two friends taking the bus up to New York City for a marathon of Broadway shows; I plan to join them at the bus station in Washington."

"Oh my God," he murmured, making Abby laugh. A whole bus of Gladys Dixons? He was happy he wouldn't be heading north with *that* bus.

"Stewart's waiting, kids." Mrs. Dixon grabbed her purse. "I wanted to make sure I dropped off this last batch of costumes for you to go over with a fine-toothed comb. I ran out of the smoke gray crystals you were using on Prince Phillip's vest, so I used some of the black diamond ones you used for Antonia's dress in

Troilus and Cressida last fall. I think they're stunning mixed in."

Abby hugged the older woman and held the door for her. "I already know that's going to look great. I'll see you in a couple of days."

Chapter Twelve

Back in 1978, when Quincy Sykes was a freshman state senator, only five thousand people called Apex home. Last year it had been named *America's #1 Town*, and it lay in the middle of a county that boasted the largest school system in the nation. Now, nearly ninety thousand people packed into this beautiful patch of heaven.

With all that growth, and as close as it was to the booming technology hub surrounding a few world-class universities, Apex claimed only one shit-hole chain motel and one super expensive bed and breakfast. Because Steven shared a small historic home on downtown Main Street with a whining wife and two rambunctious brats, Quincy preferred the B&B.

"I like to support my hometown when I have the opportunity," he often boasted to the local media, with a smile big enough to showcase his dimples and silver fox good looks that only got better each year. What he really meant was, "There's no way in hell I'm staying with my lazy-assed son and his snotty kids."

Because there was a God in heaven, this morning's church service had been followed by Homecoming. Instead of having to suffer through an irritating lunch at Steven's house in his tightly-packed neighborhood, where Jennifer liked to have them sit outside so their neighbors could gawk at him and get her brownie points with the Mommy's Morning Out crowd, they ate like kings at the church.

With a stomach filled to bursting, the SUV pulled up outside the B&B. Knowing Martha would have everything already set up, Quincy was more than ready for the nap calling his name. After a credible series of death threats six years ago, which came to a head when some whack job from eastern North Carolina slipped into the U.S. Capitol building during a congressional session and stabbed Quincy with a fountain pen, he'd retained personal security. Most legislators were protected by the Capitol Police while they were in Washington. Normally that was enough; Quincy felt his situation called for extra measures. Mark Grissom had been with him from the get-go, but this new kid, Ed Parker, was exhausting.

"I don't know about you, Mark, but I'm thankful for today's Homecoming service," Quincy said, leaning forward to pat him on the shoulder.

Mark snorted with good humor and winked at Quincy through the rearview mirror. "You're right, sir."

Ed unhooked his seatbelt and shifted sideways in his seat. "Right about what?"

"You haven't met the senator's family yet," said Mark, "but his daughter-in-law is a terrible cook." Mark tilted his head to the door, and Ed jumped out like his ass was on fire. It was charming, really, how starstruck the new agent still was with him. The younger man could be annoying at times, but Quincy never forgot the benefit of blind loyalty. The detail flanked him while they walked up the sidewalk, and before Ed could get the door, Shirley and Richard Womble, owners of the B&B, stepped out on to the porch to greet the group.

"Senator, it's so nice to see you again," Richard said, reaching out to shake his hand. "You're looking hale and hearty, sir."

Quincy chuckled with a practiced charm and wit. "I can say the same for you, Richard. Shirley, dear, you're as resplendent as these gardenias. My Margaret would be over the moon with their scent." He kissed her hand, and she giggled like a teenager.

Glancing over at Ed, he noticed the color high in the younger man's cheeks and swept his hand in an encompassing gesture. "Ed, this is Shirley and Richard Womble, owners of this beautiful B&B and our hosts this evening. If we played our cards right, Shirley's already got us stocked with peanut butter cookies."

She laughed and nodded.

He clapped and tilted his head to Mark, who stepped closer. "Senator, sir, we need to get you checked in with Martha," Mark said, using his big body to shift the group through the front door and into the wide foyer. The Wombles hadn't noticed they'd been herded yet.

"Oh, right you are," Richard said. "Well, don't let us keep you. Dinner will be ready around seven o'clock, as usual. That okay?"

"That sounds wonderful," Martha Scott said from the bottom step. She must've headed down when she heard them come inside. The Wombles moved to the side hall and headed toward their private quarters off the back of the house.

It was a pleasure to watch Martha work. She had the same herding instincts and talents as Mark, but where he physically shifted people around, Martha psychologically moved them around. And they always came around to her way of thinking. She fiddled with her slacks and made sure her hair was in place before turning back to him, unaware that he'd been watching her. Discretion, as much as brilliance, kept her in his good graces. Plus, she really was beautiful. He was about to take her upstairs and show her just how much he appreciated her when the doorbell rang. He sighed.

"That must be the mayor," she said, smirking as she walked casually to the door and opened it with a regal flourish. Her smile was warm for Helton. "Brandon, so good to see you."

The mayor leaned to kiss her on the cheek, while Ed puffed up his chest and stepped in front of his boss. Quincy gave a charming chuckle and patted the newest member of his security detail on the shoulder. "It's okay, Ed. This is our mayor, one of the good guys." He then shook Brandon's hand. "Ed joined the team since I was here last year. How're you doing?"

Helton accepted the handshake with a smile. "Great, Quin. Hope you are, too." At the slight flush coloring his cheeks, Quincy knew Apex's mayor was trying to look non-threatening. He also knew the other man considered him a dick but was probably more worried about being sized up by a scary-looking bodyguard.

Good ol' Martha broke the tension by tucking her hand into the crook of Brandon's elbow and leading him out of the foyer. He let his breath out in a whoosh. "It's so nice to see you, Martha. I figured I'd run through a few talking points for tomorrow before I head back home. We've got a little work to do in the garden before it rains later in the week."

"Perfect. I was just reading through the salient

points our local office put together for the senator. Apex is growing by leaps and bounds!"

Because Quincy's team always rented out the entire B&B, they had full access to the two upstairs bedrooms and connecting loft, plus the living room and sunroom on the side. It was private and served their purposes well. Martha walked with Brandon to the sunroom, where she had a makeshift office set up on the fussy veranda.

"I've put together an agenda that should be easy to follow. Nothing crazy, just a good news visit, you know?" She handed him a printed copy and sat down in one of the two plush Queen Anne chairs. He sat and read it over while she gave an overview. "We'll start by opening the time capsule. Everybody seems so charmed by the idea of it, so we want to make sure we give it a little attention. How nice it is to lead with something fun, right? Next, the senator will discuss some updates on what he's been working on in Washington this last session, and then he's going to announce his ideas for North Carolina. We'd like you to chime in and give an update on the community to close us out."

Brandon nodded. "Sounds good. I'll open with a reminder of Apex being number one, and then discuss a few of the challenges of managing such a boom in population and, well, popularity. The town is focusing on smart growth this year, and we've just finished our ten-year development plan. It calls for expanding infrastructure budgets for roads, schools, parks, and bike lanes. We've approved one additional fire station, and an expansion to the police department. We're also trying to woo more businesses to prevent this from becoming a total bedroom community."

Quincy grabbed a bottle of water from the table in the foyer and watched as Martha took notes and nodded occasionally. He was ready for her to wrap up the meeting so they could burn off some energy, so he sent her a quick text message.

"This is good, Brandon. There's a lot to talk about, and to build on here. You're making such great strides. Excuse me," she said when her phone buzzed. She glanced at the screen and cut her eyes over to Quincy. "I don't have any other questions, so let's wrap this up. The senator will be in his office around six forty-five in the morning, and we'd like for you to be there by seven o'clock. Media will be arriving shortly thereafter, and we're going to try and open the time capsule around seven-ten. His statements should be wrapped up by seven-twenty; you'll have ten minutes to talk about Apex and the points you've got planned. With questions and answers, we want to have everything wrapped up by seven-thirty. Sound good?"

"It does. I appreciate the platform, Martha. It's nice to have the attention of the media *and* the senator."

She stood, then shook his hand and herded him toward the door. "You're doing good things here, Brandon. It's a pleasure to share the stage with good, non-contentious news for a change."

Quincy shook hands with the mayor in the doorway. "See you tomorrow, Brandon."

"See you, Quin."

He stood in the doorway and watched Brandon amble down the sidewalk to his car, stopping and shaking hands with the neighbors as he went. That familiarity was one of the reasons Quincy hated being in Apex. He had to look over his shoulder every second he came back home. The older he got, the more likely it was that people from his childhood had died or moved on, but he remained on constant alert for those who were acquainted with him *B.M.* Before Margaret. When he was a different man.

Ed broke into his wool gathering. "I'll check upstairs for you, sir."

Mark snickered and shared a grin with him. "Yes, that sounds like a good plan, son," Quincy said. "But I'll race you to the top."

Without waiting for Ed to react, he bounded up the steps, belaying his weariness to security and keeping his heart rate up—he had to get his steps in wherever he could while on the road. Ed matched him step-for-step and split off when they reached the landing so he could check out the rooms while Quincy stopped at the small fridge next to the antique sidebar.

Martha always had it stocked with food while they were traveling, along with a bottle of his favorite whiskey. He plopped a large square ice cube into a highball glass and poured two fingers of his favorite small batch, sipping it with relish as Ed investigated the nooks and crannies upstairs, looking for bandits and marauders, and whatever else the young man could think of. He picked up one of the small plastic containers sitting on the windowsill and handed it to the stern younger man when he was done.

"Shirley always puts together a separate package of goodies for me to send downstairs for you guys. Everything look good up here?"

Ed stood taller and nodded sharply, accepting the homemade goodies. "Yes, sir."

"Good, good. You and Mark can rest for a while.

I'm sure Martha has your rooms ready. I've got some work to do for the next couple of hours, but I'd like to go for a run around five o'clock, so we'll be back in time for dinner. Who's joining me?"

"I'll go, sir," Ed said, and headed down the stairs.

Mark rolled his eyes. "We'll both go. I'm not passing up dessert from Mrs. Womble. It smells like chocolate chess pie in here. I'll work off the calories before I take them in."

It was rare that Quincy and his team let down their guards, so he'd learned to take a breather when possible. He leaned against the sideboard, lazily sipping his whiskey, when he caught Martha's eye. She slowed her pace on the top of the stairs while he threw back the rest of his whiskey and licked his lips.

Just like that, he knew she was ready. He felt it, deep in his bones. A sly, womanly grin spread on her fuckable mouth, and she added a little sway to her hips as she stepped onto the landing. Neither of the agents would come upstairs unless he called to them, and really, what better way could he spend the afternoon than fucking his mistress? At sixty-four, his libido hadn't slowed down. He didn't even need pharmaceuticals to aid in his ardor.

He only needed this pliable, private woman with a dirty streak that matched his own.

Chapter Thirteen

"How far did you run?"

Yelping, Abby sucked in a startled breath and snatched her headphones from her ears. She hit the emergency stop button on the treadmill and faced off with Ben, fists raised in a fighting stance. "Woo! You startled me. Uh, just a 5K. Yesterday was my long run." She nodded her head toward his running shoes and shorts. "Feeling a little cooped up?"

He snorted.

"I'm sorry you're stuck on babysitting duty."

After Gladys Dixon left, he'd spent the bulk of the day texting with McGee about Lawson and researching Senator Sykes. Now he was crabby and tired of feeling caged up like a tiger in a zoo. "Nah, it's nothing. It's been years since I've done desk duty, but as much as I hate to admit it, this forced research time has been productive. If you don't mind, I'd like to get a run in on the treadmill before fixing us a quick dinner. You've got a pretty well-stocked kitchen." He grabbed an ankle to stretch his quads while they talked, then shifted to the other foot after a ten-count.

"I live out in the middle of nowhere, so it's necessary. Plus, Mrs. Gladys brings me stuff all the time. I finally convinced her that Mike and I were *not* going to marry, but she said she'd still make sure I was well-fed. I'm going to change into a bathing suit and get in some laps, and then just chill in the water. When you're done, head outside if you'd like. I'm taking advantage of these lingering hot days as long as I can."

Bathing suit? A *whoosh* of air escaped before he could clench his teeth. God almighty, he'd seen more of Abby Markham's skin the last forty-eight hours than his good intentions could handle. And it was sure as shit more than he'd seen on any woman in the last year.

"Okay," he croaked, walking stiffly toward the treadmill. He was at a full sprint by the time the door shut behind her.

Over the next half hour, he worked through the handful of facts he knew. Quincy Sykes was a private man, bordering on secretive. He didn't date—at least, not in public. He came home to Apex twice a year like clockwork and attended fundraisers and social events in DC. He accepted interviews on public radio when big legislation was coming before Congress and had made it a point to visit every military base in the United States during his four decades of public service. Hell, he'd even joined two presidents on three goodwill tours scattered around the Middle East to visit the troops overseas. On paper, he was an effective senator. For the supportive constituents who reaped the reward of Quincy's focus and attention, life was good. Coffers were full, pockets were padded, business was booming. Anyone on the opposite side of the aisle, however, felt the bite of the nation's top politician.

In all the publicity photos Ben reviewed, Sykes never smiled. He didn't necessarily scowl; he just held himself a little aloof. In most candid shots, his eye was on the crowd. He was the physical embodiment of sitting in a room with your back to the wall so no one could sneak up. Suspicion seemed to dog him, but with all the war and violence inherent to his committee's charter, he supposed paranoia was a warranted reaction.

Six miles later, Ben had a plan of attack for the next few days. First off, he needed to question Sykes about snooping around Abby's house because something was hinky. No way would that man ever be a wallflower; his ego was measured in epic proportions, so the idea of him sneaking around his old homeplace didn't jibe. The only way to get a true reaction was to catch the man off guard. He'd had forty years to perfect his public persona and was an expert at tempering his reactions. Ben needed to talk with Quincy Sykes before the press conference started, while he was distracted. The local office, where he'd be surrounded by staff and media, was the best location, preventing any possibility of retreat.

Sweat pooled beneath him on the floor by the time he started his cool-down, but he felt better knowing he had a good plan of action for the senator. He bent at the waist and grabbed his ankles, stretching his lower back and hamstrings, groaning. Knowing how to move forward with Abby was another issue. She wasn't a suspect and she wasn't really a witness, but considering her a victim didn't add up, either. If she was any of those things, the line of demarcation would be clear: no touching. No attraction, no flirting, no fraternizing. She was more like a temporary team member. Receiving the flash drive made her part of the fray.

If he was a bodyguard, she would be off-limits, too, but he wasn't guarding her body here in Apex. He was accompanying her to Washington DC, hundreds of miles away, where he'd be pursuing new angles of an investigation while she was working on her thing. Stretching his arms high overhead and pulling in a deep breath, he finally settled on friend. And that meant the sky was the limit, right?

Ugh, this waffling was getting on his nerves. She was a beautiful woman; he was a young, healthy man. He wasn't going to think it to death anymore. He was starving, so he walked through the studio into the main house to make sure the front door was locked. Diverting through the kitchen, he grabbed a couple bottles of beer and found enough things to put together a nice cheese and charcuterie platter.

Abby was treading water in the deep end and smiled when he walked out onto the slate patio. "Hold on—I'll help!" She ducked under to smooth her hair back and climbed up the ladder. Jesus, that made his heartbeat faster than when he'd been sprinting earlier. Every time he saw her, she wore less and less. He focused instead on setting up their light meal. And rather than watching her walk across the pool deck, the very picture of health and beauty and grace, he opened his bottle and took a long pull of the ice-cold beer.

Friends. They were friends, and he was a professional.

She grabbed a strawberry and bit into it. "I'm starving."

"Yep. Me, too." He copied her and grabbed a strawberry.

Abby snorted, hip to his discomfort. But bless her heart, she didn't call him out. Instead, she nibbled through the tapas with him and listened as he laid out his plan for Monday morning.

"Will you have problems getting into the office?"

"Nah. Ninety-percent of being a successful investigator is looking like I know what I'm doing." He winked when she laughed. "Well, maybe it's not that much, but it's pretty high. I'm sure there'll be lots of activity while the staff gets everything ready tomorrow, so I'll just slip in with the crew. By the time anyone notices, they won't be able to ignore me."

"That makes sense. Are you worried?" She made a little stack of Manchego cheese with a slice of chorizo and popped it in her mouth. "He'll have security, right?" She licked her fingers and tipped back the rest of her beer.

"I can be charming when I want." He didn't want her to worry about things she couldn't control. There'd been enough of that in the last few days. "Come on, I'd like to get in a few laps before I call it a day."

She grabbed a long, yellow float and dropped it into the water. "You go right ahead. I've already done half a mile, so I'll anchor myself to the ladder and get a little sun while you finish. Are you staying here tonight, or will there be another officer?"

He tilted his head to the side and watched her for a moment. "I'm staying. That okay with you?" He had a go-bag in the trunk with everything he'd need overnight.

A pretty blush crept up into her cheeks from the hollow of her throat, and he had to look away. All that beauty was too overwhelming to take in at one time.

"Yeah."

****

A beautiful, cloudless sky greeted Ben the next morning when he parked and walked up to the small historic brick bungalow housing the local office for

Senator Sykes. He took a moment to admire the Masonite siding that looked to be original to the house. All of the old homes along this stretch of the Main Street corridor were built in the mid-nineteen-twenties, and they'd been well-maintained or renovated over the last hundred years, so it was no surprise Sykes had chosen one of the tried and true emblems of his hometown for his own little fiefdom. How could he truly represent his vintage hometown from a tract house in a packed neighborhood or a shop in a strip mall?

Ben straightened his navy-blue bow tie and adjusted the sleeves of his classic blue and white seersucker blazer as the hustle and bustle of press conference preparation buzzed on the other side of the door. It was going to be hotter than the hinges of hell in another couple of hours, but the breezy mid-eighties of the morning felt comfortable.

A few people stopped on a dime when he knocked on the door, watching him with irritation as he interrupted the flow of the day. He fought the urge to stop and fix his hair. He hated being in reporters' cross hairs and recognized a popular anchor from the largest local affiliate checking him out, like she was trying to figure out his importance to the day's events.

An attractive, sharply dressed woman who looked to be anywhere between thirty-five and forty-five answered the door, looking down her nose at him even though he towered over her by a good foot. "I'm sorry, sir, but the senator doesn't have office hours until eight o'clock." She moved to close the door, but he stuck his size twelve boot in the void, stopping it in its track.

"I'm not here for that, ma'am. I'm Detective Ben Owens from the Apex Police Department. I have a couple of questions for Senator Sykes." He held up his badge case which showed the tin and photo creds. He even hit her with his "good old boy" smile…the one he reserved when he wanted to charm old ladies—or calm nervous witnesses.

It didn't work for this one. She glared and looked back over her shoulder. The shrewd reporter must've noticed the quick flash of his badge because she was making her way toward them. Inwardly he high-fived himself; outwardly, he tilted his head toward the media and said, "I just need a couple minutes of his time. How about if we head back to his private office?"

The woman frowned, but stepped aside to let him in. "I'm Martha Scott, the senator's executive assistant. Can you tell me what this is about while we're walking?"

She moved briskly through a group of young aides who busied themselves by setting up a podium with a tablecloth and an easel with an elaborate portrait of the Sykes family. They were staging a homespun, apple-pie scenario that would hit the senator's constituents like a two-by-four to the forehead. Ben stopped to check out a small, birdlike man with ruddy cheeks and thinning jet-black hair who made a business of dusting the weathered time capsule. The *object du jour* rested on an ornately carved podium, beside a vase of pink peonies.

Martha followed his line of sight and smiled. "Margaret, the senator's deceased wife, favored peonies."

He nodded. They'd been his mother's favorite, too.

She turned and led him through the foyer and a small, fussy sitting room, where they stopped at a closed door. It was probably a bedroom when the house served as someone's home but now appeared to serve as the main office. Martha knocked sharply and cracked the door, poking her head inside. "Senator—you have a visitor."

A muted conversation came through the door and then Martha squeezed through, closing it behind her. "Just a moment, Detective Owens. I'll be right back."

He shrugged and stuck his hands in his pockets. She couldn't see him, so he didn't say anything. With a house full of reporters and the mayor, and whoever else cared about seeing what Sykes had buried nearly forty years ago, he wasn't worried about anyone slipping out the back.

After a minute, Martha opened the door and invited Ben inside. A young woman wearing a black apron with brushes tucked into pockets smiled and excused herself. The senator wore a crisp white shirt with tissue paper tucked in the neckline; his slate gray jacket was folded over the back of his chair. He stood and shook hands with Ben.

"Officer Owens, what can I do for you?" He gave him a shit-eating grin combined with a calculated wink. "Steven's talked about you. It's a pleasure to finally meet you."

Ben smiled and shook his hand and pulled out his phone. "Actually, sir, it's Detective."

"Oh, my. Apologies for the slip…my mind is focusing on the box out there. Between you and me, it's probably full of love letters I exchanged with my Maggie, and some baby things of Steven's. I was sedated in the initial days after the fire, and then in a haze for weeks afterward…I just don't remember what's in here." He clasped Ben's shoulder and gave it a companionable squeeze, shaking his head sadly.

"It's okay, sir." It was hard to resist the urge to roll his eyes. "Sorry to interrupt, but I have a couple questions that won't take long." He unlocked his phone and pulled up the Lawson folder in his photos. As he turned the screen around, the senator said, "Oh, please, Detective. Call me Quincy."

Ben smiled. "Thank you. Quincy."

"Now, what can I do for you? I've got to let Samantha back in to get this hair under control so I can face the reporters. It was windblown when I arrived, but by the time she's done, it'll have enough hairspray for a cat-five hurricane. It's a rarity nowadays when I get to initiate contact with them, and to tell you the truth, I'm rather excited to face them with something lighthearted."

"Well, sir—ah, Quincy—someone got a couple photos of you looking over the fence at your old homestead about two months ago. We figured you were checking out where the new homeowner had found the time capsule, but I need to make sure everything jived on your end." He held the phone out of Quincy's reach and used his finger to flip through the half-dozen images, with no doubt who was looking over the fence.

He didn't flinch or blush or look even remotely ashamed or alarmed. He clucked his tongue and shook his head abashedly. Very much for show, Ben thought, because Martha straightened across the room, shifting her gaze to the parking lot outside and squeezing her fists at her sides. Very interesting.

"You caught me, Ben," he said, in an *"aw, shucks, it's just us good ol' boys"* kind of way. "When I heard about the box or, rather, the time capsule, it brought so many memories to the forefront. It's like my sweet Maggie was calling me home. I haven't been back since we sold it. I was so happy to hear someone bought and renovated it. I think Ms. Markham's done a wonderful job with the old place."

Shazam!

Ben nodded, looking earnest while telegraphing an *I feel your pain* look as best he could. "I understand, sir. It must be difficult to revisit such a traumatic setting."

Sighing, Quincy leaned a hip against the desk, crossing his arms across his chest. He had maintained a strong, streamlined physique through the years and constantly made ridiculous lists like Washington's Most Eligible Senator. "After the fire, I never stepped foot in the house again. I was in the hospital for nearly a week, in and out of consciousness."

He flexed his right hand and looked down at his forearm, likely visualizing the injuries as they once were. "When they moved me to a rehab facility, Steven was with me. Something had to be done about the house, decisions about what should stay, what should go. It was uninhabitable in those early weeks following the fire. I asked Maggie's brother to clean out whatever heirlooms he wanted from their side of the family, and box up her personal things for me. He was a rock, which was remarkable since he'd spent most of his youth in and out of a mental health facility in the town of Buntner. But he could only handle so much, too. Someone from the recovery company working the scene in the following days boxed up everything else."

He looked genuinely haunted for a moment, offering a glimpse to the man behind the curtain, who was always on. "Really, I've got no idea what's in the box because when I got out of rehab, I moved Steven and I into the little bungalow he and Jennifer live in now. I went back one time to say goodbye to Margaret, and to bury the damned box."

"Your grief is understandable," Ben said, torn between pushing Quincy for a reaction and backing off because of the other man's palpable grief. "Next time, though, just ring the doorbell and introduce yourself. I'm certain the homeowner would let you inside. I mean, it's not like you're some random man walking around. You've got security with you all the time, right? That would be as identifiable as my badge." He grinned, sharing an inside secret with the older man. One only recognized by people with a modicum of power over another.

Quincy sighed and stood. "You're right. I hope I didn't scare the poor girl. I'll have Ed drive us by on the way out tonight to apologize for trespassing. Maybe she'll let us have a look around inside. I think she's added a barn on the back."

Ben gave himself a mental high five. "Actually, these photos came from Ms. Markham's security system because she wasn't home at the time of your little visit. Since the department took the line she'd been filing false reports, we didn't put two and two together. But after the alarm triggered again last weekend, and she was home for that one, we looked at her security footage. And we found the proof that you'd been out there at some point."

Martha made a strangled sound and walked briskly through the door, holding the phone to her ear to cover the reaction on her face. But Ben saw it. She was pissed all right. Her face lost all color at the mention of security footage and, rather than snapping at the men, left the room. The senator was dead meat.

Showing no reaction, Quincy shrugged. "I just heard someone say we're live in sixty seconds, Ben, so I've gotta hustle. I'll look for you at the station when I stop by to see Steven later. I appreciate your discretion in coming here to question me. Perception is so goddamned important to those reporters out there. I tell ya, I don't mind shaking hands and kissing babies when I'm out for legislative functions or in my office on The Hill, but just running around town or to the grocery store? I wish they'd leave me alone and let me relax in my jogging shorts and unshaven face."

Ben laughed and shook his hand again. "I can't even imagine, Quincy. Thanks for your time. And don't forget…next time just ring the doorbell."

"Ha, right you are."

Ben grinned and made his way to the front door, using his peripheral vision to monitor Martha's reaction. Either she was a great actress, or she honestly had no idea her boss had come back to Apex to snoop around. Either way, she now stood pouting in the corner, working overtime on deep breathing exercises to control a temper tantrum. He wondered if she was the reason Quincy had remained a bachelor. She was timeless in her beauty, though Ben was confident she fell somewhere between his own thirty-five years and Quincy's sixty. She was pissed.

And pissed-off people make mistakes…eventually.

****

Rene Morgan, lead anchor for Channel Five news, headed him off at the door. After bumping against Ben, managing to rub a pair of conspicuous breasts against his sternum, she squeaked, “Oh!” She lowered her chin and looked up at him through her lashes, like a nineteen-forties siren in a film noir detective movie. “Excuse me, Detective.”

He opened the door and stepped aside. “No problem, ma’am.”

She held onto his forearm for balance as she descended the stairs and gave him a squeeze, the kind that made his molars grind. Sexual harassment went both ways. An unwanted touch was an unwanted touch.

“You’re either too early for the press conference, or too late for coffee,” she said, glancing over his shoulder at the office foyer. Her expression said, tell me everything, but he had no intention of divulging why he’d been talking with Quincy Sykes. She was fishing for information and doing a bad job of masking her intentions. He tugged free of her grasp and proceeded to his car.

He set a course for the French Café a few blocks away and called the chief who answered on the first ring. “Randolph.” His voice was brisk, the stress of the situation evident.

“Hey, Chief, I’ve got some updates,” Ben said without preamble. “I just finished with Quincy Sykes. I baited him with our *assumption* that he was just trying to get a look at where the time capsule had been found, and he jumped right on it.”

“That’s not surprising. Whatever his reason for being there, he’s not stupid.”

“No, sir, he’s not. He mentioned Abby by name, unprompted, and called her Miss Markham.”

The sound of the chief’s chair creaking came through the phone line, like maybe he was sitting up straighter. “That’s bad.”

“Yeah. Everything about the encounter raised my hackles. He spoke a bit about the fire, though I know it was mainly because I questioned him about the actual house. Everything he shared was basically stuff I could get from his online biography. One thing gave me pause though—he mentioned asking his brother-in-law to help sort things out with the house while he was in the hospital.”

“We haven’t turned up anything about a brother-in-law. Steven is the only family mentioned,” Randolph said. “Did Quincy give you a name?”

“No sir, but he said something about Margaret’s brother being in trouble most of his life and having been in and out of a mental institution in Buntner. I’ll work on that lead later today. I’m heading to my place to pack. Unless you want me to stick around here to work on Jason Lawson’s murder, I think I need to stick with Abby in DC.”

“Agreed,” said Randolph. “You know, at first I figured you could just chauffeur her there, then head right back, but the fact Sykes knows her name gives me pause. As does the fact he jumped right on your prompt.”

Ben checked the rearview mirror and changed lanes so he could turn into the parking lot of the restaurant. He was going to grab a couple homemade chocolate croissants, and some of the little lilac macarons he felt Abby would probably like. They were sweet and delicate, and packed a punch, like her.

“He acts like a man’s man, know what I mean? Like he and I are members of the same club because I’ve got a badge and he’s got a security detail. When I mentioned he should ring the doorbell next time he wants to look in someone's back yard, he said he'd have his detail drive him by Abby's house this afternoon so he could apologize. I never confirmed her name, and I sure as hell never told him I've been staying with her. I don't want him to see me there, but I don't want her to be there by herself if or when he chooses to show up."

"Me, neither," Randolph said. "Does she have a garage?"

"Yes, sir."

"Good. Park your car in it and stay out of sight during his visit—if he visits. But listen closely. See what her feelings about him may be. Sometimes civilians, and women in particular, pick up on different vibes than we do. Could be he's just nostalgic, and the box is stirring up memories."

Ben scoffed. "Yeah. And could be he's a serial killer looking for single women living out in the middle of nowhere." His mom always said Ted Bundy was a babe. It was how he was such a successful predator. Quincy Sykes wasn't getting near Abby, regardless of the reasons behind his interest in her house.

"Son, that's so true it's not funny. There's no need for you to run by the station today. Check in with me when you get to DC; I'd like details on your hotel and schedule. I know Miss Markham's got everything planned already, so let's try not to get in her way."

"Okay, Chief. Keep me posted on Lawson's case."

Chapter Fourteen

A box truck parked in Abby's driveway looked close to bursting when Ben pulled in behind it a little after noon. Garment bars, running the length of the truck bed, were packed with fluffy tutus, elaborately detailed jackets and long, skinny tights. Two big, burly men kept busy tightening rods and strapping boxes into place. Despite their size and bulk, neither looked out of place in the middle of all the frou-frou.

Abby met him on the other side of the door, both hands filled with ballet slippers colored as brightly as some of the tights already in the truck. As he passed through the entryway, she stood on tiptoe to give him a quick peck on the cheek before bounding past him and down the steps.

Stunned, he watched one of the men grab her by the waist to heft her into the back of the truck. Her laughing response carried on the breeze. Instead of going inside the house, he sat on one of the rocking chairs to watch the activity. The loading was well-choreographed, with Abby and the two men moving in a groove that broadcast an easy familiarity with one another. Ben figured staying out of the way was the best help he could offer.

Once the packing was finished, the three headed back onto the porch. Ben came out of his chair to open the door for Abby who introduced each man as they passed. “This is Bruno.” He was about six and a half feet tall, with more freckles dotting his pale complexion than hair on his bald head and looked like he could bend steel bars with his bare hands. “He’s been with the Capital Ballet Company since I started working with them. About ten years, right Bru?”

Bruno shook Ben’s hand. “Yep. You hadn’t yet gone to the Sorbonne.” He gave her a half hug and headed into the kitchen.

“I was still dancing then,” she interjected. “And Pierre here, is the technical director. He designs the lighting schematics.” Pierre was shorter than Bruno by an inch or two, and had a deep, mahogany complexion. He, too, looked like he could bend steel bars, until he grinned and deep dimples split his cheeks.

After shaking hands, Ben pointed to the truck. “You guys always on pickup duty?”

“Only when we’re coming here,” Bruno said. “My brother lives in Chapel Hill, so we bring the truck down a day or two before and spend the night with him.”

They followed Abby like a line of ducks into the kitchen. She’d made sandwiches for the guys and was in the process of putting them into a cooler. “Bring those over, Pierre.” She nodded toward the two bottles of blueberry-flavored carbonated water on the kitchen table.

Bruno walked into the kitchen from the studio hallway. “I ran through the studio, and I think we got it all. Sarah said you were bringing your new boyfriend with you, so I’m guessing you won’t be having dinner with the crew tonight—ooh! Blueberry fizzy water!” He bounced on his feet, bringing an eye-roll from Pierre.

Abby snorted. “I don’t know if we’ll call him my *boyfriend* yet, but he is certainly my *man* friend. And he is coming with me.” She winked at Ben, who winced at the double entendre. “Sarah’s the director of the ballet, by the way.”

He cleared his throat. “It’s fine with me if we have dinner with the crew.”

She added a tin of brownies and chocolate chip cookies to the supply. “I figured, but it’s getting close to one o’clock and I’ve still got to pack my stuff. I’d rather get us checked in and settled, if that’s all right. Will you tell Sarah we’ll join tomorrow’s crew dinner instead?”

Pierre grabbed the hefty cooler with one arm and hugged Abby with the other. He shook hands with Ben on the way to the door, and waited for Bruno, who pulled her into a big bear hug and kissed the top of her head. “You know anything’s fine with us. She’ll be excited to see you in the morning.”

Ben stayed in the kitchen while she walked the men out to the truck, using the time alone to read through e-mails on his phone. There was nothing new on the Lawson investigation and no other fires to put out, so he started pulling sandwich makings from the fridge.

“I already made sandwiches for us,” Abby said when she walked back in. “They’re on the top shelf.”

“Excellent. I’m starving.” He shifted gears and grabbed the sandwiches and a pitcher of water and met her at the table.

“If you want mayonnaise or cheese, grab some before you sit down. I don’t eat either, so I made your sandwich like mine.”

"Honey, I can eat anything." He tucked into his sandwich while she put fruit and snacks into a small cooler.

"I'm going to have mine on the road, I think. When you finish, will you make sure the back gate is locked and then lock up the studio? I can check it when I get back down, but I'm afraid of forgetting. I don't use that fence often, and it's had a lot of traffic lately with all the officers responding to the silent alarms."

"Understood," he said. "We're in no rush and I want you to make sure you don't forget anything. Lots of weird things have happened around you over the last couple of days, so it's natural for your routine to be a bit off kilter. Since you don't have a dinner meeting tonight, we can leave whenever you'd like."

He'd been checking the fence for days now, so this last round went quick. Nothing had changed, no new footprints or rustled up leaves, which meant that Abby's peeping senator hadn't been back since Saturday. Ben returned through the rear studio door, locked and dead-bolted it, and was walking through the kitchen when the doorbell rang.

He dropped into a low crouch before he remembered you couldn't see the kitchen from the front porch windows, though he still had to prevent Abby from answering the door. Moving through the living room on his hands and knees slowed him down, but when he got to the staircase he scrambled up to the landing, then sprinted into her room. Deep male voices rose up from the porch, echoing through the house and amplifying his tension.

With one hand over her mouth, Abby stood next to the bed, a T-shirt dangling from her fingers. Her eyes, wide with shock, betrayed any reaction to fear.

He reached her in three strides, pulled her into his arms, and spoke close to her ear. “It’s Senator Sykes and his security detail. You don’t have to answer the door if you don’t want.”

With one blink of her eyes, he saw the instant she had herself back under control. “God, no. I don’t want to see him right now. What if I blurt out something important? No—let’s just pretend we’re not here.” Her body still trembled, though it seemed to be more from adrenaline than fear. “I dropped off his property, so there’s nothing we need to talk about.”

He gave her shoulder a light squeeze. “I forgot to tell you, he mentioned this morning he’d stop by to introduce himself and apologize for scaring you.”

“What?” She stepped back, anger painting her face. “You told him I was *scared*? I didn’t even know it was him until McGee showed me the pictures.”

“Hey, it’s not what you’re thinking.” He held up his hands in apology. “Remember I mentioned that I was going to ask him about the photos? I mean, there’s no denying he was looking into your backyard. I played dumb and told him it would have been better had he just rung the doorbell and ask to check out the spot where you’d found the time capsule.”

Stepping away, she swung her arm in a wide arc. “Under the circumstances, of course it would have.”

“I know. When I pointed out sneaking around was scary, Quincy admitted he hadn’t considered that.” He sat on the edge of the bed while she resumed packing. Two huge suitcases lay open on her king-size bed. A large duffel filled with shoes ranging from spiked heels to tennis shoes sat on the floor between his feet.

"There's one more thing."

She wrapped a slinky-looking evening gown in a large garment bag while an image of how she would look donning that sexy dress popped into his head and gave him a momentary jolt. She stopped folding to look over her shoulder. "What?"

"Um." He blinked and rubbed his eyes. "Well, he knows your name."

"Of course he knows my name. I gave them my contact information when I dropped off the time capsule."

Feeling ridiculous, he sighed. "Well, damn. It set off alarm bells in my head when he said, 'Miss Markham's done a great job with the house.'"

"That part *is* weird," she said, "because I never gave him pictures of the house. The only way he would've known about any changes is if he was here…so I guess he did kind of give himself away. I still don't want to see him. You're right about the coincidences with Officer Lawson and these pictures. I'm too spooked to deal with him right now. I have to keep my head in the game."

"Nothing's going to happen while I'm with you. You know that, right?" He willed her to believe him. After a moment, she nodded and zipped up the bags.

She stepped into the space between his knees and rested her hands on his chest. "I feel awful you got stuck with this stupid babysitting assignment. I know you'd rather be out looking for Lawson's killer."

He took a deep breath and placed his hands over hers. "Full disclosure—at first, I was a little pissed. But my spidey-sense is kicking in with Sykes. I think there's something there, and you need someone to keep an eye on the situation. Chief Randolph and I can work remotely if need be, and I've got everything I need to do some research on Sykes. While you're working with the ballet during the day, I'm going to reach out to Mike Dixon for support. The chief is going to allow me to read him in on the situation. Being in the District will actually work to our advantage."

Chapter Fifteen

"Well, boys, it looks like nobody's home," Sykes said. "But before we head back, I'd like to do a little adventuring in my old neck of the woods. We're only about half a mile to the White Oak Creek entrance for Lake Jordan, and I think there's a marina where I can rent a little bass boat. Whaddaya say—want in some sightseeing before we hit the road? Shake out the cobwebs?"

Ed Parker shifted on his feet, but before he could say no, Quincy held up his hand to cut him off. "Actually, Mark, I know you don't do well with the humidity, and since you're not chomping at the bit for a ride, I'd love a little bit of *me time*. Let's rent the boat for an hour—or two, depending on what their process is—and you can grab a bite of lunch at the Lake Café. I'll just tool around my old cove for a bit, and we can call it a day."

Dazzling them with the usual good old boy smile and an "aw, shucks" lift of the eyebrow, he knew he had them. He stepped off Abby Markham's porch and headed back to the car. "It's a workday, guys. There's nobody out on the lake today. Nobody knows we're here. You're seeing me off, and I'll re-dock here at the marina. I'll be fine."

Quincy knew his men well. Mark hated being in North Carolina. He was a northerner through-and-through and couldn't bear the southern heat and humidity. Ed was younger and newer, but when Mark balked and then took the alternate lunch option, Ed went with Plan B like a champ. That boy was hungry all the time.

Quincy sat in the backseat and waited for Mark to come around to his way of thinking. They were backing out onto the highway when the agent glared at him through the rearview mirror. "Sounds good, sir."

Half an hour later, Quincy was in his workout gear and pushing away from the bank. Mark and Ed were happily ensconced at the Lake Café and were bound to have already gotten their chicken and dumplings. He plastered an amicable smile on his face and looked up to the sun every now and then, the very picture of bliss and enjoyment. Anyone watching would assume he was just an old man relaxing on the lake. On the off chance someone actually recognized him, they'd see a stressed-out senator puttering over the lake his family had made possible.

Inside he seethed. How dare that bitch keep the second box? He hated the idea of someone else pulling his strings. Until he had a direct confrontation with her, gauging her reaction to a battery of questions, he'd worry about the fucking birth certificate he'd buried with the box. Fucking Terrence. His brother-in-law had never been anything but a thorn in his side. Hadn't he told him to take care of things?

The land surrounding the lake was beautiful. Fishermen pulled twenty-pound bass from the waters on a regular basis. The millions of dollars that brought recreational opportunities to a once-totally-agrarian state all came back to his making it possible. *Him.*

The light haze from earlier in the day had burned off hours ago, and now it was just oppressive. A triple-digit day like this would be hot way after the sun went down. Washington could get hot, but it was nowhere near as humid as this part of North Carolina. He made steady progress around the big peninsula that separated the rear approach to Abby Markham's home from the main body of water. As he entered the mouth of the deep-water cove, he turned off the outboard motor and switched to a paddle so he wouldn't make so much noise.

After a few strokes, he rested the paddle across his lap and drifted forward, listening for evidence of anyone else in the area. He drifted so slowly there was no wake to give him away, and he was so quiet the din of tree frogs and cicadas gave a synchronized pause but lapsed back into their deafening music a moment later. A great blue heron flew close to the bow of his boat, landing in a batch of tall reeds off the starboard side. He forced his breath to steady and after a few minutes, confirmed he was alone. Straight ahead, a lone dock jutted out into the shallows, breaking the perfect arc of nature. He paddled to it and climbed the stairs, tying the bow line to one of the cleats along the edge.

When no one came to greet him, he walked to the back of the fence. "Hello—is anybody home?" He held his hands out wide, palms facing the front, trying to appear non-threatening. "I got turned around in the lake and was so thrilled to find a dock…any chance you could help with directions?" He knocked on the gate, then backed up two big steps to wait. Judging from the photos the detective had showed him, the surveillance cameras didn't reach this far back on the property.

Nothing. No one was home. He'd learned the hard way she had an alarm and didn't intend to trip it today. But just as a general "fuck you," he picked up a rock and scraped it along the fence as he walked, leaving a long gouge in his wake. He hurried back to the boat, grabbed the metal detector, then made a sweep around the back of the fence. He'd already been gone for fifty minutes, so he had to hurry.

The house had originally been built in the mid-eighteen-hundreds and once flanked Oak Creek. When the Army Corps of Engineers bought the land from him in the seventies, they'd damned the creek that eventually led to the creation of Lake Jordan. Because of the way the land perked, most of the lake's volume had formed more toward the north and west. The old homestead had only needed to be relocated about a hundred yards straight forward. There had been little deviation from the left to the right, so theoretically not too much should have shifted between the lake's banks and the back side of the house in the last forty years…unless through human intervention and a troublesome woman named Abby Markham.

Setting up a grid layout in his head, he worked methodically from the fence line to the dock, from the left corner of the fence to the right, trying to imagine how the soil may have shifted and the original placement of the house. Nothing showed up but a handful of nails and construction debris, half a mason jar of moonshine or some other foul-smelling alcohol, and a crumpled pack of cigarettes with a matchbook. It looked like the construction crew had enjoyed a view of the lake during break times.

He checked his watch—that back sweep had taken

twenty minutes—then picked up the construction debris and followed the curve of the bank from the dock to the north, toward the woods. Again, nothing. Dejected and pissed, he followed the bank back to the dock, but the sound of gravel crunching beneath tires almost gave him a heart attack.

"Shit!" he hissed, turning to run as fast as he could back to the boat.

He threw the metal detector into the hull, untied the line and jumped in. His left foot slipped off the side and splashed in the lake, but he started paddling with his foot trailing in the water. Stupid, because that was the perfect way to get bitten by one of the copperheads that liked to drift in the shallows. As soon as he gained momentum, he pulled in his leg and re-situated his hips in the seat. Preparing his little parting gift for Markham slowed him down some, but as soon as he lobbed it, he focused on paddling. Voices trailed behind him as he increased the distance from the old homeplace. He turned on the motor as soon as the banks of the cove opened up and finally took a deep breath.

"She's got the box," he assured himself. There was no other explanation. *Shit*.

Abby Markham would not care for the retrieval process.

Chapter Sixteen

By Tuesday morning, three days after Lawson's murder, the Apex Police Department still buzzed. Even though shifts started and ended at their usual times, sworn and civilian staff made serious efforts to arrive early and stay late. It was like the building took a collective breath, holding it until it was turning blue in the face. Tension made the entire force cranky; the longer it took to bring in viable clues, the more volatile the situation became.

Steve Sykes slunk into the station, dreading another day. With Apex being a small community, it was common knowledge he and Jason had grown up together, that their wives and children were best friends. Both families spent holidays together. Hell, they even vacationed together each summer. The stress of the situation weighed heavily upon his shoulders—and it showed in his body language and pronounced dark smudges beneath his hollow eyes. To make matters worse, once the main door to the building shut behind him, all noise and activity halted.

Everyone looked at him. He felt their stares aimed at his back, his head. He took a deep, shuddering breath and forged ahead. He was halfway to the bullpen when Chief Randolph called his name. And just like that, activity in the station resumed as he veered off to the right.

"Close the door, son," Randolph said. "Come in and sit down."

Steve would've rather stayed on his feet, but he didn't feel like bucking the system today. He shrugged off the small backpack that contained his street clothes and laid it over his lap when he sat. He was so fucking tired. Jennifer had stayed with Sally Lawson the last three nights to help with the kids and keep up with the usual house routines. Both sets of kids were jacked up on adrenaline and trying to make heads or tails of the new normal. Between the investigation and helping Sally clear out the backyard of equipment and timber, Steve found himself burning the candle at both ends.

Randolph let him sit in silence for a few minutes. He was thankful for the small respite. Everywhere he went, people whispered under their breaths and watched him for…who knew. He wasn't suicidal; he was processing the death of his best friend and partner. He was tired of the whispering. He was tired of the casseroles people brought over. He was tired of the renewed episodes of profound grief that came with words and gestures of comfort.

"I meant it when I said to take the week off, Steve," Chief Randolph said in a gentle but determined voice. "We've got the investigation covered."

"Sir, if it's all the same to you, I'd rather be here. I've done everything I can for Sally…we never got the deck finished, but it's cleaned out and should be ready for her to receive guests." He took a deep breath. "Staying home is driving me crazy."

Randolph nodded. "All right. We've got three detectives working the investigation angle, but what I really need is someone to shake out the bushes.

Everyone on Lawson's beat liked him. None of the kids at the high school made complaints. Hell, even the sparse gang activity y'all have been monitoring never pointed to any retaliation or violence toward him."

Steve looked down at his hands and struggled to swallow. It was true; everyone liked Jason. He'd been the golden boy, the high school football quarterback who married the head cheerleader. But he'd always had the gift of making a connection with the poorest, roughest, most dangerous people in town.

"I'd like you to start at the school—work with the vice principals responsible for behavior and look into any kids Lawson might've been watching. Then you can focus on the Highway 64 corridor. I know you'd been out to Abby Markham's place for the silent alarms, but she's less than a mile away from where Jason was shot. There are half a dozen houses that flank hers. Any one of those homeowners might have observed something. The proximity of those properties to the crime scene might yield some results."

Steve took a small notebook from his uniform pocket to make notes. "School or highway first?"

"It's up to you. The state police have been combing the murder scene since Saturday, but some folks weren't at home when the troopers stopped for interviews. I don't think anything will come from the high school, but it's a good spot to check out."

"I think I'll knock out the school this morning, focus on the neighbors this afternoon."

"Good, good. Take Fletcher with you. We want to do everything by the book with this, and that means everyone works in pairs."

On most days, Scott Fletcher could talk the ears off

a saint, but today, blessedly, he was quiet. Like he sensed Steve wasn't up for idle chit-chat. They'd spoken with both vice principals and made quick work of checking the school off the list. As expected, none of the kids had any issues with Lawson. Even though Apex had been named the number one town in America, it was still a small community and the high school had been lucky to skip much of the gang activity plaguing the surrounding communities for the last five years. Lawson had always treated the kids like adults, so even the most troubled of the lot were able to find common ground with him.

They were fortunate to hit the houses along Highway 64 at lunchtime, so two of the homeowners were available to talk. The Saunders family land abutted the wildlife preserve where Jason was killed. Yes, they'd been home on Saturday morning; no, they hadn't noticed anything out of the ordinary. They were old and not likely able to overpower a young, strong police officer. Plus, they'd been asleep and hadn't even been aware a murder had occurred, so they were off the list. The Andrews family lived on a dozen acres across the highway from the sanctuary. Sam Andrews was the Apex town manager, but he'd been out on his tractor Saturday morning. His usual practice was to wear headphones, making him unable to hear anything. His wife and their two daughters were visiting family on the coast, so they were off the list as well.

Abby Markham's place was next door to the Andrews. Scott eased the cruiser into the driveway and parked next to a vintage black muscle car. He whistled and looked at it longingly through the windshield. "That's a thing of beauty." His wife had just delivered their third child, and insisted they sell Scott's roadster so they could trade it in for a minivan. Everyone in the department knew how much it broke Scott's heart to keep the new mother happy and applauded him for it.

"Look away, man," Steve said with a clap on his shoulder. "Staring at it'll only break your heart."

As he approached the front porch, Steve hesitated. He'd been out to the Markham place five times now, between the false alarms, taking molds of the shoe prints, now this. He dreaded seeing her again—didn't want to let on that it was his dad who was looking over her fence—but it was unavoidable. Hell, she had no idea who'd done the peeping. Unless she mentioned it to him, he'd play dumb.

The door opened, and a large man stepped out before he could knock. Steve moved back and tipped the bill of his cap. "Afternoon, sir. I'm Officer Steven Sykes, Apex PD. Is Abby Markham home? We've got some questions about an event over the weekend."

The guy seemed unruffled by two police officers showing up out of the blue. It was kind of admirable, really, because out in this neck of the woods with so many preppers living on substantial acreage, most folks were wary of the law. But this guy? He stood right at six feet tall, broad shouldered, and dressed in an expensive-looking suit. A woman's voice drifted toward him from somewhere inside the house; Steve saw her trying to look around the guy's shoulder.

The man gave an exasperated sigh, stepping to the side and further blocking Steve's view. "No, Officer, she's not. I'm Special Agent Michael Dixon." He grabbed the badge from his breast pocket. "Maybe I can help you."

The FBI? Oh, shit!

Silent alarms. His father's fucking voyeuristic habits. Jason's death. Sweat broke out on Steve's brow while he struggled to get his shit together. Good thing for Fletcher who stepped up and saved the day. He shook Mike's hand. "Nice to meet you, Agent Dixon. I'm Officer Scott Fletcher. We're investigating the murder of an officer on Saturday morning. Jason Lawson was killed just down the way, on the road leading to the wildlife refuge. We were wondering if Ms. Markham might have seen or heard anything."

Steve took a deep breath and cleared his throat. "What's your relationship with Miss Markham? Are you two in a romantic relationship?"

Dixon turned his full attention on him, glaring. "That's none of your bus—"

"You watch your manners, Mike," the older woman snapped, breaking free from the blockade of his body and making her way onto the porch. "No, young man, Abby is not dating my sweet Peanut. He's here to help me."

"Mom!"

While Fletcher barked out a laugh, Steve nearly choked, even felt a little sorry for the Fed. Dixon easily outweighed his mother by a hundred pounds, but she still thought of him as her "peanut." Worse yet, she called him that in front of *strangers*.

"And you are?" prompted Fletcher.

"Gladys Dixon. I work with Abby and Michael is my son."

She shook the hands of both officers, then crossed her arms across her chest. Steve smiled because she was about a foot shorter than her son and mirrored his same stance. In truth, the intimidation factor didn't fall far from her tree. Whereas the clean-cut Dixon wore a snazzy dark suit, his mother walked on the wild side. Her purple yoga pants and gray top clashed with her bright pink running shoes. The whole getup was topped off with a tie-dyed cape thing, and crazy eyeglasses from back in the 1950s.

He scribbled something in his notepad. "Dixon…is that any relation to Chief Stewart Dixon?"

"Stu is my husband. Chief Randolph took his place when he retired ten years ago."

"That's right," said Fletcher. He shook her hand again, much less rigid than a moment ago. "Wow, Chief Dixon's a legend." No wonder she wasn't intimidated. She'd have to chew nails to hold her own with such strong men in her household.

She beamed, which brought out a smile on her son. "What made you go with the Feds instead of something local?" Scott asked.

"Nothing in particular. I joined the marines when I graduated from high school and had a couple of embassy postings overseas. Traveled the world. I liked the diplomacy piece of it rather than the politics. After my eight years were up, I enrolled in the academy and never looked back."

"That's cool," Scott said, still making notes. He glanced at Steve but kept on talking. "Were either of you here on Saturday?"

Mike shook his head again and looked at his mom. "No, but when Stu and I came by on Sunday afternoon, she and Ben were just finishing lunch."

Steve's head snapped up. "Ben Owens?"

Gladys wrapped her arm around her son's waist

and leaned into him. She looked tired, so Steve gave his partner an elbow nudge, signaling him to wrap it up. "Yes, dear," Mrs. Dixon said. "What a nice boy that Ben is. He's like Mike—went into the FBI rather than following in the footsteps of their fathers with the local police force. Well, Ben works with you now, of course, but he started out with Mike."

"Did you two work together?" Fletcher asked.

Steve glared at his partner. Scott had to stop asking stupid questions that had nothing to with the investigation. He didn't have time to shoot the breeze, but his brain shut down right after he learned the man in front of him was with the Feds—and that Ben Owens wasn't here the other day for strictly business. He had some sort of *thing* going with Abby Markham.

"We went through the Academy together," Mike Dixon said. "Ben was assigned to the LA office; my posting was in DC. Are you guys almost done? We need to wrap this up."

"Sorry to hold you up, ma'am. One last thing—do you know when Miss Markham will be back?" Scott asked. "We'd love to talk to her."

"She and Ben headed for DC yesterday," Mike said. "She's scheduled to be there for the next week though they may decide to extend their stay."

Steve swallowed convulsively; his eyes watered as he fought the urge to vomit. Mrs. Dixon and Scott Fletcher scattered, but the big Fed grabbed him by the shoulder to help him remain standing. His ears rang like fire alarms; dark spots swam in front of his eyes. Worst of all, his voice still wouldn't work.

"You okay, man?" Mike applied enough pressure to urge him down into a porch rocking chair. "Mom, run get him a glass of water."

Steve covered his face with his hands and used the moment to get a hold on his emotions. *Oh God, oh God.* Dixon was on to his dad. A cold glass was pressed into his hand, amplified by Mrs. Dixon's cool hand as she laid a wet washcloth across the back of his neck. That made him even more shaky. His mom had died when he was an infant, and his father was always the farthest thing from a caregiver. It was all too much, and he was almost at a breaking point.

He finally found his voice. "Sorry about that. Think I must've had a bad bird this morning." He took a long drink of water and gave them a weak smile.

Fletcher smiled at Mrs. Dixon and thanked her for the kindness. "Officer Lawson is—uh, was—Steve's best friend. Their families are close."

Mike's shoulders dropped, and his mom gasped. "Oh, dear. I'm so sorry to hear that. I'll have Abby call you, if that helps. Can you interview her over the phone?"

"Yes, ma'am," Fletcher said. "We'll make that work. Thanks for the water. We'll be heading out now. Give our regards to Chief Dixon." He tapped Steve on the shoulder, and they walked out to the cruiser.

Mike stayed on the porch while they backed out, watching them leave and telegraphing doubt through the air. There was nothing Steve could do about his erratic behavior now, but if he could undo the last ten minutes, he would. Because as soon as the cruiser turned onto the highway, he saw Mike Dixon walking toward the back yard.

****

Chief Randolph was in the bullpen when they got

back to the station, adding new details on the white board. He turned and nodded, then finished what he was writing. Fletcher headed to the john, but Steve stopped to give a quick report. “Nothing new from the high school, but the veeps were sorry to hear about Jason.”

“Thanks for crossing that off our list.”

Steve swished his hand in the air. “It was nothing. We had success with two houses along the highway. Did you know Sam Andrews, the town manager, lives out there? He took advantage of his family traveling out of town by doing some lawn and garden work. He didn’t hear anything on that old tractor of his. The Saunders family didn’t hear anything, either.”

Randolph turned and made quick notes on the board. “I think that catches everybody.”

“Not everybody, sir. There’s still Abby Markham. She wasn’t home. Her assistant—former Chief Dixon’s wife—was there, though, and said Miss Markham had gone to DC.”

“That’s true,” Randolph said, turning to a pile of shift reports. “She came in with Owens over the weekend to give a statement.”

“Oh. Uh, do you know why she was traveling?”

“She’s a costumer for opera and ballet productions—artsy stuff like that—she’s heading into town to take stuff for *The Sleeping Beauty*.”

“My dad’s got plans to attend that ballet next week.” Then he looked at the ground, fighting the panic that clawed its way up the back of his throat. “Guess it’ll be the same one.”

“Interesting guy, your dad.”

He looked up, knowing his face was flushed.

"Yeah?" He was tired of answering for his father's actions. Sweat ran down his back and pooled along the waistband of his uniform pants. *Keep it together, keep it together.*

Randolph looked around, like he was checking to make sure nobody was close enough to hear their quiet conversation. "We have some pictures of the senator snooping over Abby Markham's fence. Looks like he's the one who's been setting off the silent alarms. She wasn't crazy after all."

Steve's mouth dropped open. "No shit?"

"No shit. I had Ben swing by his home office yesterday to ask what he was looking for. The senator said he was curious about the updates to the house, and that her turning over the time capsule had made him nostalgic."

A little choking sound escaped Steve's throat. "I didn't realize he'd questioned my father."

"He wasn't questioning him, really. Just reminding your dad to knock on the door next time. We didn't ask you to handle the reminder because it needed to be formal."

"I understand, sir."

"I know he's your dad, but he's a handful."

Steve barked out a laugh. "You don't know the half of it. I'll remind him to stop snooping, sir."

"Nah. No need. I think he got the message."

Steve started to walk to the locker room at the back of the building, but stopped and asked, "Why did Ben go to DC with her?"

"His former FBI team requested his assistance on a project."

"Even with this murder investigation going on?"

Steve's stomach started churning. His nerves were getting the better of him. Guilt weighed him down with every passing moment.

The chief turned back to the board. "Even with this murder investigation. I'll be working in the field, so it balances out."

Steve hustled to the locker room and managed to get inside the first stall before vomiting everything he'd eaten over the last few days. After the first purge, the dry heaves set in, so bad his ribs began to ache like a sonofabitch. It took a few minutes for the muscles in his stomach to unclench and the nausea to pass. When he could finally draw in a full breath, he stumbled to the nearest sink to splash his face with cold water.

In the mirror over the sink, he saw the toll this latest stress had taken on his body and mind. How did the department get the photos? When he met with Jason on Saturday morning, he'd pleaded with his friend to give him more time to figure out what his dad was up to. But By-the-Book Lawson refused to budge. It was like Jason had an imaginary hourglass in his mind for snitching on Quincy, and when Steve hadn't confronted his father after weeks of them arguing about it, the final grain dropped. It wasn't like his dad was going to do anything violent to Abby Markham; he was just a nosy old man.

In every other instance, Jason's rigid sense of right and wrong had been one of Steve's favorite things about his best friend…but this? Jason's ridiculous surveillance of his father had been more of an annoyance than anything. And how the fuck had the department recovered the flash drive? How much was on it? He rested his head against the cool glass of the mirror, trying to visualize the worst day of his life. There was no stopping the tears now. Waves of pain slamming at him were like a shovel to the head.

Jason said he was tired of holding the evidence, even though it put Steve in an awkward position. Steve wanted to wait for his dad to come to town for the press conference, but Jason had put a time limit on his own patience, for whatever reason, forcing the altercation. They'd fought, and in their struggles Jason's hand brushed against the old revolver at the back of Steve's waist. It had been his grandfather's, unregistered, old, and without a safety. It went off, blazing a path down the back of his right calf and out through the fabric of his pants. He'd been able to wrestle it away from Jason, who was momentarily stunned before exploding back into action. A few more violent punches took them to the ground, and then the fucking gun went off again, striking Jason in the chest, just below his vest. For a second after the loud report, they'd lain belly-to-belly, staring at each other. Then Jason closed his eyes, and his arms dropped to his side.

As the five-inch strip of skin from the bullet graze began to burn at the memory, Steve Sykes lowered his head once more and retched again until everything inside him was gone.

Just…gone.

Chapter Seventeen

Since they got on the road around three o'clock, they were able to avoid rush hour traffic in northern Virginia and DC. It was the perfect day for traveling, with clear skies, unseasonably cool temperatures, and low humidity. Abby didn't argue when Ben suggested they take his jeep. It was larger than her sporty coupe which made his broad shoulders happy—plus he figured she would close her eyes if he drove.

They weren't far from her house when his cell phone rang. He hit the hands-free button fast so as not to disturb her sleep. "Ben Owens."

"This is Mike Dixon."

"Hey, I was just thinking about you. When you get back to DC, I want to read you in on a couple things, maybe pick your brain before Abby and I head home."

"Sure thing, man. Why're you whispering?"

"Abby's asleep. What's up?"

"I'll keep this brief. Steve Sykes and his partner came by the house. Said they had some questions for your girl on the Lawson investigation."

Ben swore under his breath, but he couldn't deny how much the sound of "your girl" pleased him. "That guy's a dick. And Abby's already talked about it until she's blue in the face. Chief Randolph questioned her, too. It's one of the things I wanted to talk to you about."

"Sounds like we need to do this face to face."

"Yep. Do me a favor? Abby's had a Peeping Tom the last couple of weeks, and I have a strange feeling. Would you mind walking around the house and down to the dock to see if anything looks suspicious to you? I've gone over the ground so many times I'm afraid I may have missed something."

"I'm out back. Nothing looked off up at the house but…wait a minute." He broke off and Ben heard him walking through the natural area.

"What is it, man?"

"Maybe nothing," Mike said. "But there's a gash running the length of her fence, about eight boards long."

Ben swore. "That's new. Do you think someone cut it with a knife?"

Mike was quiet for a moment and Ben imagined he was looking closer. "Nope, looks like it was done with a rock. I bet we could find one around here with bits of wood clinging to a sharp edge." Leaves rustled in the background as Mike walked the property. "Y'all got any little shits around here who'd like to punk her?"

"It's not kids," Ben said, careful not to raise his voice in frustration. "I'm sure of it. Do you see anything else?"

"I've walked all the way down to the dock and don't see anything out of the ordinary. Did y'all go out on the lake before you left?"

Ben turned down the radio. "No, why?"

"There's a big splash of water across the end of the dock, near the stairs. Abby's property backs up to a real remote section of the lake. I don't think anybody would land at her dock on accident," Mike said. "Think she's got alligators on this side of the lake?"

Through the windshield, Ben glanced at the sky. The entire drive up I-95 had been clear and dry, so that splash was fresh. "Maybe to the 'gators question. When I fish, it's over in the next cove and there's a ton of snakes this time of year. I think she keeps a couple kayaks lashed onto the decking down there. Are they still there?"

"Yep." Mike huffed out a breath. "Hold on a minute—I'm going to look around."

Ben heard Mike rustling through the woods, muttering an occasional curse. It was hard to remain quiet while the man worked, so he tapped his fingers on the steering wheel as a distraction.

"Looks like fresh prints," Mike said after a few minutes. "Leading all the way from the wet spot on the dock up to the back fence, near this odd-looking gash. That splash came from the lake—that's the only explanation because it's been clear and sunny all day. The prints are still wet along the water line. Closer to the fence, they muddy up some."

Ben sighed. "Can you tell what type of shoe left the prints?"

"Looks like a running shoe of some sort."

"Not fancy wingtips?"

"No, these are definitely athletic shoes." Mike's voice broadcast curiosity.

"Damn. Can you scoop up soil from a couple of prints for me? If we can match the soil to what we collected from a pair of wingtip prints from another visit, it'll help build the totality of circumstance."

"Of course—wait a minute…oh, shit!"

"What?" He switched his gaze to Abby, made sure she was still asleep. "What's going on?"

“Looks like somebody tried to make a Molotov cocktail, but it didn’t ignite.”

Ben’s blood pressure shot through the roof. “Are you fucking kidding me?”

“Nope. This looks like the redneck special. An old mason jar with moonshine and a dirty paint rag. The end of the rag is burned, but after it was thrown, it must have rolled off the dock onto the bank. Guess it’s a good thing we’ve had so much rain lately, huh?”

Rage left him speechless. Blood rushed through his head so fast he had to concentrate to make himself calm down. Even though Abby was with him now, there were a handful of hours she’d been alone on that big property. He lived in a world of ‘what if’s’…What if Sykes had cornered her when she was alone? What if he wasn’t the only person watching her? What if the cop killer had set his sights on *her*?

“Ben, you still there?”

“Yeah, give me a sec.”

He got his anger under control by watching two kids in the backseat of the SUV on his left laughing at some cartoon playing in the DVD player attached to the front seat headrests. Traffic was in a good groove, everyone whizzed along at about ten miles an hour above the limit. They were about to shift onto the business bypass, but for the next three or four miles they’d be on this small state highway, surrounded by overgrown canna lilies and crape myrtles bursting with fat blooms thanks to the pattern of late summer rain they’d been in for the last week. The kudzu vines were as thick as his thigh and cascaded to the edge of the road like a volcanic lava flow.

He cracked the window in order to smell the

honeysuckle. “Package up the jar and bring it with you. Photograph the dock, but don’t call it in.”

“I’m guessing you have a reason you’d like me to keep this quiet?”

“We can’t do this on the phone, but when you get to DC, we need to meet.”

After they made plans to meet and Ben hung up, he turned the radio back on, using the music to fill in the blank spaces while he ran the conversation with Mike through in his head. He called the chief to give a quick update.

“He defaced her property and then tried to set it on fire?” Randolph croaked.

“Yes, sir. But think about it—Molotov cocktails aren’t intended to obliterate targets, really, they’re just a bit of mayhem. He was pissed and throwing a tantrum.” He glanced over at Abby, offended on her behalf. “I wonder if his security detail helped him.”

“I doubt it,” Randolph said. “Whatever’s going on with Quincy Sykes, it’s something he wants to keep secret.”

“That’s true.”

“I guess it’s a good thing Abby wasn’t at home for *that* tantrum. Think Mike Dixon can expedite the bottle through his lab? I can reach out to his director if y’all need me to.”

“We’re going to meet in the morning. I don’t want to risk this conversation over phone lines. I’ll let you know if his team needs any justification from you, but it seems like we’re on to something big. If Mike and I can frame it the right way, we should be good.”

“Put the pressure on that asshole, Ben, but do it strategically. Until we have real evidence of him doing…whatever he's doing…we have to be smart. Otherwise he'll shut us down and the investigation may die a horrible death."

****

Dusk settled in as he merged onto highway 395 North at Tysons Corner. Ben sneaked in a few glances at Abby. She looked comfortable for travel in stretchy yoga pants and a tank top. With her chestnut-colored hair in a loose ponytail, face free of makeup, her true beauty struck him once again. Nothing flashy, just young and fresh and healthy-looking.

A quiet sigh broke the silence in the car just before the big SUV in front of them stopped in the middle of the road. Ben stood on the brakes and swerved right, going up and onto the shoulder. "Shit!"

Goddamn, they hadn't even been going fast, but adrenaline coursed through his body with a vengeance. He threw his hand up to wave at the guy behind him for letting him back in and noticed a couple more cars had ended up behind him on the same shoulder. Man, were they all lucky.

"What happened?" Abby sounded groggy, but otherwise hadn't even noticed the danger.

He choked out a laugh. "I almost slammed into that SUV."

Yawning, she sat higher and looked through her side window. "Sorry I conked out on you."

"No worries—you needed it. Plus, I've been enjoying your audio book." He grinned. "I haven't seen *The Sleeping Beauty* since I was a kid. My mother loved that fairy tale."

"My mother was a prima ballerina for the national ballet in Paris. They performed many of the classics while I was growing up. I love them all."

"You were a dancer, too, right?"

She nodded. "I studied at the Paris Ballet School, like her. Well, until I broke my leg eight years ago."

"So, no more dancing?"

"Not for a long time. During physical therapy, my goal was to walk without a hitch in my gait. Then I pushed myself to run again. I could probably dance in smaller roles, or shorter pieces, but I don't think I would be happy knowing I'd never progress beyond company member."

No, he couldn't visualize her settling. "I'm sorry, sweetheart. How old were you when that happened?"

"Twenty-one, but I've made my peace with it. Really. I discovered a penchant for costume design and stayed in Paris to finish up my fine arts undergrad, and then a master's degree in history and costume design. The university was near my father's place, which was nice because I was able to live with him. I've found my niche in the arts, and I'm good."

Her smile and the lack of stress around her eyes indicated she wasn't placating him. "Anytime you'd like to dance with me, you just let me know." The top of the Washington Monument in the distance let him know they were close, and sure enough, their exit was up next. He whistled when the hotel came into view. "Have you, uh, stayed at the Windsor before?"

She leaned closer to the windshield. "Every time I come up. Most of the work I do in Washington is with the Capital Ballet Company, and they perform at The Carter. It's expensive, I know, but they typically have a block of rooms for visiting artists and dignitaries. Plus I write into my contract that *they* provide the lodging."

He shook his head as he stopped the jeep in front of the valet entrance. "Not bad."

"Nope. They offer a great burger in the lounge. Do you mind if we grab dinner before we call it a night? I'm starving."

He snorted. "You're always hungry. And blessed with skinny genes."

"That's true."

The valet opened Abby's door and offered his hand for assistance. Ben gave the kid a ten-dollar bill. "Can you take our luggage up to our room? We're going to grab a quick bite before calling it a day."

"Yes, sir."

Since it was so late, there was no wait in the restaurant. They ordered burgers and a bottle of wine and chatted while they waited for their dinner.

"While you were asleep, Mike called. Someone was messing around in your backyard again."

"Someone?"

He shrugged and gave her a pointed look. "Most likely the same Peeping Tom."

"What did he do this time?"

"Scratched your fence. Tried to set your dock on fire with a Molotov cocktail."

Her eyes bugged. "What?"

"It didn't work. Mike will take the jar to his field office to check for evidence. We don't want to run it through the local forensics lab in case something bigger is going on. This might help us prove it."

"Do I need to worry?" She nodded at their waiter and waited for him to set their meal on the table before continuing. "I mean, more than I already am?"

"Whatever's going on, it's in North Carolina.

Getting away for a bit is a good thing."

"I've got enough to worry about right now with the production, so until you tell me to panic, I'll stay calm." And that, it appeared, was that. She popped a French fry into her mouth, then sighed. "This is so good."

He moaned through dinner, too, because it really was that good. Abby chatted up the waiter each time he checked in. After a bit, she discovered he spoke Spanish. At one point he stood at their table and carried on a lengthy conversation with her in his native language. She was so open and friendly; the man looked bewitched. When he walked away to check on another table, he nearly walked into the wall.

Ben laughed. "Spanish, huh? Are you fluent?"

"I am. Though we lived in France, we traveled a lot through Spain when I was younger; it was easy to pick up the languages in the region. Half of my ballet instructors were Russian, so I picked up enough of that while I was training. I'll tell you what—when an angry Russian yells, telling you to tighten up your *grand jeté*, you do it."

He took a long sip of his wine, and he noticed that her eyes were glued to his throat. Her distraction was charming, and he gave her a cheeky grin. "Did you ever perform professionally, or only as a student?"

"Both, because I started my professional career young, like most dancers. My mother was a prima ballerina. It gave me an inside glimpse of the rigors of professional dancing, but it also lent me a leg up on the competition. I still had to bust my ass like every other dancer."

He leaned over to refill her wine and tipped his glass toward her. "Did you always want to be a professional? You didn't want to be, I don't know, a veterinarian?"

She shook her head, then sipped. "No, not really. My mother started taking me to the studio with her before I was two. When I was about three, she started me in ballet classes. Dad said it must have been genetic, since it always came easily for me. I mean, it was hard…just the sheer physicality of it—the jumping, the concentration to keep muscles locked and *en pointe*…but I could generally do anything I tried. I joined Mom's company during a production of *Giselle* when I was thirteen and caught the eye of the director. He enrolled me in the Paris Ballet School. It was tough. Professional dancers take a ballet class *every* day, for an hour and a half just to warm up their muscles. Then they spend the day at the theater, have dinner, and then the performance in the evening. And *then* they get up the next day and do it all over again."

His eyes widened. "Holy crap." A fresh wave of late-night customers came in. Between the din of conversation and clanking of dishes and silverware, the noise was nearly deafening. He leaned in closer. "I don't know anything about the Paris Ballet School, but it sounds pretty rigorous. You trained as hard as any professional athlete."

"Mm-hmm."

"I don't know the right phrases but, like, what was your favorite role? What was your hardest position?"

She squeezed his right bicep and shook her head. Sparks of electrified lust danced down his arm, but she seemed oblivious. "You've got a question for everything."

When he tensed, she dropped her hand and a pretty

blush spread across her cheeks. He could tell she appreciated his curiosity and that, correct lexicon or not, his interest was genuine.

Nearby a piece of silverware clattered sharply on the floor, breaking into their lassitude. “Uh, without a doubt, my favorite role was also the most difficult thing I’ve ever danced—Kitri in *Don Quixote*. Her *grand jeté* is a killer; it requires a lot of flexibility and power. After the accident and all the physical therapy, I can’t land on my leg like that anymore. My femur can’t take that much pressure.”

“But you’re able to run, right?”

“That’s because the pressure isn’t as jarring when I run as if I were to leap across the stage. Repeatedly. Even when I sprint, I’m only so high off the ground and hitting my leg at an angle as opposed to four feet of vertical space in a *grand jeté* and catching my full weight on the toes of a single leg. Make sense?”

He nodded. “Do you run every day?”

Squirming in her seat was a clear sign she was tired of talking about it. “I try for two miles every morning but try to push it to eight or ten miles once a week. I’ve got a bit of a compulsive personality and do better with repetition.”

“I run every day, too. It’s a holdover from my Army days.”

“You were a soldier?”

“Right out of high school.” He let the swirling wine in his glass mesmerize him for a moment, knowing she would see right through him if he wasn’t careful. “I went for the GI bill, so I’d have money for college. I was good at soldiering and for a while considered going on to become a Ranger, but my convoy was involved in a brutal...situation. My, uh, injuries were pretty bad, and a lingering effect of a traumatic brain injury I had was the loss of peripheral vision in my left eye." He looked away when he told her because he hated to see pity from anybody, much less a woman to whom he was wildly attracted.

But he shouldn't have worried, because the beautiful woman sitting across from him had suffered her own life-altering injury. She didn't want people to commiserate with her either. "Is that when you decided to become a police officer?"

He poured the last of the wine, splitting it between them, grateful she didn't linger on the suffering and try to baby him. "No, I got my degree and went into the FBI academy."

"Where did you meet Mike?"

"At the academy. I was sorry when our assignments took us to opposite coasts, because he's a lot of fun. I loved California, though. My experience in the Army made it possible for me to be part of the FBI's SWAT team, which was a big deal in Los Angeles. But then my dad got sick, and I had some really hard cases with the Bureau, I knew it was time to come home." He drained his glass and closed his eyes for a moment, forcing a couple of deep breaths. Abby squeezed his hand, pulling him back into the present.

He signaled for the bill and enjoyed Abby's giggling as he choked through a hideous broken-Spanish conversation with the waiter. An elegantly dressed woman walked in with a tall, younger man who had to be some type of security detail or cop. The way these guys carried themselves gave it away every time. Ben tilted his head in greeting when she glanced his way. At first, she smiled, then narrowed her eyes and pursed her lips. The man with her jerked his head around and glared. Ben shrugged and was trying to place where he'd seen her when the waiter brought the credit card receipt for him to sign.

The woman called out, "Excuse me, young man."

It hit him: Senator Sykes' assistant.

Abby followed him over to the table and smiled at both the woman and the younger man. The guy gave her a wolfish smile that made her shoulders hunch. Ben slid an arm around her waist and pulled her closer. "Hello, Ms. Scott. What a surprise to see you here."

"Ben Owens, right? I thought that was you. You've got a great memory."

He flashed his most dashing grin. "I guess you and the senator are back on your regular stomping grounds, huh? Time to legislate and all that?"

She let out a charming laugh and squeezed his fingers before dropping her hand to her lap. "That's right. The government machine never stops." She tilted her head none too discreetly in Abby's direction. "What brings you to the city?"

"A bit of sight-seeing, a little research. And the ballet. Martha, may I present Abby Markham. Abby, this is Martha Scott. I met her through Senator Sykes."

"It's a pleasure to meet you, ma'am." The women shook hands; the man across from Martha did not offer up his name or position. Neither did she.

Martha tapped her chin and repeated Abby's name a couple times under her breath, as if she was trying to place the name. It wasn't a long shot to believe the senator's assistant had no idea who she was. "Abby Markham…now why do I know that name?"

"I bought the old Sykes home last year, though I had no idea the local historical significance at the time. You probably know my name through the senator. He was in town this week to collect the time capsule I dropped off a couple of weeks ago."

"Yes, yes! That's right. Oh, how fun. There were some sweet books of Steven's. I had no idea the grape soda would still have any fizz left." She clapped her hands twice and sighed, though she had a real *fuck-you* sarcasm to her tone. "Did you attend the ceremony?"

"I've been on a deadline," Abby said. "I enjoyed reading the newspaper accounts of the love letters between Senator and Mrs. Sykes. So romantic. Reminded me of my grandparents, who kept the post office in business while he served in Vietnam."

Martha stopped laughing and pursed her lips again before relaxing the muscles in her face. *Bullseye*. This was why ol' Quincy never remarried. Ben squeezed Abby's waist in a message to wrap it up.

"I can't imagine someone loving me enough after I died to stay true to me," Abby said sweetly, then elbowed him in the ribs.

He chuckled for the show of it and kissed her sweetly on the temple. "Who knows? Maybe Abby will be singing my praises before the week is out," he said and watched Martha's left eye twitch. "Martha…uh, sir…it was a pleasure to see you again. Our dinner was marvelous, but we're pooped. Y'all have a nice evening."

They made it halfway across the lobby before Abby snorted. "Did you see her face when I mentioned the love letters?"

"Oh, yeah. She was pissed. I'd say *handsome,*

aging senator plays better with his constituents than *playboy screwing his staff*, wouldn't you?"

She laughed out loud this time. "What do you bet she's already called to let him know we're in town."

Chapter Eighteen

The next morning Abby led Ben into the lobby of the Carter Theatre. She spotted the security guard, stopping so abruptly Ben nearly mowed her down. “Oof,” she said, thankful his reflexes were quick enough to save her from going down face first.

But she just laughed, happy to see her old friend. “Andy, it’s so good to see you.” She hugged the older man who was built like a tank. He was always so careful with her and handled her like she was made of spun glass.

“It’s great to see you, Marky Mark. Looks like the south’s been kind to you.”

“It’s hot, that’s for sure,” she said with a laugh. “Looks like retirement didn’t take.”

He chucked her on the arm. “I was bored. Who’s your fella?” He shook Ben’s hand.

“Andy, this is Ben Owens. Ben, it’s a pleasure to introduce Andy McNeill.”

“Nice to meet you, sir,” Ben said and shook the man’s hand. “Marky Mark?”

Abby snorted. “I used to love that music back in the day. Markham…Mark…Marky Mark. It just stuck.” Andy laughed and slapped the desk. He always loved to be part of the inside joke.

“Ben will be coming and going this week,” Abby explained. “I was hoping to get him a badge that’ll get him in if you're not at your desk."

Andy led them back to his desk and glanced over his shoulder, watching Ben taking in the details of the lobby, like the doors and emergency exits. "What branch?"

"Sir?" Ben gave Andy his full attention and tilted his head.

"Son, every man who lives in the capital who's built like you is in some branch of law enforcement or government work."

"Ah, gotcha. I'm a detective with the Apex Police Department, but I'm former FBI out of the LA office, and before that Army. I'm doing some research with an old colleague."

Andy coded two cards and put lanyards on both, then handed them over. "This key card will get you in the far-right door at any time. As a general rule, this building is only open during regular business hours, but for visiting and performing artists with active productions, around-the-clock access is permitted."

Ben thanked him, then followed Abby down the hall. She kept up a steady narrative about what was behind this door or that one. She pointed out posters and talked about the different roles she'd danced or costumed. They finally went around a corner and down a ramp that took them into the costume shop. Sarah Winslow looked up as the door clicked shut and let out an excited squeal before running to greet her friend.

"The costumes are beautiful. We started fittings yesterday when the guys got back and have about half a dozen left. Antoine and Misty are coming in at four o'clock to work directly with you. Mrs. Gladys called to let us know she'll be here by lunchtime."

"Good, good. Did you see where we had to do a little ombre effect with the black and gray crystals in Antoine's jacket?"

"It's beautiful. Honestly, I was never worried. It looks stunning with the backdrops and set pieces. When Bruno called from the road, he said it gave it more depth, and he was right. I love it."

Ben cleared his throat and touched Abby on the shoulder, drawing the attention of both women who had been off in their own world. "I'm sorry to interrupt, but I've got to head out."

Sarah made no secret of checking him out. "Hello, tall, dark, and dangerous-looking. I'm Sarah."

He blushed and for once seemed at a loss for words. "I'm Ben."

Abby bumped hips with him. "Sarah is the artistic director...and Bruno's *wife*." She glared at her friend. "Sarah! Geez."

"I'm married, not dead." She gave Ben another once-over. "You really are gorgeous."

With a laugh, Abby looked up at him, wondering what was going through his mind. He looked incredibly uncomfortable, but she couldn't help making her own perusal. Ben was hands-down one of the most handsome men she'd ever met, and despite having spent most of the last decade being handled by some of the strongest, well-built dancers in the industry, she'd never been tempted. The dancers were artists, and their bodies were more purpose-built, with strong thighs and bulky arms because they were constantly leaping and throwing hundred-pound women across the stage.

But Ben...ah, Ben was confident and intelligent, and his body was built for menace. His strength and bulk came from sheer power and heavy amounts of testosterone. Well, there was probably more to it, but never had she been struck mute and immobile by a dancer.

He broke the spell when he cleared his throat and tightened his fingers on her waist. “Tell me your schedule so I can adjust.”

Sarah sighed out loud, and Abby glared at her. But her friend grinned, approval beaming in each look. “I’ll be in the costume shop all day, right, Sarah?”

“Yep. We’ll also be doing press today and tomorrow. The schedule is pretty tight, but Mrs. Gladys can keep us on track while you’re busy. Starting at eleven-thirty, *Inside Washington* will be here to get the skinny on the production, with a focus on the President and his family attending the opening. *Pointe Monthly* will be here at five o’clock for an interview; they’re interested in the connection with your mom and *The Sleeping Beauty*. A full-circle kind of thing. They’ll be talking to you about building costumes with an eye on kinesiology, and I’m sure there will be some tie-in about your shift from dancer to production staff. They’re also interested in your arts career 2.0.”

When Sarah’s phone buzzed, she paused to read the screen. “Mischa Abernathy—you should recognize her name from the company—has a dentist’s appointment at nine thirty, so we’ll start with her measurements. Uh…where was I?”

“You just finished up the *Pointe Monthly* deal,” Ben said.

“Right. Tomorrow morning at ten o’clock the *Washington Observer* is sending their arts editor because they want to talk to you about…you guessed it, your mom and your ties to Paris and the Capital Ballet Company. The local public access TV station is sending a crew to get some B-roll for this week's Sunday morning program. That's at one o'clock tomorrow afternoon. I think you'll be in the background with the costumes for that one, because they're more focused on the production than your affiliation. They'll also be on hand Friday night to grab footage of the performance with a side piece on the Prez."

Abby nodded, expecting the tie-ins from the media since this was the role that made her mother famous in Paris, initially introduced her to the stage, and now put her behind the scenes. "Why is there such interest in your mom?" Ben asked. He ran his fingers through his hair and rubbed the bridge of his nose, like maybe he was working on a headache. While she spoke, he took out his phone and responded to a text.

"Most of my professional work was in France," she said, "but I danced in three productions with the CBC at the American National Theatre in Manhattan. *The Sleeping Beauty* is the production that made my mother a star in the ballet world. It was also my first role on stage with her. It's unusual, for a mother and daughter to dance together, as much today as it was twenty years ago. And…I was dancing the role of Princess Aurora when I broke my leg. The connection is too ingrained in the ballet world to forget." She sighed and rubbed her thigh, shifting her stance a bit. Whenever she let her mind drift to the accident, her old injury hurt like a bitch. Phantom pain, she supposed.

Ben stopped texting and looked down at her. She refused to let the tears gathering in her eyes to fall. She'd spent the last eight years rebuilding her life and her career and was happy with her accomplishments. She had an amazing career. But when all of the facts of her life and legacy were laid out in one statement, the sense of loss returned, and it always took a moment to regain her composure.

Sarah put her phone in her back pocket and took both of Abby's hands. She smiled first at Ben, then at Abby, her friend. "One last thing before I head downstairs. Andre Petrov will be here on Friday. He's currently dating a *Manhattan Post* reporter who'll be here also. I'm pretty certain she'll ask the 'having to settle for something else when your life's dream is shattered' kind of question, because she's a clueless bitch. One of the CBC dancers working with us for this production overheard Andre talking about it at a bar and told Bruno about it last night." She cut her eyes at Ben and nodded.

Abby muttered something foul and dropped her shoulders.

"What does that mean?" Ben asked. He pulled her back, settling her against his chest. "Who is Andre Petrov?"

"He was Marky's boyfriend all those years ago," Sarah said. "He's a dancer, too. Well, *was* a dancer. He was driving the night the accident happened. We were celebrating her twenty-first birthday."

"Was he drunk?"

Sarah nodded. "We'd been at a bar. When it was time to leave, Andre put her in the passenger side of his car before we could stop him." The audible hitch in Abby's breathing caused Sarah to pause. After a second, she continued. "We were all kind of trashed, but he was young, and stupid, and macho. After he got in the driver's seat and closed the door, Abby bolted out the other side, so she could hail a cab. Only, she was in such a hurry to get away, she jumped in front of a cab passing in the other lane. It threw her into a light post—God, it was awful. Broke her femur…compound fracture…she was conscious the whole time."

Ben's glare at Sarah told her to wrap it up. "Anyway…I'll see you later tonight for dinner," she mumbled. "Okay Abby?"

He wrapped his big arms around Abby and brushed a kiss across the top of her head. His pounding heartbeat gave away his fury, but she didn't have it in her to soothe him. Not yet. She took a moment to pull herself together. Andre hadn't crossed her mind in years. Fucking Andre. His father had tried to pay her off to keep her quiet, but she gave her statement to the police. Since he'd never actually put the car into gear, he wasn't charged with DWI, but he was culpable all the same. The Capital Ballet Company canceled his contracts on the spot, and because he was all but blacklisted in the States, he hadn't danced in anything substantial in years. Last she'd known, he'd picked up small regional company work when he was stateside; everything else was in Europe, and he hated Europe.

"I'm so sorry, honey." Ben kissed the top of her head. "I had no idea the accident was so horrifying."

She laughed without humor. "I appreciate it, but it's over. It's in the past." She pushed against his chest until he loosened his arms. "Really. I hated him so much for years after it happened, but hate is exhausting. I had to let go of the rage so I could move forward." She took a deep breath and let it out. Breathing away the distress settled her.

He brushed the hair off her forehead and then rubbed his thumb gently along her left cheekbone. His hand came to rest on the side of her throat, fingertips brushing through her long hair. There was something comforting in the feel of his hands on her. They were so strong and warm, and she hadn't let anyone take care of her in a long time.

"I haven't seen him in almost eight years. Haven't really even given him a passing thought in half that time, but this brings it all back up. My circumstances have nothing to do with the current production. Neither Andre nor I are breaking news anymore."

"If you don't want it to happen, I'll make sure it stops now. I've still got connections in the bureau and Mike will be more than happy to help."

She wrapped her fingers around his thick wrist. "Nah, they need this coverage. Plus, any waves I make will have the media all over me like jackals. If I let her ask her questions and ignore the drama, there won't be anything to watch."

He looked like he wanted to argue, but instead he said, "You're a better man than me."

Then he leaned down and kissed her sweetly on the lips, lingering just a moment, long enough to make her pulse rate spike and all of her girly parts tingle. His eyes were glazed when he lifted his head, which was entirely flattering. Ben had been right about the current situation forcing a relationship façade, but everything about him called to her. She had no doubt they would have ended up together on their own time, which was why she was happy to let the attraction go where it wanted.

"I'm headed to Mike's office; we'll do a little more

investigating into Sykes."

Nodding, she traced along the lapel of his suit jacket. "Have you ever interrogated a US senator before?" She didn't have to add that Sykes was rumored to be on his party's ticket for the upcoming presidential race, though it was well-circulated gossip on the morning news shows.

"Ah, no. This is definitely a first for me."

He cupped the back of her head tenderly, lacing her hair around his fingers, while the other one rested on her hip, holding her close against him. His erection grew between them, prodding her belly, but since he didn't seem embarrassed about it, she didn't mention it, either. His reaction, as much as the realization he was going with the flow, too, made her pulse race.

"I think you need to tread lightly." She gave him a quick squeeze, grabbing one last bit of comfort she didn't realize she'd needed. "Okay, enough wallowing in misery. I'm a big girl. Plus, if Andre or his reporter pull a fast one, Bruno will knock them into next week."

He snorted. "I knew I liked that guy. Want me to leave the car here, or should I come back later to pick you up?"

They walked toward the stairs. "Go ahead and take it. I doubt I have time to even breathe today, but I'll grab a cab if I need to go anywhere."

"Tonight is the crew dinner, right?"

"Yeah. It'll be fun. You'll be amazed at how much food a tiny ballerina can put away in the days leading up to a production run."

"Now I can't wait. What time should I be back?"

She leaned up and kissed him quickly on the lips and patted him on the chest, because she could. Now that he was walking out the door, she couldn't stop touching him. "I doubt we'll be ready until close to seven. Oh! I almost forgot…do you have a dark suit?"

He tugged the bottom hem of his sports coat down and looked down at his battered old brown leather boots. "I don't, but I can try to find one this week if you need me to."

She had to kiss him again because he looked so cute, worrying about his perfectly fine work clothes. But the theatre required something way more formal than a sport coat and worn boots, particularly since he was going to meet the President. "Nope, don't worry about it. We'll figure it out in the costume shop. I'll see you tonight."

The corners of his lush mouth tipped downward as he focused on his clothes, so she nibbled the sexy curve of his bottom lip. He opened up, practically inhaling her. He tightened his arm around her hips and stood, lifting her straight off the ground. Tilting her head to the side, she licked into his mouth, twining their tongues together, her body shivering with arousal. Hands shifted restlessly against the side of his neck and back of his head; fingers tangled in his hair, making it stand on end. It went for long minutes until his phone buzzed in his front pocket, and she leaned back, sucking in a breath. Looking around the lobby, they were still alone, thank God. If it were a busier time of day, someone could've gotten a good show.

When she looked back at him, Ben was reading something on his phone. "Chief Randolph wants me to text him ASAP," he said. He turned the phone around so she could see the screen.

A shiver passed up her spine. "Oh."

"I need to touch base with him, then swing by to pick up Mike. I'll see you around seven, okay?" He bent and gave her a gentle kiss, holding her close and breathing in the same air for a moment.

"Okay," she whispered.

Licking his lips, he took an exaggerated step back. "Woman, you are distracting."

He was pretty distracting, too, but she was happy to not be the only one with trouble concentrating.

Chapter Nineteen

"Come on, Dad. We're going to be late."

Ellie Sykes ran in circles in the front yard, laughing and chasing their little beagle, Junie. Every couple of laps she opened the front door and yelled for Steve to hurry, then slammed the door and took off again. Her mother was going to kill her.

Instead, Jennifer was waiting by the door the next time Ellie popped her head in, grabbing her around the waist and swinging her high in a wide arc. His little girl howled with laughter, which eased some of the tension that had been squeezing his heart for the last two weeks. Hell, even Jennifer was laughing, which was a miracle these days.

"I'm coming, Scooter. Just gotta find my sneakers," he called from upstairs.

He'd been sitting on the side of the bed for the better part of an hour, staring off into space. Everything ran together; when he wasn't moping around in a depressed, catatonic state, he was filled with barely controllable rage. Fury swept through him in a heartbeat, forcing him to focus on Jason's ultimatum, his father, his guilt. It all consumed him. He blinked, and forced his breath to level out, practicing deep breathing exercises the department shrink taught him a couple years ago.

Fuck!

He'd thrown his shoes into the dumpster last week after he'd taken out the yard waste. He hadn't been thinking; he'd just reacted. About everything. He dug around in the back of his closet and found his old indoor shoes that he'd had for ten years but didn't want to throw away because he was lazy. He laced them up quickly and hustled down the stairs, grabbing his whistle and team jersey from the back of the couch.

Jennifer had already packed a cooler with juice boxes and orange slices since it was their week to provide snacks for the Vipers—even the coach's daughter had snack duty. Today was the last game of the season, and Ellie's team was poised to be champions of the league's twelve/thirteen-year-old category. He had to keep it together long enough to get through the morning; then he could have his nervous breakdown. Along with the shoes he'd tossed into the dumpster were the floor mats for his father-in-law's car—and any hope of freedom in his future.

"Nice shoes," Ellie said giggling. He looked down and forced a nonchalant laugh. They were dated and the right one had two holes along the outside seam. He'd wrapped it with duct tape last year, but even that was beginning to wear thin. Those shoes were a metaphor for his life right now. She grabbed his red baseball cap and ran out to Jennifer's minivan, scrambling in the back seat. His youngest son Joe was already at the park with his team. He'd ridden over with Sally and her middle son, Judah. Their game was starting fifteen minutes before Ellie's, but since their six/seven-year-old team had lost all but one game, there was no way they were going to make it past the first game in the round-robin tournament.

"Figured I'd wear my lucky shoes today. You knuckleheads could use it." He looked away from Jennifer. He couldn't bear to face her these days.

She barked out a laugh. "We'll take it, Daddy."

Jennifer patted his knee and backed out of the driveway, and they were on their way. The old beater sedan they'd inherited from Jennifer's dad sat on the swing-out driveway he'd made by laying bricks into the grass in an arc. It taunted him; a reminder of what happened the last time it was driven, and it made him sick. He must've made a noise because Jennifer quirked an eyebrow his way, but he shook his head *no* and watched the neighborhood whiz by through his window. Since Jason died, she'd had trouble sleeping. Between helping Sally with everything and the visceral reminder of how dangerous the life of a police officer was, she was closed for business—physically and emotionally.

Tears sprang up in his eyes and he blinked them away. Fortunately, people around him—even Jennifer—assumed he was thinking about Jason when they noticed the tears or a faraway gaze glossing his vision. It was also fortunate, he supposed, that they didn't realize he was the reason Jason was dead.

****

Three hundred miles away, the senior Sykes was still seething about the local cops barging into his office and questioning him. As soon as Martha mentioned that she'd seen Owens at dinner the night before, he'd been on a tear. He'd alerted his security detail of the unwanted attention and headed for the Hill. He was presenting to the Joint Chiefs today and needed his full attention on that matter. He'd left Martha manning the office, so he grabbed one of the Senate pages to run notes for him.

General Wellesley finally signed off on the additional capital expenditure, thereby expanding support for clandestine services in Germany for the next two quarters to aid in tracking an active terrorist cell. Quincy was gloating. He deserved to gloat—getting the general to concede had taken months of persuasion, and he was going to bask in the glory of this hard-fought win. The page stepped up to his chair just as Martha's text came in.

—owens is back and he's got an fbi sidekick—

Sweat broke out along the small of his back, making him shift in his seat. He pressed his phone against his chest so nobody could see it. Fucking busybodies. He had to maintain his usual implacable expression when dealing with this committee. If they smelled fear, how would they trust him worthy of their support? They were a bunch of jackals, and any scent of blood put them into pounce position. He understood the game; they were as ruthless as him and he loved it.

When the senate page cleared her throat, he hissed, "What?"

She titled her head toward the galley where a throng of reporters pushed toward the podium to get their quota of sound bites for the day. He blew out a breath and slipped the phone into his pocket, taking a moment to breathe deep.

Johnny Mercer from the *Times* asked why they had to expand funding for clandestine services rather than extending additional units to Rhineland Air Force Base.

General Wellesley replied, "We don't give out details of clandestine operations." Then he got up and walked away.

It was all Sykes could do to not snort. God love the military and its privacy. With a nod in the general direction of the press pool, Quincy took his leave, as well. He loved an easy exit.

Martha called as soon as he was through the door and hurrying down the hall to his office. He answered without the usual amenities. "Did you tell them I've been as cooperative as I'm going to be—that I was just looking over the goddamned fence to see what changes she'd made?"

"Yes, sir," she said calmly, but he heard the tension in her voice. "Special Agent Mike Dixon is with Detective Owens. They have new questions and state they won't leave without speaking to you."

He stopped in the middle of the hall. "Do I need to call Joyce?"

Joyce Dupree had been his personal attorney since the year after the fire. He'd needed help setting up the trust when the money from the state came in for Lake Jordan. She was loyal, discreet, and as efficient as a surgeon's scalpel.

"Yes, sir," Martha said, sending a new jolt of panic through his system. Shit, maybe they'd found the second box. Paul Pope's box.

"I'll be there in ten minutes." He hung up, nodding and waving at a group of high school kids touring the Capital. One of the adult chaperones in the group asked if he'd take a group picture with them, and as much as he wanted to tell them to fuck off, he needed to maintain a semblance of normalcy to deflect the unwanted attention from Owens and Dixon.

He held up a finger, signaling a request for

patience, then called Joyce. She picked up on the first ring. "Can you meet me in my office in ten minutes? I can't explain it right now, but I need you to get me out of answering any questions about Paul Pope from the two men who'll be meeting us there." He said as many important words as he could in one breath to alert her to the situation, because brevity was always powerful.

"Okay."

He took a deep yoga breath, forcing his belly to fill with air, then let it out in small increments. After a moment, he was back in control and ready to face the demons of his past. First, though, he was going to have to schmooze. The school group cheered when he walked their way, bringing the first genuine smile to his face that he'd had in a long time.

Chapter Twenty

Quincy's power office in Washington was vastly different than his quaint homespun space in Apex. Ben whistled when he and Mike walked into a fancy outer office, where Martha's antique desk sat in front of two comfortable side chairs. The senator's private office was, presumably, behind the carved wooden doors.

The space was close to the Senate floor with huge windows overlooking Constitution Avenue. Ben bet a month's salary that Quincy's peers coveted this space which screamed "look how big my dick is." He and Mike sat in the salon, watching Martha Scott work hard at ignoring them by giving the appearance of typing something important.

Childish, at best, Ben thought, and rude because they'd been waiting for the last fifteen minutes.

He and Mike stood when the door opened, bracing themselves for another brushoff. Instead, Senator Sykes walked in and offered his hand. "Detective Owens, why am I not surprised to see you…again?" He tried to sound lighthearted, but his eyes flashed with irritation.

"Sir, this is Special Agent Mike Dixon out of the DC field office, helping me with a new element of the investigation. I was happy he could shift his schedule this morning to lend his expertise." Earlier Mike and he had decided that Ben would handle the questioning since the Apex PD had opened the investigation.

As Quincy and Mike shook hands, a tall woman in a dark blue power suit walked in, followed by two uniformed Capitol Police officers.

"Gentlemen, I'm Joyce Dupree, chief counsel for the senator. He's been very accommodating in regard to Ms. Markham's fence and her trespassing charges, but we won't be answering any more questions today."

"That's a shame." Ben tucked his hands into the front pockets of his slacks and rocked back on his heels. "What do you think, Mike?"

Mike nodded and spoke directly to the senator. "Ben's team has a new development that requires further discussion."

"Looks like my guys have another opinion on that," Quincy said. "We're done here. Martha will see you out." He gave a smug two-fingered salute and allowed the DC cops to hustle him toward the inside office.

"All right, sir, if that's what you prefer," Ben said at the threshold to the hallway. "But I thought you'd like to know the investigation's been expanded to include a couple new pieces of evidence. Like, the fact that someone defaced Miss Markham's back fence yesterday. Then they tried to set her dock on fire. It's a good thing the Molotov cocktail fizzled out; I was able to send it to the lab this morning. We're waiting on fingerprints now. You wouldn't know anything about either of those developments, would you, sir?"

Quincy huffed out an irritated breath. "Young man, I can't believe you're suggesting that I would damage the property. I want nothing to do with that house. It's the house my Margaret died in. It changed the trajectory of my life...*all* our lives...forever. But neither does that mean I want her to have my time capsules. I buried them with the intention of laying that part of our lives to rest. And I intend for it to stay buried."

"Capsules?" Mike asked. "As in more than one?"

It became immediately clear the senator realized his fuck up when he tried to backtrack. Before he could sputter more lies, Ben broke in. "And there's this—"

He pulled up the photo of Paul Pope and turned the screen around for Sykes' view. "Chief Randolph received a photo earlier today with a note that said, 'Paul Pope is not dead.' No name, but a return address from Buntner, North Carolina. What do you think that means, Mike?"

Quincy jolted like he'd been struck by a cattle prod. Ben fought the urge to pump his fist into the air. Finally, a crack in the senator's armor.

"Who knows," Mike said, shrugging.

Ben clicked the power button on the side of his phone and tucked it into the inside pocket of his jacket. He followed Mike through the door and turned back to look at Martha, who stood in the middle of the room, her mouth gaping. He almost felt sorry for her. Almost.

He waved his hand and said, "We'll see you soon."

****

As soon as Joyce stepped into his office, Quincy slammed the door shut. He didn't want anybody—*anybody*—to hear this conversation. His security detail was well-trained and discreet, as was Martha, but Joyce was the only other living person who had knowledge of the second trust—this one in Paul Pope's name—which kept Terrence Pearson conveniently stashed in a private mental institution. And he intended to keep it that way.

"What the fuck is going on?" He wanted to punch

something, but Ed would burst through the door if he had any inkling Quincy was in danger. "Why is Paul Pope even on the FBI's radar?"

She walked over to the bar in the corner and poured them each two fingers of bourbon, then handed a glass to him, before answering. She sighed after the first sip and leaned a hip against his desk. "I don't have much to go on, but after you called, I checked on the trust to make sure payments were still processing. Everything looks good on that front, but when I contacted New Horizons, they told me law students from the Innocence Project have been working with several of the mental health hospitals across the nation, including New Horizons."

"Christ," Quincy snarled, "isn't it enough for those people to work with prisoners?"

Joyce took another sip of whiskey. She held the same opinion on institutions as him—out of sight, out of mind. Tuck the nut jobs and felons someplace safe and throw away the key.

He threw back the whole glass in one swallow and began pacing. "And?"

She met his wild stare without flinching. "And what? Your brother-in-law is a model patient. Terrence takes his meds like a good boy, helps the nursing assistants keep the rec room clean, leads daily walks through the grounds. For all appearances, he's sane and compliant. But you already know that."

He made a choking sound and stalked over to the bar to pour another shot.

"Quincy, three months ago, they enrolled Terrence in a program that allows him to leave the grounds one weekend a month so he can begin integrating back into society. They outfit him with an ankle bracelet and a volunteer chaperone who checks in with him a couple times a day."

"Let me get this straight," Sykes interrupted. "We have paid millions of dollars over the last thirty-five years to keep that crazy asshole locked up and monitored, but because he cleans up after himself, they let him leave the facility and have two days unaccounted for each month?"

Ed knocked on the door. "Everything okay, sir? We can hear you yelling out here. Unlock the door and let us inside, please." The door rattled for emphasis.

"Everything's okay, Ed. I need a few more minutes of privacy with Mrs. Dupree."

"Sir, I don't think—"

"It's all right, Ed. I'll be there in a moment."

"Yes, Quincy," Joyce said, walking over to the window and looking out, pausing for a moment as if she were weighing her next words. "Terrence only has four hours of private time, but the volunteer approves his agenda, drops him off and picks him up, and stays with him overnight. It's a pilot program, and apparently he's a model participant."

"Do they keep a record of where he goes and what he does?" His fists clenched and unclenched, waiting in agony for her response.

She nodded. "His first trip was to Apex. He wanted to visit Margaret's grave."

"Was that all?"

She looked out the window and paused. "No. He also went to the old homestead." He made a choking sound, but she continued. "He was there for two hours, wandering through the woods."

"Where he and Margaret used to play." On a roar, Quincy punched the window, shattering a small panel of glass.

The office door slammed against the bookcase. Ed barreled through, weapon drawn and yelling orders over his shoulder to Mark. Martha's voice drifted through from her office, requesting back-up from the Capitol Police.

Ed grabbed Joyce by the arm, yanking her away from the senator and throwing her against the wall in his haste to clear the situation. Mark grabbed Quincy and threw him on the floor, using his body to protect his boss from danger.

"I'm okay, Mark. Let me up, goddamnit!"

But Mark didn't budge. Ed raced around the office, checking behind curtains and clearing the bathroom. Martha crawled into the office on hands and knees, her face was pale as death as she took in the action. Her attention split between her boss and the rough circle knocked out of the windowpane.

"Clear," Ed barked to Mark, who rose and grabbed Quincy by the shoulders, hauling him to his feet.

"What happened in here?" Mark glared at Joyce, who rolled to her knees to stand on shaky legs. She rubbed her arms and winced, which further pissed off Quincy.

"Help her up, Ed, for fuck's sake! Why did you throw her to the ground?"

Christ, his oldest confidante manhandled by his own security staff? She might be a badass in the courtroom, but she was half the size of his guys. His hand throbbed where he'd punched the glass, and the mottled appearance of his knuckles made him queasy.

Martha ran to the bathroom to grab a towel. A couple police officers met at the midpoint of the office, leading two EMTs through the melee.

Joyce plopped down into a chair. Mark leaned in and yelled, "I say again, lady. What happened?"

Quincy watch her rear back from Mark, inwardly cheering at her gumption to stay silent. If it were possible for Mark to spontaneously combust from her fuck-you-glare, he would have.

Small chunks of glass stuck in random spots along the back of Quincy's hand, and a long gash split his middle knuckle. Parts of his fist were numb, but that big cut hurt like a bitch, and now that he was through the surge of adrenaline it throbbed like a toothache. The EMTs sat him on the couch and laid a protective blanket across his lap before rinsing it with saline. He howled as it trickled down between his fingers.

"Do you have any allergies to pain meds, Senator?"

"No. And I sure would appreciate if you'd administer all of them. *Now*, if you don't mind." He made a concerted effort to be calm. Friendly. The tough senator whom America loved, and who loved America in turn.

Martha stood at his other side, her hip abutting his left shoulder. After all the years she'd been with him, doubling as his lover almost from day one, neither relied on the other for any kind of emotional support. But in this moment, when his past crashed into his present, her presence was comforting. Joyce sat silently on the other side of the room, ignoring the questions both Mark and Ed were hurling at her, without flinching, not even a blink.

"Boys," Quincy said, surprised at his composure.

"I was upset at something and pacing. I tripped on the damned rug. Joyce couldn't catch me in time."

Ed walked over to the window and looked down at the rug, which was indeed flipped up on the corner. In reality, it flipped up when Quincy recoiled after punching the window, but for now it served to back up his story. And it was obvious that glass shards had exploded outward, rather than from a shot or some other projectile coming into the office.

Everyone held a collective breath when Mark got back in Joyce's face; when she nodded, the room exhaled. She was worth every penny, every emotional investment he'd made in her through the years. And right now, he could've kissed her.

Yes, she knew the secret of Terrence Pearson, and yes, she knew Quincy had buried two boxes all those years ago…but even with all those secrets, she'd had no idea what really happened to Paul Pope.

It had been so long ago, he nearly had, too.

Chapter Twenty-One

Thank God for the return address on the envelope sent to the Apex PD; there was no way this connection was insignificant. Mike and Ben spent the rest of the afternoon researching everything they could find on Terrance Pearson, younger brother of Margaret Pearson Sykes. The older man, age sixty and never married, now lived in Buntner, North Carolina.

He'd had a troubled childhood, strung out on weed and cocaine for most of his teenage years. He'd dodged the draft in the seventies, which probably didn't sit well with his war hero brother-in-law Quincy. In the days following the pivotal fire, Terrence had been the one to box up personal items that survived the blaze and shipped them to Quincy at his request. By all reports, this was so traumatic, he'd suffered a violent breakdown and thereafter was institutionalized in Buntner where the state ran its mental institution. Terrence lived in a private neighboring institute called New Horizons, though, which was where the wealthy stashed their embarrassing kinfolk.

"They won't tell me much with HIPAA laws in force," Mike said. His phone rested on his shoulder and he turned away from his monitor to talk to Ben, who worked at the desk behind him. Mike's partner was on vacation for the week, so his desk was vacant and situated perfectly for this investigation. "But I do know he hasn't had any visitors in thirty-six years."

Ben shook his head and shot off a quick text to Randolph. "Thirty-six years? Damn, that's cold." Terrence might have been bat shit crazy, but he'd lost his only sister. Rich people were so weird.

"Yes, ma'am," Mike said into the phone. Ben turned his chair and listened to the one-sided conversation. "I understand. Um-hmm…the Innocence Project?" He paused and looked at Ben. "If they'll help us get permission from Terrence, can we talk to him directly?"

Ben shot to his feet and paced along the length of the desk. Mike said, "Thank you. Most likely Chief Ward Randolph will accompany a member of the local FBI office to talk to him in the next day or so…uh, of course *if* we get his permission. Thanks so much."

He ended the call and held up a hand before Ben could ask what happened. "Come on." He led him into a walled office across the hall and closed the door. "Three months ago, the Innocence Project started working with Terrence Pearson. As you know, they're best known for working on behalf of prisoners in the penal system who've been unjustly incarcerated, but they've recently begun looking at long-term residents of mental institutions. Some of those folks were institutionalized rather than serving jail time."

"Where do you think Terrence falls?"

"Mental issues, for sure. He's one of the long-term residents. His situation flagged the Innocence Project because of the number of *decades* he's gone without incident, or visitation. Anyway, he's had two weekend getaways from New Horizons so far, both times accompanied by a volunteer legal guardian. We're not the only people who have asked about Terrence today."

Ben slammed his hands on the desk. "Sonofabitch. Do you know who called?"

"Joyce Dupree."

"Chief counsel to Senator Sykes?" He texted the name to Chief Randolph while Mike searched the browser on his phone for information on her practice.

"The one and only." He flipped his phone screen around. "She's part of Wickett, Blanchard, and Pearson, a big name law firm, here in DC. They represent any number of US senators and business magnates across the nation."

"Can you tell if she's got any connection to Sykes beyond his work on the Hill?"

"I can't see a fucking thing on this phone. Come on, let's use your computer." He followed Ben back to their shared desk space, and while Ben pulled up Dupree's firm, Mike looked into New Horizons.

The private institution housed ten patients. Photos of the place showed elaborately landscaped gardens surrounding a Georgian-style mansion. It sat on five-hundred acres of privately held land and boasted a board of directors of a dozen local physicians, lawyers, and government officials. It looked as rich as the people who paid to house their family members there instead of in prison.

"Found her," said Ben. "Joyce Dupree, partner and chief attorney for Senator Quincy Sykes, chairman of the Senate Arms Committee. He was introduced to her by the North Carolina attorney general, who was dating her at the time, a couple years after Margaret died. She handled the business end of the sale of the family property to the Army Corps of Engineers. Plus…here it is…she set up the family trust with the funds he received from the sale."

Mike whistled. "She knows where the bodies are buried."

"Yep. She's not going to be easy to get past. What'd you find out about New Horizons?"

"If you're rich and crazy as a shithouse mouse, your family can make sure you live out your days in luxury—and far from the family hearth."

"Damn." Ben's stomach growled, and he checked his watch. One-thirty. They'd been at it for a couple of hours, and he was curious about Abby's day. "Let's grab a quick lunch while we check out the Innocence Project. If we can get their cooperation today, Chief Randolph and Teddy Barnes can head to Buntner tomorrow."

Mike drove them to his favorite mom-and-pop sandwich shop in a little alley off the National Mall where, he claimed, they made the best cheese steak sandwich in the universe. Turned out, he was right. Everybody seemed to know Mike, which made it easy to get his regular table in the back corner. The WIFI was free, the corner was private, and the food a slice of hole-in-the-wall heaven.

Mike ordered an extra serving of homemade sea salt and black pepper kettle chips while Ben talked to the people at the Innocence Project. It didn't take long to set everything in motion.

"Charlotte Jackson is the law student assigned to Terrence. She's focusing on civil liberties this semester and working with the Innocence Project fills her volunteer requirements for the next two years," Ben said and glanced down at his phone. "Charlotte said that after lunch, she'd drive over and ask him if he'll meet with us. After so many years of no outside interaction, he really enjoys talking with her in person. Plus, she brings him chocolate chip cookies."

The chips arrived while he and Abby exchanged texts: Yes, the day was going well. She and Sarah had made their way through almost all of the fittings; she'd had a nice time with the arts editor from *The Post* and was looking forward to talking with *Pointe*.

She sent a photo that Sarah had taken of her and Mrs. Gladys stitching garments and laughing with a hungry-looking ballerina. Both looked happy. And safe. He turned the screen around so Mike could see his mother.

"Your mom is a pistol," he said, then sent a farewell text, letting Abby know he was looking forward to seeing her for dinner. And he was—beyond the investigation element, he was looking forward to seeing *her*.

"She was so disappointed when she figured out Abby and I didn't click."

Ben glared at him, which made Mike laugh again. "Seriously. She loves Abby like a daughter, and they've become great friends. She never looked at me like I'd hung the moon." He tilted his head to Ben. "Relax, man. I can see something's brewing between you two. Just be careful with her. I might not love her, but I like her. And my mother will kill you if you hurt her."

Yeah, he didn't have a death wish—Mrs. Gladys was one scary lady.

****

Charlotte Jackson called as he and Mike were wrapping up for the day. Mike's basketball league had games tonight, so he wouldn't be joining the group for dinner. "I'll swing by the hotel and pick you up in the morning, that way Abby can have your car tomorrow."

"Sounds good." Ben picked up on the third ring. "Hey, Charlotte—any luck today?"

"Yes, sir," she said a little breathlessly. It sounded like she was walking. "Actually, I didn't worry about it at all because Terry is great. I'm not sure why his family socked him away with no contact for so long. He's a great storyteller."

"I'm in Washington, DC, for the next few days, so my boss, Chief Ward Randolph from the Apex PD, will be the one to talk with him. Teddy Barnes from the North Carolina State Bureau of Investigation will probably accompany him. They've got information for Terrence, but I'm also passing along your info, too, if that's okay."

"Absolutely. As Terry's attorney, I'll need to be present since this is a law enforcement visit. Think they'll object?"

"For now, we're keeping this informal—which means we're trying to keep the conversation private. It's part of a larger investigation, and we're not broadcasting all of the moving parts."

"I understand, but I have to ask you, is Terry in any trouble, or in any danger?"

"No, ma'am, neither. But because of a potential connection he may have with the case, we need to keep things quiet. Chief Randolph will be able to share more with you in person."

He climbed into the car and gritted his teeth when there was a hiccup in the line as the call transferred from his handset to the Bluetooth connection. She had gotten quiet for a moment, and he figured she was weighing her response.

"Okay, I'll allow this to happen off the record until I have more information. Please tell the chief that my first availability isn't until Friday or early next week."

"They'll be there Friday." They'd lose a day or two waiting for her, but it was worth it. Plus, they needed to coordinate between his department and the SBI office. Though it seemed like secret meetings would be easier to navigate than anything on the record, they were walking a fine line between discreet conversation and political nightmare.

Ben dialed the chief while navigating the congested streets in downtown DC. Traffic in the capital was a perennial nightmare, and times like this reminded him how happy he was to live in a rural area where it didn't take an hour to drive two miles. He turned onto Virginia Avenue and was working his way to the left lane when Chief Randolph picked up.

"Chief," Ben said, "I've got a new lead for you."

"I hope it's good news. We've stalled here."

"Mike Dixon and I had a talk with Senator Sykes today. It did *not* go as planned."

"Hold on a second. I'm heading into my office." Someone spoke in the background as the chief excused himself. After a moment, he said, "Okay, give it to me."

Ben told him everything, from running into Martha Scott over dinner, to the bizarre interaction with Sykes and Janet Dupree in the senator's office.

The chief's keyboard clacked across the phone lines. "A secret brother-in-law? That's great!"

After Ben turned into the north entrance of the garage, he turned off the car and settled in while they finished their conversation. It was nice to be able to sit still for a few minutes.

"Yes, sir. His name is Terrence Pearson. He's Margaret's younger brother. He was troubled as a kid, and the family sent him to a private institution in Buntner when he was a teenager. The week after Margaret died in the fire, Terrence was able to get a temporary release, so he could help Quincy pack up the house and grab some of Steve's toys, things like that. He says he never went back to the house after the fire."

"I don't think I could have, either."

"No, it would've been hard."

"Why doesn't Terrence show up in any of the biographical stuff for Quincy?"

"Mike figured it was because rich people just socked away their embarrassing kinfolk." The chief barked out an unexpected laugh. "Plus, he's Margaret's family, not Quincy's. But it makes sense to me, I guess. He goes by Terry, and he's been a model patient. About six months ago, the Innocence Project took him on as a client, then three months ago they entered him into a pilot program that pairs him with a guardian who takes him out for one weekend a month."

"No shit?"

"His guardian is a law student named Charlotte Jackson. I've already talked to her, and she's gotten permission from Terry for us to get in touch. Apparently, he's got a lot to say about the family who pays big bucks to keep him locked up."

Randolph whistled. "Think Steve knows about his uncle?"

"It looks like Quincy's paid a fortune to keep his brother-in-law out of the public eye, so I don't think he would've helped foster a relationship between Steve and his Uncle Terry. Charlotte said that in her research with the IP, they targeted Terry because of his good record, his lack of visitors, and the self-sustaining trust that was set up for him back in the seventies. He was the perfect candidate for their pilot community release program."

"Good Lord. I'm going to call Teddy Barnes tomorrow, and we'll get out to Buntner this week."

"Miss Jackson said unless you come on Friday, she's not available until early next week. I don't think you can get in to see Terry without her."

"Then Friday it is, but it's good to know we can follow up Monday or Tuesday if we need to. Think you'll be back by then?"

"The performance with the president is Friday night. Abby said something about wanting to go to Saturday's show. I think she goes to all of the performances so she's on hand for any costume repairs. She probably likes to see her work on stage."

"Normally I'd tell you to come back as soon as possible, but in this case, the potential for her being a target in Apex makes it safer for her to stay away as long as possible."

Ben rubbed the back of his neck and blew out a long breath. Much as he needed to be with Abby, keeping an eye on her, he wanted to be there to talk with Terrence Pearson. "I'll let her choose. I'm sending the info right now."

"Check in with me tomorrow when you can."

"Yes, sir."

Chapter Twenty-Two

Ben used his badge to get into the building. Since there were no performances in either theatre tonight, the incredibly lousy boy-band music floating down the hallway had to be coming from Abby's crew.

Andy McNeill sat at the desk, bopping his head in time with the music while keeping both eyes on the wall of security screens. When Ben came closer, the older man turned and smiled. Then he stood up and did a little dance, laughing at himself. "I love this music. But if you tell anyone, I'll deny it and then shoot you."

"Ha! I can't believe you're still here, Andy."

"Load-in stretched a little longer into the afternoon, so I'm just finishing up. I'd buzz Marky for you, but I think you can follow the music. See you tomorrow, Detective."

"See you," Ben called out, already making his way toward the music. It was loud enough to make his ears throb, but the delicious aromas of hot food and fresh bread overwhelmed his senses and pushed the crappy music to the background. Whatever they were having made him happy. By the time he swung the door open, his mouth watered, but it was the throng of dancers—his girl in the middle, laughing and singing along—that stopped him in his tracks.

****

"Ben!" Sarah's greeting dimmed the sing-along

and interrupted the revelry.

When Abby pushed her way through the mass of dancers, her face flushed and her lithe body clad in a pale, pink leotard with matching tights, and jumped into his stunned arms, the crowd cheered. She had a self-conscious moment of panic, wondering how he would react to her drooping ponytail and sweaty body, but it evaporated when she got closer and noticed the look of awe on his face. Well, it was a little more dumbstruck than anything, but it was sweet.

She was having a ball, as was expected since she loved her work. Anytime the company could let off steam before a performance they took it because the final week before a big run was stressful. The expression on Ben's face made her giggle. He stood in the middle of the doorway, mouth open and head tilted to the side, like he was about to say something but stopped mid-thought. He was hard to resist, so she had danced over and jumped, thrilled that he caught her automatically. When she wrapped her legs around his lean hips, he slid those big, sexy hands down to cup her bottom.

Then she leaned in and kissed the shit out of him. Right in front of everybody. He was passive for a second, stunned by her boldness, she guessed, but his body caught up quickly and he took over. Making the sexiest sounds in the back of his throat, his breath sawing in and out of his lungs, the broad muscles of his pectorals rippling against her chest. One hand tangled in her hair, tilting her head so his mouth could open hers wider, push his tongue deeper, consuming her.

Ben kissed the breath right out of her. When she pulled back, a happy bubble of laughter trickled out.

His lips were wet and rosy, and color stained the suntanned skin above his five o'clock shadow. She rested her forehead against his and whispered, "Wow."

She was starting to slip down Ben's torso, so he hitched her up higher. "I missed you."

Her heart beat faster and she licked her lips. "I missed you, too." She laid her head on his shoulder and hugged him, then noticed the absolute silence in the room.

Ben looked over her shoulder and said, "Shit."

He set her on the floor. She tried really hard not to laugh, but his response wasn't exactly quiet. Laughter erupted from different people, and she snorted, and covered her mouth with her hand to try and be a little dignified. "Uh, sorry to interrupt…"

That was all she wrote. Abby burst into hysterical laughter and grabbed his hand to lead him farther into the room, but he grabbed her by the hips to hold her in place. "I need a minute," he whispered desperately. His lips brushed the shell of her ear, making goosebumps break out down her arm.

"What?" She matched his whisper. He pulled her flush with his body, his sizable erection pressing into her abdomen, and she got it. And started laughing again.

Bruno, bless his big, brutish heart, snapped at Sarah, "Restart the music!" He gave Ben a manly nod and just like that, Ben and his situation were forgotten. The dancers started dancing again, Mrs. Gladys raised a glass of champagne in toast, and Sarah continued her conversation with a couple of caterers as they set up buffet tables.

"I'm sorry." Abby squeezed Ben's hand. "I didn't

mean to embarrass you. I just couldn't help it...you looked so handsome standing over here by yourself, and it's been such a long day. Good but long."

He bent and kissed the tip of her nose. "It's okay. I'm a big boy. And really, you can greet me like that anytime. I doubt we permanently scarred any of these adults."

"You're right about that. Dancers are notoriously shameless. We have to change clothes in the wings so often and with so many people wandering around, rigging lights or pulling curtains or changing sets, nothing fazes us. You good now?"

At his nod she said, "Come on, I'll introduce you."

As expected, Ben was greeted with enthusiasm and camaraderie. He eased right into conversation with the group, and she realized his ability to assimilate was probably a huge asset in his career. The conversation during dinner was animated as everyone laughed and decompressed from the long day.

Mrs. Gladys was a delight, and much to Abby's relief, didn't pepper Ben with a million questions about their greeting earlier. Instead, she talked about Mike and was happy to hear crazy stories Ben told about training with her son at the FBI Academy.

Misty, one of the principal dancers, came and sat by Abby as the meal wound down. "I meant to point out a spot that pinches earlier. The boning in the corset I'm wearing for the first act digs into my hip bone on the right." Misty shifted her hips to the side and lifted the edge of the leotard.

Abby made a *tsking* sound as she ran her fingers across a small bruise. "I'll get that fixed first thing tomorrow. Since your full legs are exposed, we don't want any marks to show."

Misty gave her a side hug and let out a relieved sigh. "Thank you so much."

"No problem. I know you haven't worked with me before, but I'm not an old-fashioned designer. I want you to tell me when it's uncomfortable." Misty nodded, then grabbed a piece of baklava from the buffet on her way to the dressing room.

"Are the dancers afraid to let you know when they're in pain?" Ben slumped lower in his seat. He bit into his last piece of dessert and groaned, rubbing his hand low on his abdomen and drawing Abby's attention. He'd eaten enough for three men, so his discomfort wasn't a surprise.

"Hmm?"

"Do they keep their discomfort to themselves?"

Abby cleared her throat and sat back. "Sometimes. Back in the fifties and sixties, the Boston Conservatory designer was a genius. He retired in his seventies, but in his heyday, he was a god and unfortunately, set much of the expectations for the industry. His costumes used heavy upholstery and brocades. They were stunning, but always real elaborate. When I was a dancer, some of the costumes weighed ten or fifteen pounds and made it so much harder to leap—can you imagine the guys lifting fifteen extra pounds? I try to look at function as much as form and design. Old school designers made you suffer through it because it looked good on stage, and *nobody* ever spoke up about discomfort."

"Makes sense. The things I saw in your studio were real sparkly. I'm curious to see how they look on the dancers, and now I'm excited to see what they look like in motion. For now, though, I'm spent. I need a shower."

Abby's whole body flushed when he said *shower*, and of course he noticed.

His gaze intensified, pulling her in like a gravitational beam from the sun. Her eyes widened and she stilled, a mongoose to his cobra. "We're leaving."

Rather than going back through the group, Ben grabbed her bags and hustled her through the front door. The crisp air was refreshing after the stifling work room. It was nearly ten o'clock, and the humidity had given way to a nice breeze. Anticipation thrummed through her body. He carried the big garment bag for her and, she noticed, was paying more attention to her legs than any potential threat.

She started to tell him that men were so easy when screeching tires coming from her right brought a shout from Ben—just before he grabbed her.

In one motion, he dropped the garment bag, jerked her against his body and dove them out of the path of an advancing SUV. She and Ben hit the ground with a jarring thud, that clacked her teeth clacked together and stole her breath. He bore the brunt of the fall, whacking the back of his head on the concrete, and rolling to his left so he could whip out the gun from the holster on his right hip. As Abby landed, the pavement dug into her hipbone and thigh, tearing the fabric of her tights and scraping the skin raw. Goddamnit, that hurt.

Ben rolled onto one knee and fired rapidly at the retreating vehicle. Bullets hit the back windshield but ricocheted in a wild pattern. The SUV accelerated through the parking lot, scraping along pylons as it fled.

He took aim one last time and hit the right rear tire,

making the vehicle fishtail around the corner before it was gone. Ben surged to his feet, ready to give chase, but stopped. "Are you okay?" he barked to Abby, who still lay on the ground.

She stared at the sky, watching a pair of contrails drift in front of the moon. Fury boiled just beneath the surface, heating her blood and muffling the sound around her. Ben leaned over her face, shouting something.

She blinked. "What?" Her ears buzzed now, and a dull throb started in her hip.

"Shit." He looked off toward the edge of the parking lot, where the SUV had gone. "I asked if you were okay." He dropped to his knees beside her and winced. "Let me have a look."

She swatted at his hands. Pissed at being run down. Embarrassed at laying in the middle of a parking lot. "I'm fine, Ben. Just help me up. Ugh, this is going to hurt in the morning."

"Stop, Abby. Something might be broken."

With brusque, efficient motions, he checked her out. A swipe across her collar bones. Gentle hands down her torso and along her pelvic bone. She watched through slitted eyes as he poked at the torn leotard on her hipbone. He made a strangled sound in his throat and held up fingers. Blood. He cocked an eyebrow, like *I told you so.*

She sighed. "Just help me sit up, okay? I don't want to be lying on my back when everybody gets here." Visions of her last accident swirled in her mind. She was nobody's victim.

Bruno and Pierre raced through the courtyard, waving their arms and screaming. "We called 911.

They're on the way." They stopped just out of reach while Ben helped her stand. It took a minute to get her legs under her, but it felt infinitely better being upright.

"Thanks, Bru." She patted him on the chest and smiled at Pierre. "I'm good. Really. Ben threw me out of the way."

"Thank you, baby Jesus," Pierre said, genuflecting. He gave Ben a companionable smack on the shoulder. "What can we do to help?"

Bruno leaned down to look at her hip. He lifted the fabric away from her body and tsked. "That's some pretty good road rash, girl." She swatted his hand away. She wore nothing underneath; damned if she'd flash the crowd.

Sirens rent the air, and for the second time in a week, she found herself sitting in the back of an ambulance. If it weren't so scary and fucking enraging, she might laugh. Instead she took a deep breath for patience and looked at the EMT checking her out.

Ben flashed his badge and met two uniformed police officers as they made their way through the crowd. Sarah joined the fray soon after her husband, and stood in the open door of the ambulance, leaning against Abby's knee. Pierre had quickly corralled the company members who'd run out after the gunshots; another set of officers was walking over their way. She hoped things would wrap up soon because tomorrow night's premiere would be here in no time.

"Looks like you got caught playing in traffic," the EMT said. He grinned and flashed a penlight into her eyes. "I'm Don. How's your head, ma'am?"

"It's fine. I didn't hit it—just my side when Ben shoved me out of the way." She leaned to the right and presented her left hip. "I hit my shoulder, I think, but mostly I fell on top of him. My hip got all banged up when we skidded across the pavement."

Ben walked over and touched her lightly on the hand. She grasped his fingers and frowned. "Detective Ben Owens, Apex PD. My girlfriend was nearly run down by a black SUV six minutes ago." She heard fury in his voice.

"Sir," the first officer said and relayed Ben's badge number and name into the mic attached to his collar, then turned his attention back to them. "Ma'am, I'm Officer Donald Pike, with the DCPD. This is my partner, Arnie Wolcomb."

"This is Abby Markham," said Ben. She could tell he was working really hard at being calm. And polite. Probably because he wanted to stay in the conversation. The officers nodded, and Wolcomb made a note of her name. "How's your arm, Miss Markham?"

"It's fine," she said. "Not as sore as my hip, but it's not the worst accident I've ever had."

Sarah made a choking sound, but Abby didn't look at her. After years of reconstructive surgeries and physical therapy to put her back together, a scraped hip was nothing. She focused on staying calm.

"What happened to your hip? Were you shot?"

She blinked and looked down. Shot? That hadn't even occurred to her. She'd assumed all of the gunshots had been from Ben. She reached out and ran her hands along his arms, checking to see if maybe he'd been shot. He grabbed her hands and held them in one of his.

"Neither of us were shot, Officer Wolcomb," Ben responded. "Actually, nobody in the vehicle returned fire. It glanced off of that cement bollard, and when

Abby and I rolled out of its way, it veered off sharply."

Now that she thought of it, it was like the driver changed his mind.

Wolcomb seemed to note that, too. "Did either of you get a plate number, notice anything about the driver?"

Ben presented his gun, grip out. "I fired five times into a black unmarked SUV, probably 2015 or 2016 model. Bulletproof glass, tinted windows. I could only see one head shadowed through the back window. And the plate was blacked out."

Pike accepted the weapon and looked down at the pavement. He frowned. Wolcomb walked in a wider arc, stopping at the pylon and tapping it with the point of his pen. "I don't see any glass. You sure you hit it?"

"Yes, goddamnit. I wasn't shooting blanks. It was *bulletproof*. It didn't even make a dent in the glass—no fracturing. No splintering. Nothing."

"Ben," Abby said quietly. She wrapped her fingers around his wrist, and he rocked back on his heels. All the fight seemed to fizzle out of him. After a moment, he turned to her.

Mike Dixon's car tore into the parking lot. He was out of the door almost before it came to a halt, shouting, "Abby! Ben!"

Pike and Wolcomb took defensive positions in front of Abby and drew their weapons.

"FBI," Mike shouted, reaching into the breast pocket of his jacket to pull out his creds. Once Pike nodded, Mike surged forward and wrapped his arms around her shoulders. She yelped when his hands brushed over the many tender spots.

Ben reacted swiftly. He grabbed Mike by the

shoulder and tugged. “Hey. Easy, man,” he said in warning. “Don’t hurt her.”

“Sorry,” Mike said. He gave her a gentle pat on the other shoulder.

“It’s okay, Mike.” She gave him a fist bump so he would stop looking so pitiful. “You just pushed the wrong button. Ben saved the day, but he bounced me all around. He weighs a ton.”

Both men cut her a look; she gave them a tired smile if only to offer reassurance.

“I didn’t mean to hurt you, honey.” He looked equal parts sad and pissed. It was not a bad look on him, if she were being honest.

“You didn’t cause this, Ben. You saved me.”

“If I could go back in time, I would’ve taken the whole hit.” He ran his hand through his hair and tugged it at the end.

She pulled his hand onto her knee and grabbed his fingers. “I know.”

Don the EMT interjected when conversation lulled. “You’ve got some debris in this abrasion, and I’d like to wash it out. Okay?”

“Sure.” Her voice was as tired as her body. All the activity was distracting, but the sooner Don was done, the sooner she could leave.

He kept up a steady dialogue as he worked. Abby figured it kept his patients calm, and she appreciated it. “I’m going to cut a small patch out of this get up so it won’t brush against your raw spot.” He snipped a small square of fabric away from her hip and held up an emesis basis. The cool water stung at first and she sucked in a breath. “Woo, those raw nerve endings wake you up, don’t they? Despite the scare you suffered, this is just superficial. It's going to be real sensitive until it scabs over."

She blew out a steady breath through pursed lips. "It's good, really. Just a surprise, you know?"

"Mm-hmm, I do know. Fell off my mountain bike last month when I passed over some loose gravel and ripped my elbow to shreds. Cried like a baby."

He winked and dosed her with another splash of water. The distraction worked and with gentle hands, he worked fast and cleared the area of all the dirt and debris. She looked down and was relieved to see the patch of raw skin was smaller than her palm. It stung like a bitch, though. "You're gonna have one hell of a bruise in the morning."

Ben leaned in to look at her hip and made a sound of commiseration. It looked like he wanted to apologize again, but she held up her hand. "Are we almost done, Don?"

"Yes, ma'am. Just need a sec to bandage you up, and you're good to go." He slathered a healthy dab of antibiotic ointment onto a square gauze pad, then taped it down. "This tape won't withstand a shower but covering the area will make it more comfortable as you move around. If you can stand it and can sleep with it uncovered, it'll start to scab over. And I'd suggest you take a couple ibuprofen for the sore muscles."

"Thanks, man," Ben said, and helped her climb out of the ambulance. Mrs. Gladys stood with Mike, whispering with Sarah and Bruno. She walked over and wrapped an arm around Abby's shoulders, and patted her affectionately on the cheek.

"We want you to sleep in tomorrow morning," Sarah said. "Mrs. Dixon is going to get everything started, so if you can make it by noon, we'll prop you up and make these dancers come to you."

Abby chuffed out a laugh. Ben started to protest, but she touched his hand. Again, he quieted immediately. His natural state was bossy, but he was respectful enough to let her make her own decisions. "That sounds great. Mike, thanks for coming to check on me. If you need to talk to us, you're going to have to come back to the hotel because I want to lie down."

He and Ben used some sort of mental telepathy, and he said, "Anything we need to discuss tonight can be done by phone. I'll swing by and pick you up at eleven tomorrow."

"Yeah, that works," Ben said. He led her across the median to his jeep, walking slowly.

"Need help getting in?" He opened the door and rested a hand on her waist, like he was going to lift her.

"Nah, I'm good." She grabbed the interior door handle and hoisted herself up with a tiny grunt. She felt Ben move in against her back as soon as she stepped up and shook her head. "Really, I'm okay. Hitting the ground was more shocking than anything. Mostly, I'm so mad I can hardly breathe. How dare that asshole try to run us down."

Ben leaned in to kiss her forehead, and when he pulled back she saw his hand grasping the dashboard so hard his knuckles were white. He'd been so calm by the ambulance, so his visible anger turned out to be comforting. Who took potshots at a costume designer?

"I don't know, but we'll find out." He stepped back and closed the door. Once in traffic, he called Chief Randolph using the hands-free device.

"Someone tried to hit her?" the chief bellowed.

“Yes, sir. Well, I can’t say for certain, but it sure as shit looks that way.”

“I’ll call Officer Pike in the morning and have him fax a copy of the incident report to me. Did either of you mention Senator Sykes?”

“No, sir. It wasn’t their business, and really, why would a powerful US senator take a swipe at a costume designer?”

“Right,” he said with little conviction. “This makes too many close calls with her, Ben. My knee-jerk reaction is for you to bring her home, but it looks like she’s in as much danger there as she is here. Since she’s got plans, and I can’t imagine anybody being dumb enough to try to get to her at the ballet with all the Secret Service that’ll be there, you can stay.”

“I’m not going anywhere,” Abby said. She didn’t care if it was rude to speak over their conversation. Screw that.

The men were quiet for a heartbeat, then Ben said, “Her team has already figured out how she can take it easy tomorrow. And Mike and I are starting a little later in the day.”

“Okay.” The chief still sounded a little skeptical, but again, Abby didn’t care. She was an adult and knew her limits. “We’re going to focus on Terrence Pearson, see if we can rattle the senator’s cage a little more.”

Chapter Twenty-Three

Abby tried to be a good sport about Ben's overprotective behavior. Though, "overprotective" probably wasn't the best description. They both assumed the near hit and run was purposeful, and until Ben had evidence to the contrary, she figured she would be on a tight leash. In the parking deck, he grabbed all their bags from the day. Between her big work bag, which was a veritable mobile tailoring studio, the long garment bag holding his new suit, and his briefcase, he was weighed down.

"If I had two more hands, I'd carry you," he'd told her once he was loaded. It was sweet, but unnecessary.

Trying to get everything in one trip was his explanation for leaving his phone in the car. "I'll be right back," he told her when Abby unlocked the door. He dropped everything on the couch and ran down to the car.

She went into the bathroom to draw a glass of water and was tapping out a couple ibuprofen into her hand when someone knocked at the door.

"Coming," she said, and threw back the pills. A tension headache had setup camp on the drive over, and there was a piece of dark chocolate in her bag calling her name. The combination of muscle relaxant and flavonoids would wipe it out in no time.

She unlatched the safety bar and swung the door

wide. "Did you forget your key?"

It wasn't Ben. She jumped back and tried to slam the door shut, but a man built like a brick shithouse grabbed the doorknob and leaned in.

Terror like Abby had never known flashed through her mind, rendering her mute and paralyzed. The man gained a little more space and wedged his shoulder inside. "I didn't know," he said in a tone filled with agony and remorse.

The tremor in his deep baritone snapped her out of the lassitude and directly into hyper-awareness of her situation: a woman alone, injured, facing danger head on. "Get the fuck out of my room," she yelled, shoving at the door with all her strength.

She sucked in a breath to scream. He hissed, "Don't scream. Tell Jammin' I didn't know you were his girl." He pressed a small mobile phone into her palm. "I'll call him in tonight when I'm free. He *needs* to answer."

Then he was gone, running down the hall and dashing into the stairwell just as the elevator doors opened. Ben was there, but was looking down at the carpet. She yelled, "A man! Tried to get in. He ran." She pointed. "That door."

"Damn it!" Pulling out his gun, he took off at a run. "Get back inside. Lock the door."

Poleaxed, she stood in the doorway for a moment looking down the empty hallway. An older gentleman across the hall opened his door and peeked out. "Everything okay, young lady?"

"Sorry for the disturbance, sir. My boyfriend heard the car alarm go off."

"Oh, dear. I hope nobody backed into it. That's the

worst." He nodded and backed into his room. The door shut with quiet *whump*.

What a crazy day. She sat on the edge of the couch and rummaged through her bag until she found her little bag of emergency chocolate. Two pieces later, she leaned back and closed her eyes, feeling the tension begin to wane. Though the air conditioning soothed her frayed nerves, her goosebumps had grown goosebumps. "I gotta get out of this leotard."

She winced when she walked into the bathroom and looked in the mirror. "Whoa."

Her hair was a mess. The ponytail had long since disappeared, and the bright, garish lights made her look far worse than she felt. Turning to the right, she looked at her left side and the back of that shoulder. No bruising yet, but it was tender.

Ben was a big man, and she'd bounced once beneath him before he'd managed to roll them over. She reached in and turned on the shower, adjusting the temperature as high as possible. The best part of being chilly was not having to wrestle out of a sweaty leotard. That thing went straight into the garbage. The large bathroom was full of steam by the time she stepped under the water.

Oh, Lord, it was heaven. Definitely one of the top ten showers in her life. The giant stall; the four shower heads. Just heaven. The hot water made it easy to peel off the bandage. The abrasion stung when the water hit it, but only for a second. She was almost done when Ben knocked sharply on the door and called out, "It's me, Abby. I'm coming in."

"Okay," she said through the door, and then turned off the water. Drying off was a quick affair, even with slowing down around her hip.

The mirror was too steamy to see anything, so she eased into a pair of boy shorts and a tank top and put night cream on her face. She brushed her teeth, flossed, and waffled with the decision to ask for help with the bandage. She could only see the scrape from above, but the skin around it wasn't fevered or red.

She grabbed the antibiotic ointment and a Band-Aid and walked into the small living room. "Hey, Ben, I took the bandage off in the shower so I could make sure it was clean and wondered if you'd have a look at it for me." She walked over to the small office area where he sat and leaned against the desk.

"Sure, whatever I can do."

"Thanks." She set her stuff on the desk. "It was too steamy to use the mirror, but I think it looks okay."

"Here, let me see." He moved the lamp to the edge of the desk and gestured for her to step closer.

She lifted the tank top with one hand and folded down the waistband of the shorts with the other. Ben leaned closer an used his thumbs to press on her skin around the scrape, grumbling. The shallow, kidney-shaped scrape was about the size of three quarters squished together.

"Shit." He wrapped his long fingers around her hip and rotated her body so he could look at her back and shoulder. He poked her here and there, gauging her reaction. "Your hip looks good—still a little raw, but it looks like it's starting to dry out. Was the other bandage bloody when you took it off?"

"Not too bad. More gooey than anything, but I think that was the ointment."

He nodded and turned her again so he could look at

her other hip. "You've got some bruising starting around the abrasion, along that hip bone, but the skin isn't hot to the touch. All things considered," he said and settled both hands on her hips, "you were very lucky. How's everything else?"

The heat of his hands branded her; their weight was comforting and reminded her she wasn't alone in this. Like a strength injection, it felt good to be quiet and absorb the sensation of having someone in her corner.

"My shoulder's a little stiff, like if I overdid it with weights, but otherwise all good."

His head dropped back on a frustrated groan. He rolled his shoulders and took purposeful breaths, but it didn't seem to loosen any of the tension radiating off of his big body. As much as he tried to appear calm for her, it was impossible to mask the fury running through his blood. She could read his emotions so clearly right now. All this time he had been so comforting to her, she wanted to try and soothe him.

She ran the fingers of one hand gently along his chin, over the muscles jumping beneath his skin, silently encouraging him to loosen up. "We were very lucky, Ben. *We*. If you hadn't been so quick to react, we might've both been in the morgue tonight."

He shrugged a shoulder and looked away. "Do you want to cover it or leave it open to the air?"

She let him break the connection and considered the option. "I've had worse scrapes than this, but I don't want the waistband of these shorts to drag across it." No way was she sleeping without pajamas tonight. She and Ben may have given in to their attraction earlier that evening, but she wasn't ready to go any further at the moment—that meant pants *on*.

"Let's cover it up tonight."

He unwrapped the Band-Aid while she dabbed on a little ointment and focused on him. "How are you? Nobody looked you over before we headed back to the hotel. Can I see your back?"

He shook his head no. "I'm okay, Abby. You got banged up because you're in a leotard. I outweigh you by a hundred pounds, and I've got on a full suit."

She stepped back and pointed to his jacket. "Doesn't matter. Let me check you out."

After a brief staring contest, he stood and wrestled the jacket off. He wasn't happy, and for some reason that made her very happy. What a grumpy baby.

"I hurt you worse than the car did." Every word he punched out was grumpy. Confusion crossed his handsome face when he glared at her. Like he couldn't understand what she would have to smile about. "Why are you smiling?"

"Because the alternative is crying, Ben, and I'm done with that." She helped get his tie undone while he worked on the buttons of his shirt. "That big car barreling down on us was terrifying. But did you notice it seemed like the driver changed his mind?"

Ben dropped his shirt, and it landed on a pile with the jacket and his tie. He squinted, which Abby considered his thinking expression. "Yeah. He had the perfect opportunity with a wide-open parking lot. The only way he could've missed us is on purpose." He huffed out a pissy breath and turned his back to her.

A mournful sound rumbled up from Abby's chest when she got her first glimpse of his torso. His suit may have acted like a motorcyclist's armadillo suit for scrapes and abrasions, but all evidence of them bouncing across the pavement was written in dozens of bruises from the nape of his neck to his waist. Or maybe it was just one giant bruise. She ran gentle fingers, whisper-soft, along the long, muscular lines of his back. He had to be in agony.

"Oh, Ben," she whispered, and leaned in to press a sweet kiss to the middle of his shoulder blades. "I think this bruising goes below your belt." Her hand rested on his waist, right above the hard line of his worn leather belt. They both stood still, absorbing the moment, until she realized his whole body was trembling.

He unbuckled his belt and let his pants drop. Tight boxer briefs hugged his body, outlining every muscle in stark relief. But there was nothing sexual about her perusal, or her gasp. "How does it feel?"

"Like I almost got hit by a truck," he said. "Tell me what you see."

She walked her fingers across his shoulders, down the backs of his arms, and along his back with as little pressure as possible. "It looks like the brunt of our fall was on your left side, kind of between your shoulder and waist."

He turned and took her hand. "That's what it feels like. I'm okay, honey. I'm going to take some of your ibuprofen, though. And I'm going to use all the hot water in that ridiculous shower in there."

He pressed a genteel kiss across her knuckles when she choked out a laugh. "Even if you don't hurt too much now, you will in the morning. I'll be out in a few minutes."

Twenty minutes later, Ben walked out of the bathroom wearing a pair of low-slung athletic shorts, rubbing a towel through his hair. He seemed preoccupied as he dried off haphazardly, like men do, hitting the high spots and leaving huge swaths of water droplets along his body before calling it done, so she took a minute to admire the view. Until he turned to make sure the door was locked and bolted, and she saw the angry bruising on his skin. But she told him earlier: no more crying. She opted for humor instead. "You missed a spot."

He barked out a laugh and swiped the towel over his shoulder that was already dry, completely missing the dripping wet spots, like everywhere else. He pointed to the tablet in her hand and said, "I'm happy you're in bed, even if you're not laying down. I feel like you were already running on empty before tonight."

She took off her reading glasses and set them on the bedside table, next to her tablet. "I was, but production weeks are always intense. I'm so used to this schedule it doesn't even faze me anymore. I won't crash until after the weekend, when I'm back home."

"Do you already have another project lined up?" He grabbed a paperback that had seen better days out of his pack and sat on the couch at the foot of the bed. There was another bedroom across the living room of the suite, but Abby was happy he hadn't headed out yet. Truth be told, she was a little freaked out.

"I generally costume four ballet productions a year, which works out to be about one a quarter. In between, I have conservation work for a handful of museums. It keeps my skills sharp and feeds my love of history." She fiddled with the edge of the duvet, working up the nerve to ask him to sleep in the room with her. "How about you? You were coming off of vacation and jumped right into the fire."

He waved his hand in the air. “Detective hours are never reliable. True, I don’t have the same nine-to-five constraints as the officers on shifts since I work until a case is done, but my time is manageable, now.” He cut his eyes to the side, and Abby remembered that he’d been an FBI agent in Los Angeles. That had to have been stressful. Clearing his throat, he asked, “How are you feeling now?”

“A little sore, like after my long runs.”

“No,” he said with emphasis. “How do you *feel* about what happened tonight?” He looked at her with eyes that saw everything.

“A little freaked out.” Her voice gave away her wariness. “Would you…stay—”

He sat forward and tilted his head listening all of a sudden, and she stopped talking mid-sentence. “Do you hear a phone?” He looked on the desk at their phones. Neither were ringing. “There it is again.” He followed the sound to the side table in the small hallway. It rang one last time and Abby sat up straight. “Answer it!”

He opened the flip phone, but nobody was there. “Do you know where this came from?”

“I totally forgot, Ben. The man who came to the door gave it to me and said he’d call you tonight. And that you *needed* to answer it.” She twisted her fingers together with an overwhelming urge to hyperventilate. “I’m sorry I forgot.”

“No, no. Shh, it’s okay, honey.” He wrapped an arm around her shoulders, and she leaned against him. “Did he say anything else?”

“Yes! He said, ‘Tell Jammin’ I didn’t know you were with him,’ or something like that.”

Ben stiffened. All the color drained from his face.

"Do you know what that means?"

He sat heavily on the desk chair. "Jammin' is what the guys called me in the Army."

"Where did that come from? Did you have trouble shooting or something?"

"*Pfft.* No." He focused on the wall over her shoulder, like he was remembering. "My name is Benjamin. Ben-Jamin…Jammin'."

"Ohh. Not a lot of rocket science there, huh?" She rubbed his shoulder, trying to soothe him. "Uh, he looked really upset when he was talking to me. It startled me at first, when he stepped into the doorway, but he didn't try to come in or grab me or anything. It was more like he wanted to keep the door from shutting. It seemed like he was going to cry, actually."

He stared at the phone, like he was willing it to ring again. After a minute when nothing happened, he grabbed the phone and walked over to set it on the bedside table. "Who knows when, or if, he'll call back. Were you going to ask me to stay in here?"

Abby walked around the other side of the bed, past the couch so she could shift the bags from the couch to the floor. "I can sleep here if that would make you more comfortable."

"Uh," he said, floundering like a fish for a moment. "Isn't that supposed to be my line?" A corner of his mouth kicked up in a grin. She liked that he didn't move away from the bed.

"No. I'm the one asking you to do something you didn't want to do."

Ben held up a hand. "It's exactly what I *want* to do. Not like in a skeevy way, but if I'm in here with you, I know you're safe, maybe we'll both sleep better."

With a nod, she climbed in on the other side of the bed. He walked through the suite and turned off the lights, then headed into the bathroom to get ready for the night. A few minutes later, she felt the bed dip and rolled toward his big, warm body. He sighed, and she thought it sounded happy, so she curled on her side and laid her head against his chest. His heart beat sure and strong beneath her cheek, like a metronome, and its calming pace helped ease her nerves. She traced the wrinkles in his T-shirt across his chest and down his torso, caught in the lassitude of finally letting her mind rest. His hand closed over hers and squeezed, stilling her movements.

A couple breaths later, once he relaxed his hold, she whispered, “Maybe it can be the skeevy way tomorrow.”

He snorted. “Yeah.”

Chapter Twenty-Four

They'd just drifted off when the burner rang. Ben grabbed the phone. "Who the fuck is this?"

His fingers ached from squeezing the phone so hard. The small device made a cracking noise, and for one satisfying, berserker-crazed breath, he imagined it exploding into a cloud of dust.

"Jammin'—it's Jim. Forthmann."

The name, then the voice from the past, hit Ben like a sledgehammer. He and Jim Forthmann went through basic training together. They'd once been fast friends. *Once* being the operative word.

They were together in Kuwait when their convoy ran over an IED. Both survived the explosion, but when the insurgents swarmed their small five-man team, Ben was shot in the chest and sustained a head injury and was later discharged for diminished peripheral vision.

Forth wasn't so lucky. He took a head shot and was killed instantly. "Fuck you. Jim Forthmann is dead."

He snapped the phone shut, fighting the urge to rant at the world. Or punch the wall. Both options sounded good. Black spots danced in his peripheral vision; his hands started to tingle. He sank to the bed, working hard to get his breathing under control. He caught a glimpse of Abby's head popping up out from the nest of blankets, eyes wide with terror—and he was down for the count.

****

When he came to, he found Abby on her knees, phone at her ear. "Hold on, let me see if he can come to the phone now."

Tears streamed down her face; both hands trembled like seismograph needles, but she seemed to be holding her shit together. Fucking panic attack. Fucking Jim Forthmann.

He shifted to pull himself up against the headboard. "It's the guy," she hissed and handed the phone to him. She knee-walked over and sat next to him and dipped her chin in thanks when he switched the audio to speakerphone.

"What?" He didn't give a fuck how surly he sounded.

"Stop being such a pussy, Jam. You need to hear what I've got to say." The deep rumble of the voice was familiar. And so eerie it raised the fine hairs on the back of his neck.

"You've got two minutes to convince me."

Ben came off the bed and walked to the desk. He opened his laptop and logged in using his secure hotspot. Years of being in the military and FBI had taught him to not rely on the public WIFI because it was unsecure. No way was he going to shave off steps when something of this magnitude was happening. Jim Forthmann, back from the dead. Fuck him sideways.

He felt Abby move in close and looked over at her. Her eyes were as wide as saucers and all the color had drained from her face, but she stood by him, staring at the phone like the caller would reach through airwaves and grab her.

"I didn't die on the battlefield," the caller said.

"They pulled me out for reassignment."

"They?" Ben hissed. Their attack had been some two-bit splinter group protesting oil rights in the Gulf of Oman. It hadn't even been anything official, which is how they'd been caught with their guard down. Both Forthmann and AJ had died that night; their bodies had been recovered by a sweep team an hour later. Oh, God, was AJ alive, too? "*They* who?"

The silence was a damning response. *They* refer to anybody. Any agency.

Ben started pacing, swinging his free hand in agitation as he punctuated the conversation. "I watched Jim Forthmann die. There's no way he's still alive. No. Fucking. Way."

"I am, Jam—Ben. I am." Ben heard the man sigh, and mutter something under his breath. "Remember our third post in Kandahar, when Jerome ran across that kid who used to brag about his grandfather having some old relic from Genghis Khan?"

His heart nearly stopped, but the man went on, like he didn't know Ben's chest was cracking wide open.

"How about when we hitched a ride with that UN crew to Beirut and got a flat tire outside Hamra? That crazy Scot who plied us with Almaza and nearly got AJ's balls shot off when he tried to make out with—"

"Miss Lebanon."

Ben snorted, despite his best efforts. Oh, God. It wasn't possible. They'd been so far off the beaten path on that mission. The US hadn't been at war with Beirut in decades, but if his guys had been discovered, shit would've hit the fan. He didn't want to remember fondly. He didn't want to bend to this man's memories, but he didn't want to break, either.

He rubbed his forehead, fighting off a migraine. "Fuck."

"We need to meet, Ben."

The man Ben had counted among his best friends—had mourned for a decade—broke his heart all over again. He pressed onward, twisting the knife deeper, forcing him to remember the worst night of his life. "No."

"They'll send someone else."

Ben slammed his fist down on the heavy wooden desk and roared. He leaned against it heavily, paying little attention when Abby jerked back and stumbled over to the end of the bed to sit, covering her mouth. He couldn't comfort her now. Hell, he couldn't even level out his own breathing. "Come up now."

Three sharp raps sounded on the door almost immediately. Abby yelped and rather than saying anything comforting, Ben pulled her to her feet. "Do you think that's him?"

"Yeah, I do." Forthmann was always the most punctual son of a bitch he'd ever known. He grabbed his sidearm and motioned her toward the bathroom. "Lock the door. Don't come out until I call for you. No matter what you hear. And take your phone."

She was as white as a sheet but scrambled to the bathroom without argument. As soon as she was safe, he cracked opened the door to the hallway. A feather could've knocked him over.

Sucking in a sharp breath, he glared at his former friend. "What the fuck?"

Jim Forthmann said nothing, but the expression on his face spoke volumes. "Can I come in?"

He looked pretty much the same. Leaner and

somehow deadlier looking. His eyes were haunted, and his color sallow. All traces of the brave, loyal friend gone. The man who was quick with a joke to break the tension. The man who traded water rations in the desert for Turkish delight because of his legendary sweet tooth. Ben stepped aside to open the door a fraction.

Forth stopped in front of the wardrobe and quietly disarmed himself. Reaching to the small of his back, he pulled out a knife Ben recognized from their standard Army gear. Next came a small pistol from the custom holster under his right arm, and the revolver he called "the Judge" from his right boot.

He took a deep breath, holding his hands up in a submissive gesture, and turned, despair written over his face. "Honest to Christ, I didn't know she was yours."

It was like waving a red flag in front of a bull. The rage and sorrow and fear bubbled up so fast, Ben couldn't contain it. With a roar, he lunged at Forth, slamming his fist into the bastard's face. Forth's head snapped back as blood splashed from his mouth.

He didn't fight back or try to defend himself from the blows Ben landed on his chest, which only further enraged him. His hands ached from the impact and though Forth's utter stillness began to cut through his awareness, he still couldn't stop.

"Ben!"

From a fog-filled distance, he heard Abby call his name, but caught up in the violence, he roared out his fury and heartbreak. Forth's head dropped forward, his chin rested on his chest, passively accepting the beating.

She stepped closer, but Forth raised one palm. "Don't touch him—he's not in control right now." He turned his head to the side and spit out a mouthful of blood. “I’m sorry. So sorry.” His voice broke, and his chest heaved.

Ben’s arm was cocked back, ready to deliver another painful blow, but Abby put her hand on his arm. Finally, he blinked. As if coming out of a stupor. His eyes shifted to the spot where her hand rested, then to her tear-filled eyes. A harsh sob echoed from his chest. He took a giant step backward, mortified and as broken as the other man. Forth slid to the ground, resting his head against the wall and closing his eyes.

No one spoke. They stared at each other, like Old West gunfighters. Abby went into the bathroom, came out with wet washcloths. She handed one to Forth, but when she bent down to help him rise, Ben stepped forward.

“Don’t touch him.” He jerked his head toward the mirror hanging on the wall across from the closet, his intent clear. Jim Forthmann could clean up his own fucking cuts, where they could watch him.

Forth took a deep breath and groaned as he knee-walked closer to the mirror. His hair was out of whack, and the left side of his face was beginning to bruise. Blood flowed from a cut on his lip and a spot beneath his left eye. A cauliflowered edge popped out on his right ear, and his shirt was rumpled from the torso battering. He looked bad. But he didn’t say a word as he cleaned up with the washcloth.

Ben pulled Abby closer, positioning her so his body stood between her and her would-be assassin. After a few tense minutes, Forth rose and it looked painful. There were likely a few bruised ribs, and he’d be pissing blood for awhile. But he hadn’t fought back.

Why hadn't he fought back?

Forth spoke to Abby at first, then leveled his gaze at Ben. "I've got two weeks on this contract," he lisped through swollen, lacerated lips. "And we're already to the end of week one. You don't have a lot of time—you ready to listen, now that you've gotten the bruise to your gigantic ego out of your system?"

Ben nodded. "Fine."

"Ms. Markham, I'm not sure what you did to piss off Senator Quincy Sykes, but he put out a hit on you."

She sucked in a startled breath and grabbed Ben's arm. "I didn't do anything to that crazy asshole."

Forth's mouth kicked up on the less-damaged side. For a second, Ben caught a glimpse of his old friend and the easy camaraderie they once shared.

"I always research my assignments. I don't kill women. Ever. There's nothing tying you to criminal activity or threats against Sykes."

"That's because she's not a criminal," Ben sneered. "She's no enemy of the state."

As if Ben never spoke, Forth continued. "The way this works is I get details, then research the best ways to…complete the assignment. I figured you must've been his mistress and wanted more."

Ben growled and took a menacing step forward, but Abby grabbed his wrist. "There's no way in hell I'd let that old man touch me."

He nodded. "That's what I figured. So, I tried to scare you off."

"By running her down?" Ben growled.

"No. I was just trying to scare you…I wasn't going to hit you or do something irreversible until I was sure." He shifted on his feet and drew in a slow, painful sounding breath. "Why is he so interested in you?"

Ben cut her off before she could answer. "Enough of this horseshit. Where've you been? And why is a US senator putting out hits on American citizens?"

Forth just looked at him, no expression on his face, for a moment. He winced and bent at the waist, resting his hands on his knees. "Do you mind if we sit at the table in there while we talk?"

Ben saw he was in pain and was content to let the bastard stew in his misery. But Abby gave in, gracing him with undeserved mercy. She made a wide arc around him and headed to the table. The guys followed, with Ben taking up the rear so he could keep an eye on his old friend. No way would he be able to grab any of those weapons off the floor to pull a fast one on them.

"I've been a government contractor since I left the service," Forth admitted. "I lost track of you after your FBI posting in Los Angeles. You're a cop now, right?"

"Detective," Ben muttered. He pulled his chair around to Abby's side and squished up close to her. She rolled her eyes, but he didn't care. No way could he fall back on assumed friendship and safety.

"Ninety-nine percent of the time, I'm a data analyst and field operative. But when the situation calls for it, I take out high-level targets overseas."

As Abby sat up straighter in her chair, Ben said, "He's a spook."

"Mine is a necessary role, Jammin', no matter how you feel about it."

Ben understood the darker side of democracy. But brotherhood was stronger. "How I feel about it is pretty fucking bad, man. You couldn't reach out to let me know you were alive?"

Forth shook his head. "You know I couldn't."

Ben squinted, forcing out the question he did not want to ask. "Is AJ alive, too?"

Forth looked down at his clenched hands. "No," he said. His eyes got a little glassy, but he blinked and looked away. He set the burner on the table between them, looking at it like it was a ticking bomb. The silence in the room was deafening; the ghosts of heartache and regret threatened to drag them all down.

Finally, Ben rubbed a hand through his hair and let out a frustrated huff. "Why are you doing this?"

His old friend's smile looked sad. "I hate that cocksucker. My life is stressful enough with international projects. When he called me out of the blue last week, it was obvious something was up. He has zero integrity, but he gets shit done. He wanted me to get *you* done. I'm not okay with that."

He nodded once at Abby, then looked back down at his hands clasped on top of the table. "You're an artist. Former dancer, presently a costumer. Last regular lover a year ago, though you date occasionally. You employ a retired woman, the mother of an FBI agent. You run daily and open your backyard pool for your assistant's friends so they can do water aerobics twice a week. For fuck's sake, you're a saint in the scheme of things. Why did he sic *me* on you? Are you blackmailing him, or something?"

She got up, then limped over to the cabinets in the kitchenette and rummaged around until she found three highball glasses, then pulled out the bottle of bourbon Bruno had given her yesterday and brought the load back to the table.

She poured them each two fingers and shot hers in

a single gulp. Forth's mouth kicked up, and he followed suit. "Christ," Ben muttered, drinking his and grabbing the bottle to pour them all another round.

"I returned his time capsule," Abby said quietly.

"The what?"

"The time capsule. I had no idea who he was when I bought this old farmhouse last year—I just know I got a great deal for the house and the land. My assistant, Gladys Dixon, filled me in on its history. I moved an old barn from a spot farther out on the property and attached it to the house so I could use it as my studio. During the winter and spring, I had renovations done, including putting in a pool and a tall fence. While the workmen were digging the holes for the fence posts, one found an old metal ammunition box. It had the number one painted on top, faded but still legible. It was locked, and on the side in some kind of marker it said, 'Quincy and Steve's Time Capsule'. Mrs. Gladys mentioned there had only been the one owner, so I looked up Senator Sykes."

Forth sat forward. "Did you look inside?"

Shaking her head, she worked slower through the second glass of whiskey. "Mrs. Gladys found the address for the senator's local office. I dropped it off a couple weeks ago."

Ben leaned toward Forth, looking for a reaction. "He opened it on Monday."

"Quincy called me early Monday morning at, like, three o'clock Eastern Standard Time."

Ben slapped his hand on the table. "It's got to be the time capsule. There's something he doesn't want anyone to see."

"He opened it live on television, Ben," Abby said.

"The only thing in there was old photos of the family, love letters between him and his wife from his time in the service, and some of Steve's baby toys. There's no way he could've hidden something secret. The room was filled with people."

"Is the time capsule what brought you to his attention, Ms. Markham?" Forth asked.

She offered her hand. "Please call me Abby."

"I'm so fucking sorry." He squeezed her fingers gently. "I do a lot of tough, bad shit in my job, but I have never killed an innocent woman. Assassin maybe, not a murderer."

She paled. Ben was proud of her composure. Government and law enforcement were not in her bailiwick, but she was a smart woman and could suss out danger.

"A couple weeks after I dropped off the capsule, I started getting what I *thought* were false alarms at my house. The Apex police officers were quite nasty about having to come out so often. Steve Sykes, the senator's son and a police officer, came out once and told me if I called it in again and it turned out to be false, he'd arrest me. Turns out it was his father, sneaking around the back fence."

Ben made a furious choking sound. Son of a bitch, she was going to tell it all.

And he was going to let her.

"What was he doing?" Forth was invested now, and Ben remembered enough about his old friend to know how much he liked a good mystery. And that he was taken with Abby.

"I talked to him Monday, and he said he was just curious about the old homestead," Ben said. "Told him to just go up and ring the doorbell next time and *ask* to look around."

Forth snickered. "Bet that went over like a lead balloon."

"Yeah. Mike Dixon and I have been doing some investigating on Sykes this week. Today we went to his office with new questions about a man named Paul Pope, who was his best friend when they were kids. Quincy's tragic rise to fame and prominence is well documented online, but it's also the stuff of legends in his hometown. *Our* hometown. But one of the details I didn't know was that his childhood best friend, Paul Pope, is the guy who died the night of the big fire. Apparently, he'd been staying with Quincy after he came home from Vietnam."

"Oh, that's so sad," Abby said.

He agreed: it was sad. But in light of the current situation, it was also curious. He added, "We also got a tip about Margaret Sykes' long-lost brother, a man named Terrance Pearson, who's been socked away at a mental institution for the last four decades."

Forth took out a small notebook and made some notes. "I'm going to do a little research and see if I can help you from my end."

Abby looked to Ben, and when he nodded, spoke up. "Be careful, Jim. We found out my Peeping Tom was the senator because someone gave me a flash drive with photos of him looking over my fence."

"That's great!"

"No," Ben said. "It's not. Abby was running her usual route and came up on two men fighting in a field. One of them was a uniformed officer—Jason Lawson—who was murdered by the other guy. She tried to help him, but his injuries were fatal. Lawson gave her the jump drive before he died."

She threw back the rest of her whiskey and stood. "And with that, gentlemen, I'm going to get some sleep, if that's okay."

Ben nodded and pulled her in for a hug, pressing his face into her hair and taking a deep breath. Even in the chaos of the last few minutes, she was a calming presence. "I'll be in soon." The bedroom door closed, and he asked the painful question he'd been stewing over since his dead friend had walked in through the door. "Did you kill Jason Lawson?"

Forth didn't even flinch. He didn't look insulted or embarrassed. "No. But you can bet your sweet ass Quincy Sykes had something to do with it." He pushed back his seat and groaned.

"Why are you so willing to help Abby?"

"Like I said, most of my work is as an analyst. About four years ago, Sykes put a hit on a crooked general in Moldova. My first shot went wide and hit the wife of the US ambassador to Moldova. Freak thing—gust of wind, fate, I don't know. The ambassador was out for blood, but Sykes pulled down the veil and has held it over me ever since.

"Does that happen often—casualties?"

Forth nodded. "For some operatives, yes, but she's the only one I've had. After she died, her husband was reassigned to a small African nation and recently retired."

"Can you go to the ambassador directly?"

"Yeah, maybe after all this time. Anyone in that role understands the risks, and the rewards, of covert work. But it's not an easy sacrifice to forgive. That general was crooked, not the ambassador."

Ben was quiet for a moment, wanting so badly for his friend to throw an arm around his shoulders and laugh about this all being a big joke. But it wasn't a joke, and they weren't kids. Instead he took a deep breath and an even bigger leap of faith. "We've got an extra bedroom if you'd like to stay. I've got fresh clothes if you don't have a jump bag."

Jim looked torn. In another life, there would be no hesitation. No awkward silence. "Okay," he said quietly, standing. "My bag's in the hallway. I dropped it before I came in." He opened the door, leaned out, and grabbed a bulging duffel bag.

Reality finally kicked in. A powerful senior senator and presidential hopeful in the next election had ordered a hit on a civilian. A gentle artist with a beautiful soul and kind heart, who had already suffered so much in her life. He was pissed. Then again, so was Jim Forthmann.

"Is she in danger?" Ben asked.

"I've still got a couple days left on my contract. Sykes won't jump the gun. It's just not done."

Ben huffed in irritation; Jim just blinked.

The danger was written in blood at this point.

Chapter Twenty-Five

Friday morning's six o'clock alarm was more jarring than usual—so much was at stake—for everyone.

Abby had a fitful night's sleep which she'd attributed to pre-show jitters, before falling into a motionless sleep two hours prior. Ben suspected it had as much to do with the sudden appearance of Jim Forthmann as anything, but he didn't know her well enough to gauge if she was always on edge leading into a production.

He shifted to his side to look at her. She lay on her side, curled into a tiny, boneless ball that only someone extraordinarily flexible could pull off. Her eyelids fluttered, and he imagined she was leaping across the stage in all her former glory. Maybe she was sewing intricate costumes in her dream. Maybe she was running from Lawson's murderer. Who knew? But her breathing was slow and even, and she appeared to be in no acute distress.

He grabbed his phone off the bedside table and opened the Notes app. Making a list of the day's tasks always helped focus him and today was no different. By now, Chief Randolph and Teddy Barnes should be about halfway to Buntner. They were set to call him around six-thirty to make sure all bases were covered.

He and Forth had worked long into the early hours

of the morning, hammering out a deal with Mike and the FBI. Understandably, Forth wasn't comfortable going to Mike's office for fear of being arrested on the spot. But the lure of getting out from under Quincy Sykes' control outweighed any argument for staying in the shadows. It felt like a dream. The possibility of Jim being alive, and with him after all these years, was too much to process. Right now his old friend was asleep in the second bedroom in the suite. Unless he'd bugged out in the last couple of hours, they were set to deal with his information at seven-thirty.

He sat up and yawned and stretched his arms across his chest. He wasn't used to sleeping beside anybody, and his muscles were a little sore. Not a bad price to pay, though, to have given Abby a little peace of mind. Besides, before Forth had barged in last night, she'd asked him if the skeevy stuff—the fun stuff—could happen tonight. Far as he was concerned, things were looking up.

Twenty minutes later, showered and shaved, he stepped out of the en suite bathroom, trailing a cloud of steam. "How was your shower?" Abby asked, and he jumped.

She snickered.

"Good, thanks. I didn't mean to wake you. Why don't you go back to sleep? I'll take Chief Randolph's call in the sitting area."

She unfurled and stretched and climbed out of bed with more enthusiasm than he'd had in his entire life. Even after a lifetime of being in the military and working in law enforcement, he wasn't a morning person. He shook his head.

"Nah, once I'm awake I'm up. There's too much to

do today to be lazy." She skirted around him closely enough that the bottom hem of her tank top got caught on his chunky diver's watch. But he stood there like a bump on a log.

"Real smooth," he muttered, and grabbed his phone. He pulled the covers up so the bed was neat and was unplugging his laptop when Abby came back into the bedroom dressed for the day.

"What was real smooth?" She was brushing her hair and pulled it back into a ponytail.

"Nothing." Of course she'd heard him.

"Um-hmm, nothing." Her voice sounded happy, and her smile was contagious.

She met him at the door and wrapped her arms around his waist, watching his reaction. When he neither pulled away nor jumped her, she leaned in for a hug. It was hard to remember the last time a woman had hugged him solely for the purpose of comfort. But it was nice. He pressed a kiss to the top of her head. "Thanks for staying with me last night."

"Anytime," he said and smiled broader when she laughed. She was one of the most optimistic people he'd ever known. It was refreshing. "Okay, that's enough sweetness. I've got three minutes before Chief Randolph calls." He gave her one last squeeze and opened the door.

Forth was already working when they walked out. The sitting room was well-appointed, with two large couches and two fluffy wingback chairs connected by a giant square coffee table. His laptop teetered on the edge of a stack of notebooks.

"Morning, y'all. I ordered breakfast." He pointed to the kitchenette and a compact dining table holding probably a dozen pastries, a pitcher of orange juice, and a carafe of coffee. Abby lifted the dome off of a platter and the scent of French toast and sausage made her moan. "I nearly starved *to death.* You slept so late."

Ben snorted. Forth always did have a flair for the dramatic. And a hollow leg. That man could eat twice his body weight in whatever was put in front of him.

"Thank God you managed to feed the rest of us before you checked out," Abby said. She clearly had a flair for the dramatic, too. She also shared a hollow leg, because she piled on two of everything before sitting at the table.

Forth just blinked, and then gave Ben a thumb's-up. Then he, too, got up to make a plate. Ben's phone rang before he could get in line, so Abby gave him a little charades motion that he interpreted to mean she'd bring something over for him.

"Good morning, Chief," Ben said, and sat on the couch. He set the phone on the coffee table and turned on the speaker phone. "I've got you on speaker phone so I can take notes and we can all brainstorm."

"Sounds good, son. Morning, Miss Markham."

"Good morning, Chief," she called out from the other side of the room around a mouthful of French toast.

"Okay, we're just pulling into the parking lot at New Horizons now." He whistled, and Ben heard Teddy Barnes say, "Rich people."

"What was that?" Ben asked. Abby brought over a plate of food and set it on the table. He caught her fingers and squeezed, then mouthed, "Thank you."

Randolph chuckled. "This place is palatial, like a European castle or something. Elaborate landscaping.

Water fountains. Teddy was just wondering at the lengths rich people go to keep their people contained. We've got to go through a security check, so hold on."

Ben heard their gravelly footsteps moving across the parking lot and used the lull in conversation to fork in a mouthful of French toast. He put his phone on mute and just listened. It sounded like a pretty secure facility, but considering New Horizon was appended to the state's mental health facility, it was necessary.

Abby finished breakfast and moved around getting her bag ready for the day. Forth piled a second helping onto his plate and settled into a wingback chair across from Ben.

"Wait a minute, Ben," Randolph said. "Here comes the law clerk. Hold tight—I'm going to let you speak."

Ben unmuted his phone and sat forward. "Okay."

"Good morning, y'all. I'm Charlotte Jackson," said a young, chipper-sounding voice.

Randolph and Teddy introduced themselves, and the chief said, "Charlotte, so nice to meet you. Detective Ben Owens in on the phone. He's on assignment in Washington DC. Ben, you're up."

"Good morning, Charlotte. Sorry I couldn't be there today, but there were just too many moving pieces to coordinate."

"Oh, that's no problem, detective," Charlotte said. "Will you be joining us remotely all day?"

"No. Chief Randolph will give me an update this afternoon. I wanted to make sure you and Terrence didn't need anything specifically from me. I remember you mentioned he's a little rough around the edges since he's only had one visitor in nearly forty years, before you started working with him."

Charlotte laughed, and Ben could hear the echoey clack of shoes hitting the tile floor. "That is true, but he's also a lot of fun. Such an interesting man to have been left alone for so long. The staff here loves him."

Chief Randolph cut in. "Ben, we're about to go in with Terrence. Do you have anything to add to the notes you sent over last night?"

"No, sir."

"Good. I'll call you this afternoon when we're done here. Good luck on your end."

The call ended, and Ben and Forth looked at each other. Forth grinned and grabbed a sausage off Ben's plate. A moment of nostalgia hit Ben so hard he could only blink.

Abby broke the spell when she touched his shoulder and leaned down to kiss him square on the mouth. He groaned and tilted his head to the side so he could kiss her deeper. He stretched higher in the seat so he could get more of her, and for a stolen moment, the only thoughts swirling through his mind were how much better French toast tasted on her lips than on his.

A brisk knock made her pull away, and when he looked around her head, Ben noticed Forth was nowhere to be seen. It was for the best, he supposed, because now was not the right time to introduce Jim and Mike in person.

She looked through the peephole and laughed. When she opened the door, Mike stood in the middle of the hall in warrior pose, like he was in the middle of a yoga class. "I see you've been working on your form," she said. Then she poked a finger into his shoulder and pushed, but he didn't budge. "And your balance."

"Abby got Mom into yoga last winter when it was

too cold for water aerobics, and they both forced me to begin practicing with them," he said, and winked at Abby. She blew him a raspberry and pocketed Ben's car keys.

"Whatever. I promise you yoga is good for you. You've gotta balance all those big, bruiser muscles with agility and grace. Plus, Kegel exercises are good for stamina."

Ben choked at Mike's expression. God, this woman.

****

Ben rode to the office with Mike, and they spent most of the morning looking into Jim Forthmann's burner phone while Forth stayed at the hotel and spent the time recreating a timeline of sketchy assignments Sykes had tasked him with over the last four years. While he wasn't comfortable going to Mike's office, he'd willingly traded information for immunity.

"You realize I have to meet this Forthmann in person if we're going to work out a deal," Mike asked after they were in the car.

Meeting was inevitable, but Ben wasn't willing to rush the process until they had everything in place. They couldn't run the risk that Forth's black ops status would overshadow the investigation into Quincy Sykes. Plus, Ben wanted to make sure Mike was able to get some protections in place first. On paper, it was a no-brainer. Mike's clearance got them a remarkable amount of information.

Forth had been an excellent Army Ranger and was obviously an effective operative. He had a file packed with commendations; in general, his colleagues enjoyed working with him. Hell, even the ambassador whose wife got in the way wrote him a recommendation. Gaps in his meticulous daily logs, some as long as six weeks, stood out in stark relief because Ben knew what they meant: Forth was on assignment from Sykes.

"I did that on purpose," Forth told them by phone, probably working through a second platter of pastries. "Figured the breadcrumbs might come in handy one day. Well, in this case, the negative space."

"That was pretty smart, man," Ben said. "If I didn't know you had periodic absences, I don't think I'd notice the chunks of unaccounted time. Do you have a hidden set of books with details for the gaps?"

"I'll hand it over to you this evening," Forth said.

Ben cut his eyes to Mike, who asked, "Who else knows you've been the senator's assassin?"

"I'm not his assassin," Forth snapped. "I was doing my fucking job."

Ben put his hand on Mike's shoulder, halting whatever his friend was about to say. They'd both been soldiers on the government's payroll. "Who else, Jim? Who else knows the senator's been blackmailing you?"

Forth blew out a ragged breath. "As far as I know it's just me and Sykes, my boss at the CIA, and one of the guys I work with in the field. I'd like it to stay that way. Again, data analyst."

Ben said, "We'll keep your name out of it for as long as we can. If we can pull this off, we'll get it sealed, man."

Mike Dixon had proved himself to be a by-the-book kind of guy—fair but driven by parameters. It's what made him a good federal agent. It was also one of the reasons why Ben had left the Bureau. He couldn't live with everything being *only* black and white. Fair and just interpretation of the law, for him, meant a willingness to look at the space in between, too. Life was messy; sometimes people needed a moment of grace.

Forth didn't respond, because there were no guarantees in life. And there sure as fuck weren't any guarantees in government service. But the black ops assignments Quincy Sykes forced him to do were beyond Forth's control, and if there really was justice in the world, Sykes alone would pay for this.

Ben sat on the other side of Mike's desk working on his laptop, texting back and forth with his tech expert at the Apex PD. They hadn't gotten much further on Lawson's investigation, but the larger the gap in evidence grew, the more convinced he became in a Sykes connection. He sent a new question that he hoped would help him begin to find clarity.

—how did lawson get so far down the dirt road? Did he walk or drive?—

—walked—

—what about footprints?—

—two sets on the way in, spaced like they were walking. Only one set—leaving. The runner we think—

—defensive wounds on his hands?—

—No, sir. None—

—He knew his attacker—

—That's what we were thinking, too—

Son of a bitch. Lawson went down that road of his own accord.

Ben looked at his watch. It was nearly two-forty-five, and he had to meet Abby. He and Mike had kept an open conference bridge with Forth all day, and it felt like hours since he'd moved more than an inch. He stood and stretched while thumbing through the email on his phone. Chief Randolph sent a note about fifteen minutes ago, with a file attached. His pulse accelerated while he read the message.

"Forth, I'm forwarding this video snippet to you, but just listen to the audio so we can watch it now. Chief Randolph sent a video from his interview with Terry today. Said Charlotte recorded the whole meeting, but he wanted to get this last bit on video."

They all knew what that meant: in case Terry wasn't able to give testimony later. For whatever reason.

Ben turned up the volume on his phone. Terry was talking about how troubled he was as a teenager, running with a bad crowd and getting into drugs. Their mother helped him dodge the draft, which made Ben smirk. That would've gone over like a lead balloon with someone as pro-war as Quincy. Terry went on to say he figured if he had ever had children, he would've wanted them to be more like Margaret than him. He chatted casually about his time in the facility with an open, wistful expression, but then he scowled and leaned across the table.

His hand shot out and grabbed Chief Randolph's wrist, like he was holding him in place, and he said: "Paul Pope didn't die in that fire. Quincy Sykes did."

Ben sucked in a sharp breath and Mike shouted, "Holy shit."

Forth was silent, but Ben heard his fingers flying across his keyboard. The video went on. Chief Randolph asked Terry to repeat himself.

"Quincy died that night, along with Margaret. I don't know how it actually went down, but the man the world knows as Quincy Sykes is not my brother-in-law. He's that shiftless bastard Paul Pope who followed him everywhere. They could've been twins, and it's been decades since I've seen him in person, but somehow the man the world knows as my brother-in-law is really Paul Pope."

If Sasquatch walked into the room, it wouldn't have made a difference. Ben's attention remained glued to the video. Chief Randolph asked if there was any proof, and Terry said, "I have the second time capsule."

Bam! With one sentence, Terrence Pearson damned Senator Quincy Sykes.

Ben's imagination went into overdrive and his blood surged through his body, like a hurricane battering the shoreline. The possibilities were endless—how the fuck had some Joe Schmoe managed to masquerade as the most powerful US senator for decades?

"Jam," said Forth. Ben had almost forgotten the other man was on the phone. His voice was gravely soft and made the hair on the back of Ben's neck stand on end. "Don't let her be alone with Sykes. There's no real code in this industry. He's ruthless, and if he has an opportunity, he might take it."

"He'll have to get through me first."

Mike shook his head, like he was thinking Ben shouldn't borrow trouble. "Nobody's bulletproof."

"That's what I'm afraid of," Forth said. "I'm going to try and wrap up everything tonight so I can head back to Nicaragua."

"Will you still be here after the performance?"

Jim was quiet for so long the answer seemed inevitable. But he sighed heavily and said, "Yes."

Emotions swelling inside Ben's chest made it nearly impossible to speak past the lump in his throat. The friend whom he'd mourned for more years than he cared to think about was alive. That same friend had tried to kill his woman because he'd been living under the thumb of a corrupt senator and now worked tirelessly to make up for it.

What did you say to that?

He decided to keep it simple. "Thank you. If something happens and you have to leave sooner, find me in Apex. You will always have a place with me."

Ben grabbed his laptop and walked out of Mike's office, holding his breath the whole way to the elevator. As soon as the doors slid shut, he bent at the waist, fighting off tears. *Fuck!*

He had to take a car service to the Carter Theatre since Abby had his jeep. By the time he picked up lunch, it was almost four o'clock. He was late and stressed—and so hungry it felt like his gut was trying to eat itself. Secret Service agents were already on site at the theatre for security sweeps in advance of the president's arrival. He sent up a silent prayer to the gods of preparation for his production badge.

Mike called just before he reached the backstage door. "What?" he barked into the phone.

"Uh, just wanted to let you know that Mom usually likes me to be there by the curtain speech, but since we're sitting in the booth with you and Abby, I'll be there a little sooner."

Ben stopped walking and took a calming breath. Mike didn't deserve his ire, and it would not serve him well if he stormed the building half-cocked. "Thanks, buddy. Sorry I snapped at you."

"It's okay. It's been a stressful couple of days."

Chapter Twenty-Six

Security for the performance was tight for obvious reasons. On the way in, two Secret Service agents stopped him, despite Andy McNeill greeting him at the door as "Detective Owens."

Ben shook his hand, then let the agent do a pat down and question him. The agents were polite and thanked him for his patience once they were done. It was much nicer to deal with this team than those protecting Sykes.

"Almost done, sir," the taller of the two agents said. "Why are you here so early?"

"My girlfriend is in charge of costuming the production."

Short and simple. When you offered explanations in depth, it made people curious. He didn't want any of these agents to get a whiff of what he and Mike were working on.

"And what's her name?"

"Abby Markham."

After the agent spoke into the mic at his wrist, then nodded, the two walked away without another word.

Andy blew out a stressful breath. "I hate when the Prez is here. These guys make me a nervous wreck."

Ben tapped him on the shoulder. "I know. But they're just doing their jobs."

"Good thing you realize that, my man, because you

aren't leaving this facility until after the production ends, and *after* POTUS clears the premises." He barked out a laugh and held up both hands when Ben swore under his breath. "Hey, they're just doing their jobs."

Ben was halfway through the lobby when Abby came out to greet him. She stood in the middle of the floor, looking more beautiful than he deserved, smiling and waiting patiently for him. She wore another soft outfit that made her look tall, lean, and artsy. Her dark, charcoal-colored tights were covered by a mauve tunic that hugged her torso. Black clogs added enough height for her mouth to line up perfectly with the underside of his jaw. She pressed sweet kisses along his scruff. "I like your shoes," he murmured, "I don't have to lean down to kiss you."

She waggled her eyebrows. "Hm, I hadn't thought of that."

She cupped his cheeks and sucked his bottom lip into her mouth. Hard enough that he yelped, but then she swiped her tongue across the same space. He held still, dying to see what she'd do next. She pulled back enough for their breath to mingle, and her lips to brush against his when she spoke. "Let's test it out."

And then she really kissed him. With lips and tongue and teeth. The bite of pain where her fingernails pressed into the skin behind his ears spurred him on. He wrapped his right arm low around her hips and hauled her tightly against him, taking the kiss she offered. Like a marauder. No mercy. No hesitation. And it was glorious.

She was guileless in her affection for him, genuinely enjoying their blistering kiss and not giving two fucks about the extra security prowling in and out of the lobby. In all likelihood, though, these agents had seen it all and then some, and kept their jobs because they could avert their eyes and keep their mouths shut. When she pulled back long enough to tilt her head the other way, he dropped the bag of food and wrapped his other arm around her. Lord, she tasted good. Like she'd been sucking on an atomic fireball.

Somewhere, across the cavernous lobby, somebody coughed. Abby pulled back. "I missed you today."

"Oh yeah? I missed you, too. How are you feeling? How's your hip?"

She did a little twist and patted her hip. "Between stretching out with the dancers earlier, I've been moving and bending. My muscles are good. Plus, I've got a super-sized bandage over the strawberry."

"Good. That's good." He leaned down and pressed a kiss behind her ear. "I'm happy you're feeling good," he growled. "Because, woman, I'm going to have to walk past half a dozen Secret Service agents who will be certain to see the boner in my pants."

"Good." She gave him a cheeky grin before heading for the door.

He caught up with her before she could reach it, glaring at the agents who gave them no privacy whatsoever. He flipped them off, making one of the guys laugh outright. Abby played to the crowd, laughing now, until he smacked her on the ass and swept her up into his arms.

They walked into the costume shop like that, and Bruno gave a wolf whistle when he spotted them. And just like that, his erection wilted.

Ben passed the bag to Bruno who cheered like a kid when he pulled out a boxed lunch. The company had a light dinner coming in at six o'clock, but none of the production staff had had time for lunch. He'd discovered that nothing made this crew happier than turkey sandwiches and chocolate chip cookies.

A frantic Sarah hustled non-stop, checking to ensure last-minute details were perfect. Abby had mentioned her friend was always on edge the hours before opening night, but it was exponentially worse when they hosted heads of state. The President wasn't the only big dog who liked to attend the ballet.

"It's worse when Russian dignitaries are here," she'd told him that morning before she headed out. "In the eighties, there were so many dancers who defected after performances, and then there's the Bolshoi."

"What does that mean?"

"The Russian ballet companies dominated the ballet industry for decades, and their dancers and choreographers continue to be held in the highest esteem. Imagine if you only played piano for your mom, who has to tell you how good you're doing because she's your mom. But all of a sudden, Beethoven showed up and asked you to play one of his pieces—with him. What would you think?"

"Whoa," Ben said.

"Yeah, whoa," she said. "Most presidents attend at least one performance during their term. It's like a rite of passage for the performing arts in this area. But the first lady is a retired prima ballerina, so politics aside, there's more at stake when insiders are in the audience."

"Gotcha," Ben said. "Bruno, there's a box in there for Sarah."

Mrs. Dixon hurried over and kissed him on the

cheek and, rather than taking a box of her own, picked up half of Abby's sandwich. Abby didn't even blink, so he figured sharing was their norm.

"Oh, thank you, young man," Mrs. Gladys said. She took a bite and let out an exaggerated sigh, like it was the only thing that kept her from wasting away. "How's my boy?"

"He's good," Ben said. "We were busy, but the investigation hit a stopping point for me."

At Abby's worried look, he said, "It's nothing bad, honey. Mike is running with a different angle tied to DC, and I've got a couple things to wrap up with the Apex PD after we eat." He gave her shoulder a gentle squeeze, trying to convey through body language that he'd fill her in later.

He grabbed his lunch and headed toward Sarah's office. "Hey, Bruno—I'm gonna use the office to make a work call. Okay?" The office had a door; what he needed to discuss didn't need to be overheard.

Randolph answered on the second ring, out of breath, like he'd been running. "Whatcha got, kid?"

"It's been a busy twenty-four hours."

"Tell me about it. How about you start."

"First off, thanks for the video. Oh my God, what Terrence disclosed explains a lot."

"I know. But you first," Randolph prompted.

Ben paused to focus his thoughts and said, "Turns out an Army buddy of mine, whom I believed to be dead, is still alive. He's the bastard who tried to run down Abby last night." Even though he understood the situation now, saying it out loud still made his blood pressure soar.

"Why? How in hell did she get on anyone's radar?"

"Our *friend* hired him," Ben said, using covert language...just in case.

"Are you fucking kidding me?"

Ward Randolph's calm demeanor was a running joke at work. He never raised his voice, never issued threats, never demeaned anyone. In the nineties, he'd served as a drill sergeant, shifting into police work after retiring from the military. He led by example and instilled confidence in his department. The Apex PD had worked hard on infusing diversity, equality, and inclusion training so they could put their money where their mouths were. Randolph's people protected and served, and though it was a constant learning curve, Ben was proud to be one of the man's detectives.

"Hold on, Ben," Randolph said, and then yelled, "Hey, Teddy—can you come in here?" Ben heard a door slam, followed by some shuffling and muted conversation before the chief said, "Can you repeat what you just told me for Teddy Barnes?"

"Yes, sir," Ben said, then went on to relate the bare essentials, ending with, "Sykes hired Jim Forthmann to take Abby out."

"Your friend's an assassin?" Randolph asked.

"Not exactly. He's normally a data analyst and undercover operative, but one of his assignments went south about four years ago, and Sykes has been using it for leverage, blackmailing my friend really. Forth was just trying to scare Abby into getting out of the way while he looked into why she'd become Sykes' target. When he realized she was with me, he paid us a visit last night. I've got a whole bunch of new information that I don't want to send through email; Mike Dixon is chasing down a couple leads on his end. We're all coming back in the morning, so we should be able to compare notes by lunchtime."

"Does that timeline work for Ms. Markham?" Barnes asked. "She mentioned trying to attend as many performances as possible."

"Normally that's the case, but this is an extenuating circumstance. I'm pretty certain we would have headed home last night if the President wasn't scheduled for tonight's performance. Even though she likes to see her work on stage, she doesn't have a death wish."

"I think you're making the right choice. McGee said you figured out Lawson must've known his shooter. That makes the most sense. What do you think of the video of Terry? He has a very interesting theory that might help us tie everything together."

"I can't believe it. It's like a movie or something. I guess it makes sense that there were people after the war who dropped out of society and popped up somewhere else," Ben said, "but to take on a different identity and live as publicly as a senator? He's ballsy, that's for sure."

Barnes snorted. "That's one word for him."

"Did Terry give you any background on Paul Pope? Does he think Paul murdered Quincy?"

"Actually, Terry had a great recollection of events from all those years ago," the chief said. "Paul Pope came home from war and stayed with his friend and his young family. Margaret was young and had just given birth to the couple's first child. Terry said she was tired of having another man in the house, with no job and no home, and felt like Paul never considered leaving. The lightning strike on the house was a genuine accident, as well as the fire that ensued."

"You heard Terry say he didn't think Paul murdered Quincy on the tape. That even though Paul was always a lazy ass, he genuinely loved Quincy. They were truly friends. Nothing about Terry indicated he was delusional or schizophrenic. There's no reason to think he's misremembered anything because the circumstances revolving around his confinement in New Horizons were more related to drug use than a psych diagnosis. It's pretty clear Quincy paid to have Terry hidden away."

Ben let that sink in for a moment, but before he could ask any questions, Teddy Barnes cut in. "I keep running through my mind what must have happened during that night. If Paul and Quincy had the tight friendship everyone's convinced of, then it must have been Quincy who was struck and incapacitated by the beam. It would've been easy for Pope to assume Sykes's identity."

"No shit," Randolph said.

Ben couldn't imagine the desperate fight to get a family of three out of a burning house. The fire and the heat and the pain would have been terrifying and painful. Just imagining it nearly choked him. He sat back in the chair and shifted his gaze through the window in the office door and found the dancers milling around Abby's shop. A beehive of activity swarmed around both her and Mrs. Dixon, as several stopped to have beads and baubles added to their costumes.

Abby chatted while she worked, her face and her body animated and engaged with each person. He knew from experience that her individual attention felt like a ray of sunshine focused directly on you. At the moment, she seemed to be trimming things from the waistbands of two male dancers who slowly turned for her perusal. It looked like she was giving their jackets a haircut, which made him smile. Such camaraderie. They all looked amped for the coming performance, but at the same time so unencumbered by the burden of murder and death and deceit. He would give anything to keep that carefree expression on her face.

"We can come back now if you'd like," he told Randolph.

"There's nothing we can do tonight that can't wait until tomorrow. I'm going to talk to the D.A. in Raleigh to figure out how the hell we can get a warrant for DNA. Christ, we can't afford to tip off Sykes—*either* of the Sykes men—without more proof. But I can't get more proof without a DNA sample. This will take a little finessing. I plan to speak with Steve in the morning and find out if he was aware of Uncle Terry."

"You going to mention Pope?"

"I haven't decided how to broach the subject. Don't know if I'll ask if he knows who Pope is, or fish around and see if he has any inclination Sykes might not be his real father. My gut says Steve has no idea."

"Mine, too, sir."

Abby walked toward the office with a garment bag in her hand, smiling at him through the glass. He waved her in and motioned for her to have a seat. "We'll hit the road early in the morning. After I drop off Abby at home, I'll head into the station. I think we need to assign a unit at her house for protection until we see how this plays out."

"Agreed. Let's plan on one o'clock, so let me know if you'll be later."

He hung up and closed his eyes, drawing in a deep breath and trying to settle his nerves before he talked to his girl. *His girl.* Over the course of the week, and in between being run off the road and accosted in their hotel, he'd given in to his emotions. Even though stress had sped up what would've been a natural progression toward dating, there was no doubt in his mind that they would've eventually wound up together. He'd never crossed the professional line with a witness, but now he was so far past the line, it wasn't even a distant blur.

He pushed the chair back and invited her closer. She laid the garment bag across the desk and then, God love her, straddled his lap. "What've you got there?"

"Hmm?"

Staring at his mouth, she licked her lips, slowly, languidly, ignoring the question when he asked a second time. Slim arms looped around his shoulders, sealing her lithe body against his torso and offered a scorching kiss that sent his heartrate from resting to sprint in two seconds flat. When he flexed his hips to rock her against his erection, a deep, satisfied groan escaped his chest. It was like this every time they touched.

All the breath zapped from his lungs and he wrenched his head back, sucking in a deep breath. Pressing open-mouth kisses along the length of Abby's elegant neck made her moan, especially when he sucked at the spot where her pulse raced. "Abby." She made him pant when she pressed harder against his cock. His eyes rolled back in his head. "Baby, I can't do this with a glass door separating us and the dozens of people milling around out there." He pressed his face against her hair. "You've got to be still."

"I know. I'm sorry." But she wasn't sorry. He knew by the sexy smile on her face. "You just looked so tense. I couldn't help it. I'll get up now."

Relief hit as soon as she stood, and he couldn't help making an adjustment through his slacks. "What've you got there?"

She unzipped the bag and handed it to him. "Here. Mrs. Gladys and I altered a suit. I meant to give it to you last night but it slipped my mind."

He was stunned. "Huh?"

Embarrassment tinted her cheeks and she tried to scoot away. But he was faster. "Uh-uh." He grabbed her wrist and held her there while he looked at the suit. Even he could tell it was an exquisite garment.

"This gala has been on the books for a long time, and it wasn't something you'd planned for. Opening night at any ballet is formal, but this is the Carter Theatre and the President will be sharing our box. I didn't want you to have to worry about fashion when you needed to focus on the investigation." She tried to take the bag out of his grasp. "You don't have to wear it. Just, never mind."

He held the suit out of her reach. "Wait—I'm sorry. I appreciate it. So much. I've never had a bespoke suit before. Can I see it?"

She nodded and sucked her bottom lip into her mouth. The blood in his body had finally started to circulate, but that lip action made his pants tighten all over again. She gestured at his crotch. "We may need to do some slight alterations, but I think it's going to look handsome."

Ben had always been a believer in dressing for success, so while many of his fellow detectives wore blazers and jeans, or mixed suit separates, he'd always worn athletic cut suits. His mom had bought his first suit for him when he'd first joined the Bureau, teasing him because he'd grabbed a cheap-ass navy blue suit that fit. It *had* been awful looking, but the Feds required a dark suit. She turned him on to the designer section in the local department store, and while they'd cost a little more than mix-and-match suits, they lasted longer and were more comfortable. They weren't going to get him on a red carpet, but they made him feel confident.

"We pulled a suit from the costume department and altered it," she explained.

Ben ran his hand down the sleeve. The fine wool material was soft. The deep charcoal color was almost black. The lapels were thin and modern, the jacket shorter, with four buttons. She'd made a vest to go with it, and it had a little extra room under the right arm for his holster. The pants were flat fronted with a splash of red inside the pockets. They were cool and hip. He shrugged out of his slate gray jacket and laid it across Sarah's chair, and tucked his gun into the back waistband of his pants.

Abby stepped back to watch. The jacket fit like a glove, with enough give that he could stretch his arms across his chest with ease. "The pants were the easy part. The jacket took a little more time because I rebuilt the arms with fabric that's got a little stretch to fit over those linebacker shoulders." She grinned, pleased with her work. "Step out here so I've got good light. Mrs. Gladys suggested we also add extra space in the shoulders for your gun. She said her husband always complained about his jackets being too tight when he was on duty. I know you won't always wear your gun with this, but I figured you'd have it with you tonight. I want to adjust the right side of the jacket and the vest so the lines are true. I wasn't sure about the length of your pants, either."

He grabbed her hand as she turned toward the door, pulling her back for a sweet, gentle kiss. "Thank you. This is beautiful. I just don't know what to say." But it must've been enough, because her smile beamed and made everything around him pause. The moment was amplified by the realization he was falling for her, and he stood there for a moment longer. And when he blinked, realized he was alone in the office.

The bright lights in the costume shop made him look like a movie star in the floor-to-ceiling mirror. The garment looked rich, and he felt like a million bucks. Mrs. Gladys walked over with a pincushion bracelet on her left wrist and a measuring tape draped around her neck. She was already in a formal gown and looked lovely. It was lavender, which he figured must be her signature color. "Abby, climb down there and pin those ankles for me. I'll get this hemmed while you two get cleaned up. Young man, I need you to re-arm yourself, then put on both the vest and the jacket so we can get it adjusted."

"Yes, ma'am."

Several dancers stopped to watch them. He kept his gaze glued to the floor because he wasn't used to being in the hot seat and judging by the laughter in Abby's eyes as she and Mrs. Gladys worked fast to get everything marked, she was capitalizing on it.

"Abby grabbed a shirt for you during lunch. We shouldn't have to do anything to it."

He nodded.

Bruno walked in and grabbed Sarah by the hand, getting her attention so she stopped moving and looked at him. "We need you backstage to go over marks, and to help focus the spots for your curtain speech." He looked at his watch, then to the room at large. "Six o'clock, people. It's time to wrap it up and stretch out. Marky—time to clean up." They turned and left, and the dancers started shedding leg warmers so they could get ready for the night. The business side of ballet was as choreographed as the dance. It was fascinating.

"Give Mrs. Gladys your suit. She'll have these alterations made in, like, ten minutes. She's a sewing goddess." Mrs. Gladys waved her hand and laughed, but when Abby stood and gave her a big hug, the older woman blushed. He was happy to see their good working relationship.

"Come on, Ben. Let's get ready." She led him back to Sarah's office, then through the back door he hadn't noticed before. It led into a large private bathroom with a shower. "It's been a long day. We need a shower—I mean, we're meeting the President tonight." She stripped, and he almost swallowed his tongue. Again, he stood open-mouthed and gaping like he was on pause, while she stepped into the large glassed-in shower. As the water warmed up, she grabbed something small off the shelf by the faucet before stepping under the spray.

Water poured over the contours of her body, making all her curves and hollows stand out in stark relief. From his vantage point, no bruises were visible. The scrape on her hip had a pretty solid looking scab. They could take a few stolen moments to remember they were alive and whole. To revel in the intimacy shrouding them by the steam. She shifted close enough that he could see water droplets on her eyelashes and a siren's smile on her beautiful face.

He licked his lips and wondered, *why in the hell is this incredible woman interested in me?* She ducked under the spray, washing the week's stress down the drain. Clarity struck, and he didn't give a damn any longer. He exploded into motion, stripping and climbing in the shower as fast as he could. Abby's laughter wrapped around his heart, squeezing it tightly, as he stepped in and closed the door.

Chapter Twenty-Seven

Organizations that regularly hosted dignitaries in Washington had special event management down to a science. Since the shows routinely went on with or without special guests, the goal was to ensure the paying audience didn't get caught up in the pomp and circumstance. The President and First Lady always made everyone antsy, but Sarah was downright anxious tonight because she hoped to charm the First Lady into joining the Capital Ballet's board of directors.

Bruno walked Ben up to the box they would share with the President. He nodded at the two Secret Service agents flanking the balcony doorway, showed his badge…again…and paused while they perused his credentials. Again.

"I don't know how these important people do it," Bruno murmured while he waited for the agents to communicate through their sleeve mics.

"Do what?"

"Travel. Shop. Just, be active in public, I guess. It would make me a nervous wreck looking for goons to pop out from every corner. I don't think I'd ever draw a peaceful breath."

Ben noticed the First Lady watching them. She was a beautiful woman, but up close and in person he saw the strain of life in the limelight around her eyes. As an immigrant, she'd been on the receiving end of some really shitty press. Her husband wasn't his choice in politicians, but he was determined to ease the worry in her gaze while he was there. Ben shook Bruno's hand. "I think you do what you gotta do. See you later, man."

Bruno chuckled and walked past the agents. "I'll see you after the performance. Abby will be right up."

Ben was in the process of introducing himself to the First Lady when Mike hustled in. He grinned at the larger of the two agents, flashing his badge, and made his way over to his mother. She sat behind the First Lady and waved wildly, unabashed. The woman, fiercely devoted to Abby, loved her son and talked to him like he was a sweet little boy, not a six-foot bruiser built like a linebacker. "Made it, Mama," he said and kissed her on the cheek. He leaned over and shook the First Lady's hand, then sat next to his mom.

"Just in time," Ben said, glancing at his watch. Mike grinned, but his buzzing phone caught his attention. His eyes widened and he turned the screen for Ben to see, but Abby walked into the box and everything came to a halt.

Her long hair had been piled into a messy bun at the nape of her neck, showing off the dramatic plunge of the front neckline of the gown. The full back was elegant, but the front wrapped around her slim torso, tying at the left side of her waist and showcasing her beautiful figure. The front vee started at her collarbones and stretched down almost to her naval. It was sophisticated and sexy, and so unexpected.

And all he could think was, *I know how her skin tastes right there*. The black fabric was soft and filmy, sort of dreamy like the fabric she used in so many of the costumes. The skirt was long and fell simply from where it tied around the left side of her waist and fell open from the tie all the way to the floor. When she walked, her sleek thigh peeked through. He noticed a flash of scarlet on the underside of the fabric that matched the lining of the pockets in his suit. It was like waving a red flag at a bull.

The First Lady's chuckle cut through the haze. "Mr. Owens." Then she nudged him with her elbow, like they were regular people sharing a joke, and laughed out loud.

"You look beautiful." He put an arm around Abby's waist and kissed her temple. After their aerobic shower, it had taken her longer to get ready because she was drying her hair and going through a checklist with Mrs. Gladys, so he had gotten out of the way.

She squeezed his arm. "So do you."

"Thank you." He leaned closer and spoke directly into her ear, satisfied when he saw goosebumps race down the length of her arm. "I didn't hurt you, did I?"

"No," she said demurely. She glanced over his shoulder to a Secret Service agent standing in the doorway to the opera box, who paid them no attention.

He was torn between laughing at her bashful response and howling like an animal for everyone in the theatre to know she was his. But she saved the day by running her hands along the suit lapels, straightening the lines that were already crisp and true.

His suit fit like, well, like it had been made for him. This night, with this woman and this crowd he was sitting with, would be something he'd never forget. Abby squeezed past him to introduce herself to the First Lady. The women spoke animatedly for a few minutes about ballet and the arts; then the President came in, led by the orchestra's rendition of Hail to the Chief, and waved to the crowd.

The audience stood and applauded. Everyone in the box was introduced, and Ben was filled with awe, standing next to Abby, who stood beside the President. It didn't matter if he'd voted for this guy or not, it was impressive to meet the Man. Just before the house lights dimmed for the curtain speech, Ben looked back to check out the size of the crowd.

Movement in the next box back caught his eye, and he did a double take.

Senator Quincy Sykes glared, his face paling when he took in Ben, Abby, and Mike Dixon sitting with the President.

Mike followed his gaze to the older man, then flashed his best "fuck-you" grin.

"What are you two looking at?" Abby asked.

"Quincy Sykes is in the next box. He looks like he's going to pass out. Wait—looks like he's calling someone on his phone."

Though the two men—POTUS and Sykes—were of the same political party, it was widely reported they couldn't stand each other. Any attack he might lobby against Abby right here would be misconstrued as one against the President. Sykes was anything but stupid.

Abby squirmed against him, trying to look discreet, but it was no use. He and Mike blocked her view, but her curiosity was getting obvious. He leaned close to whisper, "I don't think he'll do anything in public. With all the Secret Service agents, he'd be a fool to even breathe funny." Not that it made him feel any better.

When Sarah Winslow walked onto stage, followed by a spotlight, the crowd quieted and resumed its seats.

"Good evening, ladies and gentlemen."

She spoke about the importance of the arts, and the audience's continued support of the Capital Ballet Company and artists everywhere before wrapping it up. The curtain speech was brief and competent, just like her. "We have the pleasure to welcome the President and First Lady tonight. Thank you all for coming—we hope you enjoy *The Sleeping Beauty*." She curtsied with grace, and the orchestra started the long introduction for Tchaikovsky's overture.

****

Steve Sykes picked up on the third ring, jerking his head back from the phone when his father barked, "Why the fuck didn't you tell me Abby Markham was going to be at the ballet tonight?"

He sucked in a breath and lowered his voice. "I can't talk right now, Dad. I'm in a meeting."

"Then step out and call me back."

In all his life, Steve never remembered a time when his father had stepped out of a meeting to take a call from him, yet he was always expected to jump through hoops for the old man. "I can't. Is everything okay?"

"No!" Classical music played in the background. "The smart-ass detective from your department is with her, and they're sitting with the goddamned President." His whisper was furious, but Steve imagined the people around him could hear most of what he was spewing.

He cupped his hand around the phone, muting his words. "Check the program. She designed the costumes."

Chief Randolph cleared his throat and sat back against his desk. Steve had just been called into the office when the phone rang, confident that any call at seven-thirty on a Friday night from the senator was not of a social nature. Still, he couldn't walk out of the Chief's office, so he'd excused himself to the corner.

He was already sweating this conversation with Randolph; the stress tipped him ever closer to the breaking point. He wiped sweaty palms on the legs of his pants and squeezed into the corner, speaking as quietly as possible.

"Yeah, so okay, she's the costume designer," Quincy hissed. "But that fucker Owens keeps looking at me. And the Fed who he's been working with this week is sitting with them. He's checking me out, too."

Steve's heart stopped beating. His vision blurred as an all-consuming terror raced along his spine. He started hyperventilating and backed out of the corner, slamming his back against the wall. He was having a heart attack. That was the only possibility; the muscles across his chest and up his throat tightened with agony, cutting off his breath.

It must have startled Chief Randolph, because he ran over to grab him by the arm, but the older man wasn't fast enough. The ringing in his ears silenced everything around him, like his whole body was cocooned in an air-tight bubble, and he hit the ground.

The last thing he remembered before blacking out was the chief kneeling over him, shouting something.

Chapter Twenty-Eight

Quincy Sykes attempted to make his way closer to the President's box to learn what the fuck Abby Markham was doing in the President's box, but the damned Secret Service agents held him at bay like he was a terrorist. Her boy toy, Detective Smart-Ass Owens, just smirked. Made him want to knock in his goddamned teeth.

"Is everything all right, Quin?" Martha only called him that while they were in the bed, so it was obvious she was trying to get his attention. She leaned in close. "Your whole body is tense. I don't know what's gotten into you, but people are starting to look over here."

She made a show of checking her phone, then her watch, and then finding a familiar face in the crowd she could acknowledge with a smile or simple wave. He paid her a fortune, but she was worth it—both in the way she fielded unwanted conversations and put up a smokescreen whenever he needed one.

Watching her work the situation helped him regain control. She was aware of Owens' interest, and still assumed it was related to the time capsule. It was getting more difficult to keep up that façade because how interesting could a time capsule be?

He patted her on the hand and waved at the same donors she'd acknowledged a moment ago. Everybody wanted to be somebody. They wanted to rub elbows with famous people and to be known and recognized by them was a quick second place. Christ, it was a huge distraction in life, but it kept him flush with cash when he smiled and stopped for photo ops with donors. It was exhausting being "on" all the time.

The house lights flashed at the five-minute mark and people filed back to their seats. Abby and the First Lady had become fast friends, their heads bent toward each other as they chatted. Both women spoke animatedly with their hands, and every now and then one or both would burst into laughter. Their lightheartedness pissed him off. Seeing Abby Markham in work mode explained her presence in town, but he wasn't going to relax until she was back in North Carolina.

Fucking Owens had been on the phone during the entire intermission but spun around to look at him when the house lights dimmed. Quincy's whole body tensed, and the fight or flight instinct kicked in. Tension rolled off him in waves, nearly suffocating him. His legs started bouncing with nervous energy until Martha placed a hand on his left knee, prompting him to make a concerted effort to quit squirming.

Owens was driving him crazy. Throughout the second act he maintained a steady text missive on the phone, passing it between Abby and the Fed sitting behind them. The one time he caught a glimpse of her face, her expression was filled with distress. By the time the curtain closed, and the house lights came up, she leaned heavily against Owens's side. Like all her bones had melted and there was nothing left but shapeless skin. The Secret Service allowed people in the box to say their goodbyes and then whisked their charges away and out the back door before the dancers retook the stage for flowers and applause.

Martha watched him intently, curious about his strange behavior. "I think something's going on at home." It was the best explanation he could offer, even though it was obviously bullshit. But she let it go and worked the small crowd that had gathered in their box. He shook hands and joined in the conversation when anyone spoke to him directly, but otherwise kept his eye on Owens.

As soon as the President's entourage cleared out of the building and the ushers opened the side doors, Owens and Abby stepped into the hallway. His FBI friend kissed the older woman sitting next to him, then the three of them hustled backstage. The men dragged Abby behind them, and she looked odd shuffling on her toes in the spiky stilettos, but she was fast.

He skirted the railing close to their exit door, but Martha grabbed him by the other arm.

"Damnit, Martha."

The complaint died in his throat after she caught his eye with the tilt of her head. Senator Alice Ruffin, one of the senior Democrats he'd been trying to woo for the last quarter, had just stepped into their box.

"Quincy, I didn't realize you were a supporter of the ballet."

Alice once reigned as Miss Alabama in her early twenties, claiming to have used the pageant circuit to pay for law school. She'd made good on that claim by becoming the state's youngest district attorney before running for the senate eight years ago. Now, in her mid-forties, she was still a knockout. She also hinted at an attraction to him on a regular basis but was savvy enough to know that Martha's reluctance to relay social calls on to him were a fuck-you to her. Still, if he could figure out a way to keep an affair on the down-low and out of Martha's scope, he'd nail her in a heartbeat.

"Alice, dear," he said magnanimously, grasping her small, graceful hand and bringing it to his lips for a genteel kiss. "Such a pleasure to see you. The ballet was Margaret's passion, so in her honor I try to take in at least one performance a season."

She melted, as he'd intended, and settled against his chest. Yes, they sat on opposite sides of the row and carried different political viewpoints, but both were attractive and single, and loved by their constituents.

"Have your assistant call my office on Monday to set up a meeting. I'd like to go ahead with funding for military families—if you can meet the requirements we've developed through focus group discussions."

She looked up at him through her lashes, a feminine gesture as old as time, but it made him rock hard. They'd never get away with this physical proximity on the senate floor, which was why public outings were so important.

Alice's succulent mouth turned down in a sexy little pout when Martha cleared her throat. The crowd jostled them a bit, so he wrapped an arm around her waist. Together they stepped farther into the booth, forcing Martha to back up and rest her bottom against the railing. Alice was playing with fire, and he would pay for it later with Martha. Sadly, it was time to end the encounter. Sighing, he stepped to the side so Martha could shift out from behind him. She shot right to his side, looking down her nose at Alice.

While both women were beautiful—and an old

man like him would normally think he'd died and gone to heaven with their cattiness—Martha could suck the chrome off a tailpipe. In the long run there was simply no comparison.

Martha dismissed her with a dead-eye stare. "We'll be in touch on Monday. Senator, you have a conference call with the Joint Chiefs at ten. We need to get going."

Alice's face flushed red before she regained her composure. Beautiful people did not suffer dismissal attractively. "Of course. Quincy, it's *always* a pleasure. And Martha, so good of you to be on top of things. As usual. I can't seem to keep a good executive assistant. I guess I'm too demanding."

She looked over her shoulder and gestured for a muscular younger man to step closer. He stood well over six feet, was gorgeous to look at, and dressed like a cover model. "Quincy, Martha, this is Jackson, my new assistant. He was an Army Ranger before being injured and has decided to try something new. A lateral entry foray into politics, if you will. He's going to have great input on this military families bill you want me to co-sponsor."

After Jackson shook hands, he placed one hand just above the curve of Alice's shapely buttocks, leading her through the doorway. No way was this one a simple "administrative assistant," Quincy decided acidly. This one was a straight-up fuck buddy.

Jackson winked at Martha as he and Alice passed, smirking broadly when she grunted in irritation. Yeah, he had her number, too. It took one to know one.

Chapter Twenty-Nine

By the time they made it to Ben's SUV, Abby wanted to scream. During the performance Chief Randolph let Ben know Steve Sykes had suffered a heart attack during an interrogation. No further information was shared until the finale, and Ben hadn't wanted to share anything that might be overheard.

"Steve didn't have a cardiac arrest," Ben said, and turned out of the parking lot into a steady stream of heavy traffic. "It was just a panic attack."

Abby was relieved to be out of the theatre and the fray of what felt like a thousand bodies. It had taken about half an hour for the Secret Service to get POTUS out of the building and clear the area. Waiting to find out what Ben had learned was torturous.

"Thank God. I don't want anything bad to happen to the man. I mean, I don't want him to come to my house again, but neither do I want him to be hurt." She twisted her fingers together in her lap, running through a thousand what-if scenarios. "Why was he interrogated?"

He squeezed her fingers before turning into the hotel parking lot. "I don't know. The only update I got was that it was a panic attack rather than a heart attack."

"Do you think his father knows?" Everything she'd discovered about both of the Sykes men was underwhelming, but she didn't wish a child dying on her worst enemy.

"Chief Randolph reached out directly."

"Oh, dear." She looked down at Ben's larger hand holding hers and welcomed the weight of his arm on her lap. It grounded her. Kept her in the moment rather than drifting away on a cloud of worry.

Ben broke into her musings. "I'm sorry we had to rush out after the show. Will anyone be mad at you?"

"Nah. We just missed the after-party. It can be a little wild…the dancers are probably going to have more fun without a cop in the mix."

Ben parked and grabbed the keys before climbing out. "Hey! I can be wild."

"I'm sure you can." She was laughing when he opened the door and helped her climb down. Stilettos and tall vehicles did not mix well. She winced when her feet touched the ground because stilettos and walking didn't mix well, either.

They held hands through the lobby and into the elevator. Ben stared off into space, and she took advantage of his distraction to watch him in the mirrored doors. He was so handsome. Tall and broad with a swimmer's build…the suit she'd made him highlighted all his yumminess. Long legs with thickly muscled thighs, slim hips and flat abdomen. Rounded biceps bulged just enough to show his strength without making him look like a pumped-up gym rat.

She was intimately aware of how it felt to drag her lips across the soft skin of his throat, from the smooth skin around his Adam's apple up to where his whiskers began to tickle along his jawline. He was the definition of masculine beauty, and he was hers. At least for the time being. Anything could happen when they got back to reality, and she wasn't going to waste this opportunity.

She was lost in a daydream, staring in the reflection when his gaze shifted. Like he knew she was thinking about him. The heat in his eyes scorched her, shocked her, and she jerked backward, slamming into his chest. Before the elevator could ding on their floor, his hand shot out and pressed the STOP button on the panel. Their eyes met in the mirror's reflection and the arousal tinting the hollows of his cheeks made her wet. He caught her by the hip when she would've stepped away to give him space and pressed his erection against her bottom. Slowly, deliberately, he ran the fingertips on his left hand along the side of her neck, down to her collar bone and into the deep vee of her dress, settling his big, hot palm over her right breast.

Rapid, panting breaths and helpless moans filled her chest and made it hard to concentrate. Brushing his thumb back and forth across her stiff nipple set off sparks behind her eyes and moisture pooling between her thighs, and she had to lean against him heavily so she wouldn't crumble to the floor.

She pressed her hands against the wall and ground her hips back into his. "The elevator is beeping."

He ran his teeth along the tendon on the left side of her throat, nipping and sliding his tongue along her racing pulse. When he got to her ear, he whispered darkly, "I don't care," and pulled his hand out of her bodice. "We just need another minute, sweetheart."

"Yes." Her voice rumbled out smoky and sultry, and she wondered what stranger inhabited her body.

Strong fingers smoothed down her torso and into the high slit in her skirt, dragging along skin that burned like fire. Ben growled, and pulled her closer, sliding his hand down so he could cup her pussy. "Christ, have you been bare under here all night?"

She couldn't speak. His long middle finger rubbed back and forth, slowly, across her stiffened clit, and when he gripped the inside of her thigh to push it wider, everything started trembling. "You didn't answer me." He tsked, and then slid a finger inside, pressing deep.

"What was the question?" It didn't matter what he asked because she didn't have an answer. Just rolling hips and raw nerves.

"Were you bare all night?" His finger stilled while he waited for her response.

"I took them off when I went to the bathroom—before we got in the car.

"Good girl." He kissed her temple and added a second finger. Those long, broad fingers. The other hand eased into the vee of her bodice to work her nipple, and her breath caught in her throat. "You hoped I would do this, didn't you?"

Puffs of air blew across her throat from Ben's panting, growing more erratic the faster his fingers pumped. The press of his wrist against her pelvic bone almost got her off but coupled with a sharp pinch to her nipple and the sudden way he sucked a patch of skin on the side of her throat into his mouth…that did it. She came hard. The muscles in her legs gave out, but Ben's arm clamped around her middle, holding her up. She was boneless and totally replete.

A deep groan rumbled in his chest before spinning her around and stealing her breath with a kiss. He kissed her with his whole body, until she thought her lungs would collapse, but she pulled in as much air as possible through her nose and sucked on his tongue. His erection lay heavy against her belly like a steel pipe, pressed tight between their bodies, and amplifying the subtle rock of his hips. He was moments away from whipping her into a sexual frenzy.

But the elevator buzzed louder this time, cutting through their passionate haze. Ben blinked and shook his head, looking a little incredulous. He cleared his throat and, if she wasn't mistaken, looked a little embarrassed. "I, uh, didn't plan on jumping you in the elevator, but this dress." He brushed the hair off her forehead to press a sweet kiss on the end of her nose.

"We'll have to be all business when we get back to the room. Jim's in there, so I know we'll need to get some things wrapped up. But this dress is so distracting. It's so fucking hot."

Who could resist a reaction like that? But instead of being nonchalant and cosmopolitan about a sexual encounter with a sexy man in an elevator, she let out a super dorky laugh that was way beyond a snort, but somewhat less than a guffaw.

"Come on, let's go." He pressed the "door open" button and took her hand when they stepped into the hallway.

"I'd like to have my way with you in this suit, too. The holster under your vest is really doing it for me."

"I can't believe you made me a suit. And I can't believe I'm telling you we have to wait. Like, it physically hurts."

Her eyes widened. "Your suit is uncomfortable? I've made all kinds of clothes and costumes, but I've never made a suit."

He flexed his elbow and raised his arms above his

head as they walked. "Super comfortable. The flex in it is nice. I'm going to stick to bespoke suits from now on, I guess." He dipped his chin to her, and she read between the lines: he was going to stick to bespoke suits now that he had her. "It's my cock that's uncomfortable."

Ben pulled the key out of his wallet, but the door opened before he could swipe it in front of the sensor. Forth stepped into view. "You two clean up really well."

Abby snickered and walked in, kicking off her shoes as soon as she was through the door. She patted his arm on the way by, laughing when she glanced back at Ben. Pretty sure the residual evidence of her orgasm was written all over her face. "You have no idea. Boys, I'm getting out of this dress."

Arousal still colored Ben's cheeks and she was certain they smelled like sex, but Jim was a gentleman and kept his mouth shut. She was almost to the bedroom when Ben's phone rang.

"Owens," he said. She stopped and turned around when he said, "Hey, Chief."

The conversation went downhill from there. So did Ben. As he listened to whatever the chief said, his whole body seemed to crumble in on itself. He made his way over to the couch and dropped down heavily, covering his face with one hand.

****

"Steve killed Jason. Oh my God," Ben said as tears sprung to his eyes. "He admitted he was covering for his father. Jason was the responding officer on the first call for the silent alarm on your house. Jason didn't report it."

Swinging his arm wide, Ben slammed the side of his fist into the wall. One of the framed images next to the doorway hit the ground with a loud crunch. It fell behind the couch, immediately forgotten. "He didn't report it," he roared.

"What? Why didn't Jason arrest Senator Sykes right away?" Abby asked. Her eyes were wide and frantic looking. "Why didn't Jason ask what the hell was going on? To, you know, protect the person who lives in the house!"

She made a choking sound and moved away from him. Fury washed through Ben in a flash flood of anguish. He wanted nothing more than to scoop Abby up and carry her away from this new knowledge.

"I don't know," Ben said. "He and Steve were best friends. Christ, maybe he thought he was protecting his friend. Doing him a solid. Maybe he figured that even though Quincy's a dick, he's an old man. And wouldn't be dangerous to you."

"That's bullshit," said Jim. "I'm sorry, Ben, but 'thin blue line' or not, wrong is wrong."

"How long did they cover it up?" Abby asked.

Blood pounded through Ben's head, making his ears ring. It pulsed behind his eyes and made his floaters swirl around like a lava lamp. "How long ago did you find the time capsule?"

One of her hands flew up to cover her mouth, and she paled. "Almost three months."

He had to look away. He could not bear to see her recoil from him. For her to compare his life's work to the careless, selfish coverup of two fellow officers whose friendship and secrets outweighed both of their senses of justice. "Then three months," Ben whispered.

"They kept it quiet for about three months."

Fat tears plopped on the carpet between Ben's feet. His runny nose joined in on the dripping, and he sniffed. "Steve was always a dick, which obviously runs in his family. But Jason." He took a deep breath. "Jason was a great guy. I knew him growing up, and when I got back in town last year, all accounts of his track record showed him to be a good cop. I can't believe he didn't arrest Quincy right away. I can't believe he conspired with Steve to keep it quiet." He finally looked at Abby, far enough across the room that it felt like the entire Guadalajara Desert spanned between them. "I can't believe he chose to allow an innocent woman to remain in danger."

Jim leaned a hip against the desk. "Quincy didn't kill Lawson? You believe him?"

Ben shook his head. He didn't know. "Those two were closer than brothers. You know how dangerous close-contact brawls can be. Steve said they met on that back road leading to the bird sanctuary. They argued about Steve needing more time, because he and Quincy didn't get along. Jason was done keeping it a secret. Knew they would be in a fuck-ton of trouble when it came out and was going to take it to the chief that day. Steve said he just snapped. Punched Jason, and they hit the ground. He said Jason's gun fell out of its holster when they hit the ground, and it went off when they were scrambling to get it. The second shot happened when they were fighting for control."

Jim nodded. "I get loyalty. But if Jason had taken this up the line right away or, damn, arrested Quincy on the spot, none of this would've happened."

Ben slammed his fist on the desk. "I know. Christ,

I know." He felt Abby's attention shining on him now. It was as fiery as a laser beam, and he forced himself to meet her glare. He was mortified that his department had bungled the situation. Bad cops made everyone around them culpable because of misplaced loyalty. "I'm so sorry, Abby."

She nodded and laid her forehead on her knees. She looked like a turtle in its shell. Protecting herself.

"It's only a matter of time before Quincy finds out about the coverup." Jim's tone was ominous. "Once he finds out it was Steve who killed Jason, he'll up the purse." He jutted his chin toward Abby.

Ben looked at him, then sighed heavily. He walked over to Abby and rested his hands on her shoulders, making sure she was paying attention. "Go ahead and change your clothes. We need to pack fast. I'll be in in a few minutes to get my stuff together."

"We're going home tonight?"

All the color drained from her face, and when she stood, Ben dropped his hands. "Yes." He didn't want to tell her they were sitting ducks up here.

Abby hesitated for a moment, looking back and forth between him and the bedroom. He held completely still, trying to look nonthreatening. Yes, he was a police officer. No, he was not corrupt. He wanted to rail at the world and remind her that he was a good guy, but he wouldn't push her. Her bottom lip trembled, and his heart broke right in two. She noticed when his fists clenched and reached for him.

It was enough. A grounding gesture that said, *I'm still with you.* Her gentleness settled over him like a veil, and he could breathe again. Without another word, she turned and went to the bedroom to change. Behind him, Jim's burner phone dinged.

"What is it?" Ben asked. He walked back to the desk and looked at the phone screen over Forth's shoulder.

"It's from Quincy. Looks like he's just found out Steve killed Lawson," Forth said. "He's narrowed the window on taking Abby out. Twenty-four hours or he's calling in a sweep team."

"Oh, Christ." Ben's hands fisted. He hadn't seen Forth in a decade and had no idea how loyal he'd be if shoved into a corner. If he was forced to fight for Abby, Ben would take on an entire strike team. If he had to fight Jim Forthmann, he knew he would struggle with their history.

"Stop backing away from me, Jam," Forth snapped. "I'm on team Abby all the way."

Ben relaxed enough to start packing up his shit. Forth watched him move around the suite for a minute, and said, "I looked into this Paul Pope while you were working with Mike today. He grew up poor on the wrong side of the tracks. Father was an abusive alcoholic; the mother took off when Pope was in elementary school."

Ben shrugged. "Probably got tired of getting her ass whipped daily." He moved his hotspot and laptop into his old, battered leather messenger bag and started shoving clothes into a matching duffel bag.

"Can't blame her," Jim said. "The old man died when Paul was in boot camp."

"Any other siblings? Kids…anything?"

Jim shook his head. "Nothing. When he died in the fire, all evidence of his life died with him." He looked at Ben intensely.

"Shit."

"I hacked into his military records. He was a war hero, which was one of the things his friend, Quincy, was so proud of. Pope was injured in battle; the shot in the hip fractured his pelvis. That was all she wrote, honorable discharge and a Purple Heart. He'd been at the Sykes place, recuperating for about three months when it caught fire. Evidence supported what Quincy said, that the fire engulfed everything so quickly after the house was struck by lightning that he could only get Margaret and the baby out. He maintained that it was Pope who carried Margaret down the stairs but had been hit by a falling beam that pinned and, ultimately, burned him to death."

"What a nightmare," Ben said. He popped a pod into the coffee machine and hit the start button. The little machine made a lot of noise, so the conversation lulled.

"I took a trip down a couple of rabbit holes after that," Jim said. "First, I poked around to see if there was any question about the fire, and if Quincy could've started it. But because Pope was a war hero, the Army actually sent an investigator. All evidence points to an actual lightning strike—plus, several other homes in the area were damaged during the same storm.

"I was also curious how easy it would be to assume a person's identity back in the seventies. Social security numbers were first issued in the late thirties. Quincy and Pope were both born in 1953. Pope would have had a service number for the Army, too. But it's not like AFIS was around, or Internet searches. They were similar in build, were the same age. People said they could've been twins. And to top it off, both men were in the house at the time."

Ben took a careful sip of the hot coffee and watched Forth over the rim. A quick glance assured him Abby was still occupied in the bedroom. "Terry was telling the truth. It seemed like the crazy fever dream of a madman. I know Chief Randolph was also looking into the claim, so I need to make sure he's got this information."

"I'm way ahead of you," Jim said. He keyed something into his laptop, and Ben's phone dinged. "All wrapped up with a pretty bow."

"Well, damn," Ben said. "Thanks."

Abby opened the door and sucked all the oxygen from the room. She'd changed into her artsy uniform—black tights and a long-sleeve black T-shirt. Her hair fell loose around her shoulders and her face appeared free of makeup. Gone was the tentative, worrisome expression she wore earlier; in its place was confidence and determination. She stood tall looked him square in the eye. "Let's do this."

Behind him, Jim chuckled. "Right on."

"I'm going to change before we hit the road," Ben said. He pulled off his tailored jacket and unbuttoned the vest. "Can you do a sweep of the living room to make sure I didn't miss anything? I'll double-check behind you in here."

Abby's suitcase was zipped up and sitting right inside the bedroom. The garment bag was unzipped on the bed, and her gown was already nestled inside. He hung his jacket and vest on a hanger and laid it on top of her gown, and his heart kicked in his chest. Something about the silky material of that dress against the heavier wool of his suit did something to him. Made him wonder if maybe he and Abby might be able to have a relationship when they got home. Laughter from the other room shook him out of his daydream, and he hustled to finish packing. He grabbed their bags and moved them next to the door.

"I told Abby I'm giving you a three-hour head start," Jim said, "and then I'll confirm the time frame with Quincy. He's going to Apex tomorrow morning to see Steve, but I don't think he'll bail him out. Now that Steven has admitted to murdering his partner, a magnifying glass will hover over the entire Sykes family." He gestured to the burner phone. "The countdown to close all loose ends has started, and since he thinks you have his other time capsule, Abby, you're definitely his biggest loose end."

She moved to stand by Ben, and he pulled her in close. He could feel her rapid heartbeat against his sternum and rubbed her back to offer what comfort he could.

Jim took a deep breath. "I've got twenty-four hours to take you and Terrence out. I have every expectation Sykes has already called in a sweep team, which is why you need to leave now. He has no idea that we share a connection, Jam, so the element of surprise is on our side for now. As soon as I know he's not watching me, I'm heading your way. I'll try to stave off anyone who may be gunning for you."

"Thanks, man." He wanted to ask Jim if they'd ever see each other again but couldn't make himself say it out loud.

"I'm not disappearing again," Jim said, reading his mind with the ease of people who've known each other for decades. "But I am turning over all of my records to

Mike, including a shitload of incriminating evidence I've kept on these shady assignments Sykes has sent me on the last four years. I'm done being his hitman."

He held out a hand to Abby and waited until she shook it. "Ma'am, I won't let anything happen to you. Whatever's going to happen—and believe me, it'll be something—is going to happen fast. I have a couple things for you." He rustled around in his backpack and grabbed a long metal rod. "This is a lightning strike device. It delivers a disorienting blast of light. It's not going to injure anybody, but it'll give you enough time to get out of harm's way until someone can get to you."

Abby bounced her arm up and down and twisted her hand over to look at the device from all sides, then nodded. Ben could tell she felt a little empowered having something to hold herself. Jim gave her a smaller tube that he recognized. "And this is just your garden variety pepper spray," Jim said, smiling. "Make sure you point it away from yourself if you have to use it. It stings like a bitch." She huffed out a laugh and lunged at Jim, wrapping her arms around his waist.

For a breath, he stood motionless. His hands hovered above her shoulders like he didn't know what to do with them. When she turned her cheek and rested it over his heart, Jim gave in. Ben understood exactly how that felt, that acquiescence.

Jim spoke to him over Abby's head. "Watch your back on the way home. I think Sykes will anticipate you leaving tomorrow morning, so tonight will give you a head start. Every minute counts here. Stay sharp when you get home. Get someone on Terrence, too."

Ben nodded. "It's all covered. When it's clear, come see me."

They stood nose to nose for a moment, and then Jim gave in and gave him a big bear hug. They slapped each other on the back with enough force to break bones.

"Go, now," Jim continued. "Refuel as soon as you're on the interstate, and then don't stop until you get home. Be careful."

Chapter Thirty

The sun was brightening the sky to the east when Ben pulled into Abby's garage. She'd been too jacked up to sleep while he drove, so she managed the missives between them, Cindy McGee, and Chief Randolph during most of the six-hour drive. Their first sigh of relief came when Randolph confirmed they'd put a protective detail on Terrence.

Abby yawned and said, "McGee said Rick Stone, whoever that is, has been at my house since midnight, along with three SBI agents assigned by Teddy Barnes. They're stationed inside and around my property."

"Rick is a patrol officer. He came over from the sheriff's office last month," Ben explained. "I think McGee's sweet on him."

"Aww," Abby said.

Ben popped his knuckles and stretched his neck. She could tell he was nervous. "How will they know this is us?" he asked.

She scrolled through the messages. "Uh, here we go…knock out your initials in Morse."

He turned off the car and closed the garage door, squeezing the steering wheel reflexively. Tension filled the car, ratcheting her anxiety to supersonic levels. The open road was scary enough, but if anyone besieged her house, they were sitting ducks.

"Abby."

That was the only warning she got before he grabbed her by the shoulders and hauled her across the center console and kissed the hell out of her. It was deep and wet and aggressive, and filled with promise and possessiveness that was as clear as day. He rested his forehead on hers and drew in a shaky breath. "Stay here—don't get out until I tell you to, okay?"

She nodded, tears springing to her eyes. Ben wasn't the only one feeling possessive. She grabbed onto the sleeves of his blue oxford, holding him close. "Please be careful."

"I know it's scary, but we've got to do this." He stepped out of the car and tugged her into the driver's seat. Then he pressed the keys into her palm. "If I give you any indication of danger or if something happens to me, you leave as fast as you can. Gun the engine and back out through the garage door. Don't waste time waiting for it to open—just bust through it. I programmed Forth's number in your phone; call him." She started to protest, but he kissed her swiftly. "We don't have time to argue. Promise me." With her nod, he slammed the door and walked up the garage steps. She saw him take a deep breath, and then he knocked. *dah-di-di-dit, dah-dah-dah.*

The door cracked open and the muzzle of a gun poked through, level with the bridge of his nose. Abby gasped and reached into the center console to grab the tube of pepper spray. It was terrifying. Ben raised his hands and said something; the door swung wide.

And she burst into tears. Her nerves were shot. If she had just re-buried the damned box. If she had just kept on running after the first gunshot. God, if she had just minded her own business, she wouldn't be in danger…*these* people wouldn't be in danger. Like Mrs. Gladys always said, "If my aunt had balls, she'd be my uncle." You just couldn't let the if's in life dictate your path.

The car door opened, and Ben crouched on the floor, eye-level with her. "Okay?" Thankfully, he didn't judge her for crying or point out that snot dripped from her nose. He just held her hand as she climbed out and led her inside. A handsome man with deep almond skin, a dark brown fade and the prettiest dimples Abby had ever seen, nodded when he walked past her to the garage.

"That's Rick," Ben said. "He's grabbing our bags."

"I can see why McGee's sweet on him."

She heard Rick chuckle from the other side of the jeep, so she knew he'd heard the comment. Hopefully Cindy McGee's crush wasn't a secret. The trip home was always lighter because costumes and equipment took up so much space. Mrs. Gladys was going to bring home anything studio related on Tuesday, since she had agreed to stay with Mike in Washington rather than joining the Broadway-bound bus with her friends. Truth be told, she was far happier to spend the time with her "baby." Plus, Mike had already gotten approval from his boss to be in North Carolina the rest of the week to work the case with Ben, or at least see how it was wrapped up…whichever came first.

"Ma'am," Rick said as she walked into the kitchen. "It's nice to meet you, though I'm sorry it's under such stressful circumstances."

"Thank you, Rick. For everything." She swept her arm in a wide arc, trying to convey gratitude for securing her home as much as the concierge service.

He got the gist and grinned, and then walked toward the living room. Abby was momentarily stunned because he was really handsome. And he had braces. So cute. “McGee said to tell you hi.”

“Aw, McGee,” she called out. “Thanks again, Rick.”

Ben led them to her studio for a moment of privacy. The space looked so stark with all the costumes gone. And in the light of a new day with zero clouds in the sky and nothing to obscure the twenty-foot windows or soften the concrete floors, it never failed to make her a little melancholy. Like after taking down Christmas decorations and the house looks so naked. She wondered if Ben had the same observation. He was quiet, so it was hard to tell.

Rick walked in and apologized for the interruption. “Hey, since you made such good time, Chief Randolph wants you to meet him at the station at nine o’clock. Abby should go with you, because we think together is safer right now.”

“I’ve got to close my eyes, Rick,” Ben said. “I’ve been up for twenty-six hours—I’ll be no good if the shit hits the fan. Abby didn’t sleep, either.”

Rick punched a number in his mobile phone, waited for someone to answer and said, “Can we delay until ten o’clock?” He paused for the response, nodded, and hung up. “Sorry, man, you’re gonna have to grab a power nap. The chief said you need to be there at nine o’clock. We’ll keep watch while you rest.”

Abby tried to keep up with the conversation, but she was so exhausted she was swaying on her feet. Ben checked his watch and asked, “Who’s here?” If they closed their eyes in the next five minutes, they’d have a little over two-and-a-half hours to nap. He snagged her by the wrist and pulled her close.

Rick pointed at himself, then a guy who walked up. “This is Bobby. Wes is patrolling the front and eastern side of the property, and Marcus is keeping to the western side and along the waterfront out back. Bobby’s going to stay inside with me.” They shook hands with Bobby, and Abby took a moment to thank him, too. He continued. “If I were you, ma’am, I’d grab a quick shower before lying down. You won’t have time to do it when you wake up. Bobby used to be Apex PD with us but transferred to the SBI a couple years ago. Wes and Marcus are both SBI. They’re all good men. Rest easily but be ready to head out at eight-forty-five. When we leave for the department, it’s going to be fast and hard.”

She nodded and staggered through the house and up the stairs. The men spoke quietly, but when the studio door closed behind her, the conversation ended. She made it about halfway up the stairs when Ben scooped her up. “Come on, honey. We can clean up quickly and lie down.”

“I think I’m too tired to sleep.”

He closed the bedroom door and set her down in the en suite bathroom. “I bet you’ll be asleep before your head hits the pillow. Save time and shower together?”

He waggled his eyebrows and unbuttoned his shirt. She huffed out a laugh, surprising herself. Everything about being home was terrifying. In the scheme of things, she was a nobody, yet here she was, in the middle of a murder investigation with a sociopathic United States senator gunning for her.

She turned on the water, and by the time steam began to fill the big, glassed-in shower, they'd undressed. He followed her in and closed the door and pulled her against his chest. "I'm sorry this is happening."

"Me, too. But if I hadn't turned in that stupid box, I never would have met you."

"I don't know." He squeezed a dollop of shampoo into his hands and massaged it into her scalp, running his fingers through her long hair. Suds trailed in their wake, and he shifted his body to block the water. "I have no doubt we would have found our way to each other eventually. This *is* a small town."

She smiled against his warm skin, leaning her head back for a kiss. He dipped his tongue in briefly and nibbled on her bottom lip before switching places so she could wash out the shampoo. They finished showering, dried off quickly, and climbed into her big bed. As predicted, she was out as soon as her head hit the pillow.

Exhaustion continued to plague her after Ben woke her up two hours later. She was groggy and crabby, and her eyeballs itched like they were coated in sand. He tried to be gentle at first, but when she snapped at him that she was too tired for sex, he just laughed and said, "It's time to go." Then she remembered; she was wide awake.

"Abby." His quiet voice kept her from jumping out of bed, and the hand gently shackled around her wrist made her look at him. "Take deep breaths, baby. Like this." Holding her gaze, he demonstrated slow, deep breaths that she instinctively adopted. "Good. Try to slow down a bit. We're heading out in fifteen minutes. I want you to put on a comfortable pair of yoga pants and a long-sleeved shirt, with socks and running shoes." In case they had to run. She got that. "Rick's going to take us in the squad car, because it's less likely anyone would attack a marked vehicle." She noticed he was already dressed. His shoulder harness was visible over his shirt, the sleek handgrip of his gun tucked neatly in his armpit.

"Smart." Her voice was a little choked, her breathing a little shallow. Her hands shook while she brushed her teeth and combed her hair. They shook when she got dressed and tied the laces on her shoes. And they shook when he held her hand and they walked through her house. Ben opted to go out through the front door, where Rick's cruiser sat at the bottom of the stairs running. The back-passenger door was open, and the three SBI agents flanked them as they hustled down the stairs and into the car. Marcus climbed in the passenger seat next to Rick, and Bobby and Wes hurried into a big, black SUV idling behind them. They were flying down the highway before Ben could get her seatbelt clicked.

****

Rush hour was winding down and a manageable amount of traffic remained on the road at eight-forty-five, but every car was a potential ticking bomb. Marcus held a shotgun in his lap, ready for action as he scanned the roads around them. Rick, who was typically a chatty, charming guy, was silent, hands gripping the steering wheel tight enough that his knuckles were a pale beige and the tendons in his wrists stood out in sharp relief. His body was a visual reminder of the shitstorm they were in.

When they'd jumped in earlier, Ben had strapped her into the center spot in the backseat, thinking she would have the buffer of his body on one side and open space between the door on the other if they got into some kind of shootout. It didn't seem likely, but they were prepared just in case. But as the subtle shivers ran the length of her body, he acknowledged the real reason he'd positioned her so closely was because he just needed to feel her against him. Her terror was palpable, but it was obvious she worked hard to be still and keep her breathing regulated.

He held his gun in his right hand, resting alongside the shotgun in his lap. Nobody spoke, and as he kept a constant surveillance of the road around them, he tried to make eye contact with Abby every few minutes to remind her he was present. He was proud of her bravery. She was a trooper. Actually, she'd been a trooper from the very beginning, once they'd established it was okay for her to do her job and be on site for the ballet. He focused on the road again, visualizing the Apex Police Department in the middle of downtown, and the steps they would take to get from the car to the building.

Rick had taken Highway 64 rather than the backroads, hoping to avoid too many opportunities for a hit, but it also introduced more stop and go traffic. The final turn onto Salem Street was just ahead, which meant two more miles until they could pull into the covered parking deck at the station. Two more miles until they could let out their collective breaths. Their speed lowered as they made their way through town, from fifty-five to thirty-five. The reduction hiked up the tension in the car. They were so close.

A dark SUV with blacked-out windows pulled up to the stop sign on the right, a block ahead of them. "Shit," said Marcus. He cocked his shotgun. Rick rolled his shoulders and fiddled with his bulletproof vest along his neckline.

"Right side," Ben murmured, taking the safety off his pistol. He shifted his hips and pivoted his knees to the right, balancing the pistol on the door just below the window. His left hand wrapped around the butt of the shotgun, prepared. The men were ready if they had to give chase or protect the squad car.

Abby's terror was a living thing as they pulled up even with the side street, but there was no way to comfort her now. When the vehicle pulled across the intersection right toward them, the sound of the leather bench seat bunching in her hand as she gripped it broke the silence.

"Easy," Marcus whispered. "Easy."

He turned his shoulders and pointed the business end of the shotgun at the SUV and held his breath. Rick hit a button to buzz the window down, so there was no way anyone in the surrounding area missed the threat they presented. The cars behind Rick's honked their horns, but the SUV forced its way in behind them, splitting their group. Ben and Marcus swiveled fast, aiming for the driver, now behind them.

Their pursuers gunned the engine, and at the last second, Rick jerked his steering wheel to the right and shot down the street they'd just passed. The SUV slammed into the back of a lifted pickup truck that had all kinds of winches and stupid zombie apocalypse shit all over it. All hell broke loose behind them, and Marcus called dispatch.

"Rose—we need backup. *Now*. Late model SUV with diplomatic plates pulled in and separated us from SBI. Blackout windows. Tag reads whiskey-hotel-zero-zero-one-kilo. We need an armed guard at the door."

"Roger that, Stone. Moving into place now." Urgency crackled through the airwaves. It wasn't every day that the sleepy little town of Apex, which was the reigning Small Town of America, had a gunfight in broad daylight.

Rick hit the siren and lights and gunned it. Stealth was no longer necessary, and they needed to get out of the little neighborhood teeming with morning dog walkers and joggers. They raced down the side street, drifting across the next intersection that brought the Apex PD into view. Officers ran down the sidewalk, shouting and clearing pedestrians out of the way. They closed the distance fast—fifty yards to go when the SUV barreled down the hidden street on the left, with no front bumper and a busted-out windshield.

"Gun!" Rick screamed, wrenching the wheel to the right so Abby's door wouldn't get T-boned. The vehicle clipped the back bumper and sent them spinning like the teacup ride at the state fair. Abby screamed, and Ben threw himself on top of her, covering her smaller body completely.

Marcus leaned through the seats and shot through the back glass, shattering it into a thousand pieces and rendering them all deaf. The passenger in the SUV returned fire, peppering the side of the squad car with dozens of bullets; the driver used a handgun and fired rapidly, hitting Rick in the left shoulder. He grunted and struggled to keep the car lined up with the entrance to the station's gated parking lot and deck.

Ben popped up long enough to line up a shot and fired, hitting the shooter and taking out that automatic gunfire. Abby screamed again, but then stopped abruptly, like she realized she'd been making noise and didn't want to distract anybody. Marcus screamed, "Reload!" and reached back for Ben's shotgun.

The SUV rammed the squad car again, but Rick was able to turn into the lot and race behind the rolling gate before it could nudge in behind them. Ben fired four shots in quick succession into the other vehicle, and bought the officer manning the gate enough time to hit the close button.

"Fuck!" Ben swore as a bullet ripped into the back of his left shoulder.

He'd come up too high when helping Marcus reload, but by the time he drew another breath, the gates closed behind them and he could hear sirens and shouting outside. Bobby finally showed up and drove straight into the side of the SUV, pushing it forward and pinning it against an ancient oak tree in front of the police station. The other officers surrounded the SUV and dealt with its inhabitants.

As soon as Rick put the cruiser in park, his door was wrenched open. Somebody leaned in and cut him out of his seatbelt, then pulled him out and onto the ground. EMTs and firemen descended on the scene from the emergency services offices a block over. Marcus jumped out and yelled, "Detective Owens is in back with our witness—he's been shot and needs medical ASAP."

Ben heard Chief Randolph yelling for another EMT before he opened the left passenger door. Abby stopped shaking all together and was silent. White hot agony blazed a trail down his arm when he lifted up to check on her, and he roared. His shoulder was pretty fucked up. The chief leaned in and lifted a bit, helping him sit upright. The gunshot throbbed like a sonofabitch but sitting up made it easier to breathe. He let out a roar of fury, pissed that the senator's sweep team had gotten the drop on them. Goddamnit.

JC Fowler, the fire chief for Station Two, cut through Abby's seat belt and slid her out onto the ground. Ben watched them work on her, nearly vomiting at the sight of her face and neck covered in blood. When that first hail of gunfire hit, her window had shattered—and cut her. Badly. He fought against Randolph's hold, desperate to get to her. Shock or pain, or God, trauma, had made her pass out. It was too much for him to bear.

As soon as she was flat on the ground, she sucked in a startled, painful-sounding breath and let out a pitiful scream. Her eyes darted around in confusion, taking in the fact she was lying on the ground in broad daylight rather than hunched in the backseat of the car with Ben smothering her. An EMT stretched over her head and pressed a stethoscope to her chest. He watched the rise and fall of her chest while someone else pressed gauze to the side of her neck.

"Where's Ben?" she whispered.

Randolph raised his hands, and Ben shot off like a bolt. He dropped on his knees beside her head and took her hand. Emotion clogged his throat and muddled his brain. Christ, they'd only met a week ago, but their insane experience had forged an unbreakable bond.

He leaned in to kiss her. "I'm here, baby."

The EMT working on her, Johnny Wilkins, had

gone to school with Ben's younger brother. He'd always been a good guy and was good at reading the situation because he didn't try to stop him. "How is she?" Ben asked. "Where was she shot?"

Johnny checked her pupil dilation and squeezed her wrist to take her pulse. "No bullet wound, Benji. Looks like she whacked her head good on the glass. All these little cuts are most likely from the shattered window. I know it looks like a lot of blood, but head wounds bleed like a sonofabitch. Besides, I think most of this blood is yours." Johnny patted Abby on the hand and smiled at her. "We're going to transport you to emergency so you can get these cuts cleaned out."

She nodded and looked back at Ben. Her bottom lip trembled, and once again, he was struck by how much of an effort she made to keep it together. Abby was quiet while Johnny switched out his gloves and poked around the bullet wound on Ben's deltoid. He cut away the material from the point of impact and *tsked.*

"You, Detective, are gonna need a couple of stitches. Looks like a through-and-through, but it's got to be cleaned and sealed up. You can ride together."

Under any other circumstance, Ben would delay the stitches in lieu of sitting in on Steve's interrogation. Plus, he wanted to make sure all immediate threats were dampened. He glanced around the courtyard, at the row of men in tactical gear sitting on the curb, cuffed and glaring bullets his way. A dozen uniformed officers formed a perimeter around the station and were having conversations with people on the street. He figured Abby wouldn't get herself checked out, or want to be separated from him, if he didn't go.

"I'll ride over with her, but we gotta get back fast."

It would take the department a couple hours to clear the scene, and then the SBI would come in to investigate the shooting since both agencies were involved. He figured the Feds would be there by lunchtime, and somebody would want to talk to him regarding everything he and Randolph had uncovered about Quincy Sykes. It couldn't stay quiet for long.

Johnny looked relieved that he was going with the flow, which made him realize he was being an ass. "Sorry, man," he muttered. "I need to talk to Chief Randolph before we leave, though. Okay?"

"Yeah but make it quick. The faster we can get out of here, the faster you can get back." He tilted his head toward the sidewalks flanking the station, where people sat on the curb with scratched hands and knees they'd gotten while scrambling out of the way. "We'll load Miss Markham in while you talk, and make sure y'all get priority service."

Ben leaned down and kissed Abby, then walked slower than he liked over to Randolph, who was deep in conversation with Bobby and Marcus. He stopped in front of the chief and realized they were on a video call with Teddy Barnes.

"Sir," he said loud enough to get his attention.

"Hey, kid, how ya doing?" Randolph asked. He pulled his glasses from his front pocket and put them on to look at Ben's arm. He poked and squeezed it, grunting when a trail of bright red blood trickled out. "Looks like a clean shot, and you're moving your arm. That's good."

"Hurts like a motherfucker, but I'll live. I'm riding to the ER with Abby but we're coming straight back here when we're done. I don't want to miss anything."

"Good," the chief said and nodded. He gave a sharp whistle and pointed to three officers standing close by, trying to manage the melee of gawkers. They scrambled over, faces flushed and jacked up on adrenaline. "Accompany Detective Owens to Peak Med. Demand a private room for him and Miss Markham, and don't let anybody in but the doctor. They're to be seen right away, got that? And as soon as they're done, you get them back here as fast as possible. I'm looking for less than an hour turnaround. Got it?"

"Yes, sir," they said, practically in unison.

To Ben he said, "You already know we've got Steven in custody. I was waiting for you to be here this morning to question him, but with all this bullshit, we're going to have to wait until later. I can hold it off for a bit, but more than likely we'll have to hand him over to the SBI or the Feds this afternoon."

"Don't let them take Steve before I get back," Ben said. He lifted his chin and said defiantly, "I won't be quiet about Jason's coverup, sir."

He stood tall while Randolph gave him a critical once-over, no doubt seeing the rage seething just below the surface. Lawson had been a good officer and a friendly face when he'd returned last year. But Sykes had always been a privileged asshole. A chip off the ol' block, for the most part. And he'd killed his best friend and partner, setting off a chain reaction that led to an attempt on Abby, and this wild shit today. Turned out corruption came in many forms. The bullet hole in his shoulder was testament to Sykes' duplicity.

"Be nice to the doctors," Randolph said. "They'll treat you quicker that way."

"I will. And sir? Make sure you call Mike Dixon

out of the DC field office. He can talk you through the files I sent overnight. You're going to need it in order to get a warrant."

Randolph pulled out his phone and dialed, watching Ben walk away.

Chapter Thirty-One

Abby at his side, Ben stormed into the station, barreling through the wide foyer with menace in mind. Ten stitches, a numb shoulder, and two delightful hours spent in a busy emergency room did not improve his mood. He *hated* getting shot, and he hated that the woman he'd fallen for had been placed in the line of fire.

More than anything, he hated dirty cops. He wasn't in LA and this wasn't some dumb-shit, redneck, good ol' boys club, for fuck's sake. Apex was a happy city. Crime rates were low; hell, they hadn't even had to deal with gang infiltration from the surrounding bigger cities. It was a peaceful, idyllic, sleepy little town. One dirty cop gave the whole house a stink of corruption. But two? That was a pattern. And thereby obliterated any good will a police department might hold in a community.

His angry strides ran as fast as anger pumped through his veins. When Abby stumbled, he stopped and forced himself to take deep breaths and regain control. The left side of her face was peppered with small pieces of gauze covering liberal applications of antibacterial ointment. Three tiny stitches closed a cut on the underside of her jaw, courtesy of a plastic surgeon who happened to be on ER rotation. The doc assured them both there would be no scarring.

Didn't matter; he was still pissed. "I'm so sorry."

"Stop," she ordered. Again. "We are alive and we are safe."

She patted him on the chest, over his racing heart. He discovered lately that it beat for her. He offered his arm and slowed his pace toward the chief's office. The bullpen buzzed with conversation and officers going about their day, only today they were dealing with the attack on the station on top of their regular case load of little things, like stolen bikes and speeding tickets.

As she and Ben reached Randolph's door, activity and conversation stopped for a beat, then resumed with little fanfare. Teddy Barnes greeted them. He shook Ben's hand and gave Abby's shoulder a gentle squeeze. "Sorry we couldn't prevent this."

She replied with more grace than Ben was feeling. "Perhaps if your officers had done their jobs to begin with, you would've had a better chance of preventing this." She pointed out the floor-to-ceiling windows to the pile of trashed vehicles in the front yard. "I would like to commend the team who stayed at my house last night, though. They did a great job."

Teddy had the decency to look ashamed and very likely was. Chief Randolph remained silent. Abby however did not. "At first, when we realized it was Senator Sykes poking around, I thought he was just being a nosy old man. I would've gladly given him a tour of the house or let him bring out a metal detector."

Color ran high in her cheeks, and she rubbed the tips of her fingers together in a gesture typical for her when she was anxious. She pinned Randolph with a guileless stare. "Throughout all of it, it never entered my mind that I might be in danger."

"Ms. Markham, if I—" Randolph started.

One hand shot up. "No, sir. I'm not finished. You have a problem in your department. You failed to supervise your officers in an adequate manner, and as a result, today's debacle occurred."

Emotions spent, she seemed to deflate, then leaned into Ben's side. He wrapped an arm around her shoulder and held her close. He glared at Chief Randolph and fought the urge to punch him in the throat.

The chief had been complacent and willing to fall back on the hype of Apex being the best town in America. He'd been lazy with his officers who were liked in the community and friendly colleagues. Ben didn't want to admit that the same complacency rolled over to him—he'd been so desperate to get back to his peaceful little town that he stopped paying attention.

That ended now.

Abby said, "Ben, I know you want to question Steve Sykes, but I'm done. I'm tired. I just want to go home."

Chief Randolph cleared his throat. "Ms. Markham, I want to thank you for your service to the community. Thanks to you, Officer Lawson wasn't alone when he died. He was able to talk to his wife, who was, in turn, able to talk to him. I know it's hard to see any blessings in the situation, but your presence was a gift."

Beneath his hand, he felt Abby's breath hitch as she turned fully into his arms. Her whole body vibrated as she cried, clearly oblivious to the effect her sorrow had on the rest of the room. One of the things he found so attractive was her quiet strength; she wouldn't want anyone to see her lose control. He wanted to take Steve out back and beat his ass. He wanted to turn in his badge and sidearm and drive off into the sunset. Let someone else clean up this clusterfuck. Instead he rubbed her back until she stopped trembling, knowing her exhaustion made her more emotional than usual.

"I'm sorry I'm being so sappy," she mumbled. "I think it's the pain meds."

Randolph nodded. "Nothing about what's happened over the last week is part of your normal routine. Hell, nothing over the past few months, for that matter. We're heading to the interrogation room. Cindy McGee will stay with you in Ben's office while we talk with Steve Sykes."

McGee stepped forward. "Come with me, Abby. You already know Ben's couch is comfortable. Maybe you'll get a little rest while you wait."

Ben hung back while the guys went into interrogation. "I'll let you know what happens. If you need anything, just ask McGee. I don't want you to leave my office without her, okay?"

She nodded and let him kiss the breath right out of her, until McGee cleared her throat. "They're going to start without you, asshole," she said, earning a glare before he hustled out.

By the time Ben got to interrogation, Teddy had already read Steve his rights and Chief Randolph sat in the anteroom in the role of observer.

He slammed into the room, not caring if the doorknob left a gaping hole in the wall behind. "Why the fuck would your father send a sweep team for Abby Markham? *You're* the one who killed Lawson. She did nothing to him or you. *Why, Goddammit?*"

Steve bowed his head over the table; fat tears

plopped steadily onto the scarred surface. “I told him you were in DC with her. I don’t know anything about a sweep team.”

Blind rage making him reckless, Ben struck so fast Teddy couldn’t react fast enough when his fist connected with Steve’s nose. His head snapped back, and his body slid from the chair and landed on the floor in a boneless heap.

Stone silence reigned for a few seconds. And then chaos.

Officers hustled Ben out fast, swearing and yelling as Chief Randolph hurried in to check on Steve. He hauled the weeping officer back into his seat. Steve let out a sob and laid his head on the table. His hands were cuffed to clamps extending from the underside of the table, so his face smeared through the blood and snot and tears pooling beneath his head.

Once they had Ben under control in the anteroom viewing area, Teddy went back in to speak again with Steve. “Why on earth would you do that, son?”

Steve laughed humorlessly. “All my life I’ve waited for the senator to call me ‘son.’ ” He snorted, lifting his head and then tried to wipe the side of his face on his beefy shoulder. “I thought he’d be happy I covered for him.”

Teddy leaned forward, an expression of interest on his face. “What exactly were you covering for?”

“The peeping. God, he kept coming back. Half a dozen times, I’ll bet. Jason saw him twice, you know. The first time surprised him, and he jumped out of the way so my father didn’t see him. But that second time—he got photos.”

“Why didn’t Lawson call it in the first time?” Chief

Randolph asked from where he leaned against the door. "Why cover it up? Nobody around here likes your dad. Jesus Christ, Steve, both you and Jason are better than that."

"Because he was my friend." His voice was so quiet they had to ask him to repeat himself.

Unable to stand it any longer, Ben burst through the door. "Louder, you bastard. I want to make sure we get this on the recording devices."

"Settle down, Owens," Randolph warned.

Steve never flinched. "Jason was my friend. He asked me to find out what was going on."

"Did you?" Teddy asked.

He shook his head. "Quincy and I didn't talk often; when we did, it was…painful. He hated me. My mom died because he took the time to save me from the flames. When I was a teenager, he often said he should've saved her instead of me."

Ben made a choked sound and looked at the chief. Knowing how this man had been treated all his life hurt his heart as much as it did his head. He found it difficult to maintain his high level of outrage.

"All right, let's get this over with," Chief Randolph said. "One more time, tell us what happened that day. For the record."

Steven Sykes related the same story as when they'd arrested him last night, this time on the record. It was just as shocking, just as sad, as when he'd confessed before, but his sobbing broke Ben's heart. Quincy Sykes was the biggest bastard in the world. And it was clear that Steve had no idea the man who raised him might be an imposter.

Chapter Thirty-Two

"What's left of the sweep team?" Ben asked while Steve Sykes was readied for transport to the SBI lockup by Teddy and his team.

Dejection was evident in the man's body language and demeanor of profound sadness. It was hard to feel too sorry for Steve; at the end of the day—even though they'd established the gunshot was unintentional—he'd covered it up. His best friend, and a good officer, was dead. They'd already been informed the district attorney's office planned to open an investigation into the corruption charges.

The department would likely undergo restructuring and training. Chief Randolph would likely lose his job. Hell, Ben was starting to question his own future with the department. With all that on the horizon, Ben didn't envy Steve when it was time to face the wives and children of both families.

He repeated his question. "Anything on this sweep team of Sykes?"

"One dead, two shot up pretty good," one of the SBI guys said. "They're at the hospital, under guard. A fourth is in lockup and not cooperating at all."

"Any ID on—" Ben paused when someone spoke over him.

"They're ours."

Whipping his head around, he found Jim

Forthmann, dressed in a sharp black suit and flashing a badge. Chief Randolph narrowed his eyes and leaned in to check out the credentials. “Ben—I’m sorry I couldn’t get here in time to stop the sweep team.” Anguish filled his eyes, and as pissed as he was, Ben didn’t blame Jim. None of this was his fault.

“How do you two know each other?” Randolph barked.

Ben clamped his mouth shut, unsure of what Forth intended to share.

“We were Rangers together, sir, but parted ways a decade ago. I ran into Ben when he was in DC this week.”

“That right?” the chief asked.

Ben saw the wheels turning in his boss’ head. “Yes, sir.”

Randolph, face red, bellowed, “Why is the CIA sending a sweep team to *my* town, shooting at *my* officers?”

Jim cut his eyes to the side, cringing at the number of uniformed officers staring openly at the events unfolding. It wasn’t every day that the chief lost his temper, Ben knew. Nor was it likely they often had a CIA agent in the building, either. “How ’bout we step into your office for this conversation?”

Ben couldn’t agree more. “Follow me,” he said, and led the way.

Abby stood when they walked in and broke into a grin. Jim gave her a quick hug. “I thought you were staying off the grid,” she told him.

Forth huffed out an irritated breath. “I thought you were under guard.” He held her chin in his fingers and looked over the patchwork of gauze and stitches.

She patted him on the chest and let him check her out. When Jim dropped his hand, she whispered, "What are you doing here? This place is crawling with cops." Ben shook his head, and smiled, unexpectedly happy. She winked at him.

"I want to help you wrap this up," Jim said. He patted Abby's hand and took a step back. He shook hands with Chief Randolph and spoke directly to him. "Sir, I was recruited by the CIA directly from the Army. Much of what I've done is classified, but I can tell you that I've had postings in Spain, Central and South America, and some Eastern European countries. Four years ago, Senator Quincy Sykes ordered the hit of a dirty general in Moldova. My shot missed and killed the ambassador's wife instead. He's been blackmailing me ever since."

Randolph propped his hip on the edge of the desk and crossed his arms. "Why are you telling me this?"

"Every job I've done with the CIA has been sanctioned. Even the bullshit wet work Sykes tasked me with for his committee was, in some fucked up way, supported. I'm done with him pulling my strings, though. My work is stressful enough without having to worry about him pulling a trump card like sending me on some crazy assignment such as this one." He looked at Ben. "I came clean, all the way up the chain, even talked to the ambassador. I gave a formal statement to Mike Dixon; he's also got the journal."

"What's in this journal?" Randolph asked.

"I started recording Sykes whenever he called, kept copies of payments—which are all in an off-shore account that I've never drawn a dime from. I'm done with field work. I'm too old for this shit."

Ben snorted. They were thirty-five, but he guessed being a spook added years to a man's life. His phone dinged, indicating an incoming text. "Shit." He spun the phone around so the chief and Jim could read it. "Mike's team got a warrant for the senator's arrest, but he and his security detail are nowhere to be found."

"If he's not here already, he's on the way," Jim said and checked his watch. "I have to go. I'm taking the prisoners with me, but you'll have paperwork on your desk by eight o'clock in the morning. I think it'll be everything you need to wrap up your case."

Chief Randolph opened his mouth to say something, but shut it, then shook his head. They might never know what Jim would do with them. Since they were operatives like Jim, Ben surmised their actions had been ordered, too.

Sometimes it was better not to know.

"Is Mike on the way now?" Randolph asked.

"Yes, sir," Ben replied. "They hopped on a plane and should be here in about half an hour."

"All right, then. We need to prepare for all hell to break loose at any second. Meet me in my office in five minutes." The chief jutted his chin toward Jim but looked at Abby. "I have no idea when to expect the senator to arrive, where he's going or what's going to happen, but we don't have time to get you to a safe house. Until we know what's going on, you're going to hole up here in Ben's office. Understood?"

She nodded.

"Good. Ben, five minutes." He walked out, shutting the door behind him.

Ben pulled Abby into a hug. "What's going to happen now?"

Jim sighed. “I’m taking the sweep team. All of them. I’ll turn them over to my team at Langley, and then I’ve got to wrap up an assignment in Nicaragua.”

His eyes looked hollow, and tired. Abby wiggled free of Ben’s grip and walked over to Jim. She wrapped her arms around his waist, laying her head against his chest and giving him a sweet hug. The man looked stunned. It made Ben wonder if Jim ever drew a peaceful breath. “I’m so sorry I hurt you.”

“I know.” Her voice was muffled. “But you made it right. When you’re finished with this assignment, and it’s safe for you, come back. There’s a place here for you.”

With an audible hitch in his breath, Jim closed his eyes and laid his cheek against the top of her head. After a moment, he cleared his throat, then squeezed her and let her go.

“She’s right, Forth. There’s a place for you anytime. Our town is small and normally very quiet. Seems like you need a little less excitement.” Jim snorted and they shook hands. “The offer stands, man. Come back when you’re done.”

Jim was quiet, but he seemed to absorb the rightness of Ben’s sentiment. “Okay.”

Ben figured it would take Forth half an hour or so to collect the dead, injured, and incarcerated, and that there would be no trace of the team by the end of the day. The report the Apex PD received tomorrow would be sanitized and wrap up any questions with a bright, red bow.

Ben filled his cheeks with air and blew it out with a puff. “I have no idea how long this is going to take. Shit, I don’t even know what to expect or try to plan for, but we've got to assume the senator is going to try to save face. He still doesn't seem to know Jim's been helping us, so that may give us a bit of an advantage."

"I just want it to be over," she said.

"I know, honey." He lingered as long as he could before opening his door for Cindy McGee and Rick Stone. After taking up defensive positions, they waved him off.

****

Senator Quincy Sykes loved to make an entrance. At planned events and press conferences, he took the stage three minutes after the scheduled start time so everyone would be in place to watch him walk in. But today he used predictability to his advantage. The Apex Police Department expected him to sweep in with his usual pomp and circumstance, cameras in tow, to protest the unfair treatment of his beloved only son.

Screw that. He hadn't called anyone. And that little prick could rot in prison for all he cared. Steve had been a colossal disappointment—who was still in uniform after twenty years on the force? No effort to rise to detective rank. No attempts to take the sergeant's exam. If he could go back to "The Night," he would've left the baby in the house.

In a moment of weakness, he'd broken down and told Martha about peeping over the fence at the "old homestead," then confessed to being in trouble with the Apex PD because his actions had scared Abby Markham. He'd also told her that Steve had accidentally killed Officer Lawson to keep his poking around a secret. But he had no intention of *ever* confirming his true identity.

"Do you want to try and schedule office hours

while you're in town?" she asked, steno pad in hand to keep notes. "Any press coverage?"

"No, dear," he said a little condescendingly. He was the senator, after all, and sometimes he needed to remind her of that. "I'm going to let Steve know that murder is unforgiveable. Corruption is unforgiveable. He's dug his own grave here."

She looked like she would protest but kept her opinion to herself. Good girl. Not that it mattered, but she and Steve had never enjoyed each other's company. At the end of the day, she was his employee and had nothing to do with family.

Behind the wheel, Ed Parker cut his eyes to the right to meet Quincy's gaze in the rearview mirror. Even after a year the young man was still in awe of his boss. The senator made use of it on a regular basis.

"Perhaps Steven just lost his way," Martha said under her breath, one of the few people privy to his real opinion of Steven. She had the down-low on so many facets of his life that he was going to have to walk a tight rope today.

"Yes, I'm sure that's it. After two decades in the same position, I'm sure he hit his breaking point."

"We're here, sir," Parker said.

"Oh, good. I don't want to make a huge showing of force today. This shouldn't take long—I need to make sure Steven has representation and let him know I'll be out of the country for the next three weeks. Just drop me off at the door."

"No, sir, we can't," said Ed.

"You can. I'm walking into a police station, for goodness' sake. Nobody knows I'm coming; we've alerted no local colleagues or press. I will do this task for my child, by myself."

Mark Grissom nodded from the passenger seat, but Ed struggled with Quincy's wishes for a moment. Martha, who long ago made it clear she really didn't give a shit about family stuff, smiled when he looked at her. She just wanted a paycheck, status, and the occasional lusty fuck.

When he got to the front desk inside the APD, he kept his face tilted toward the floor and made no eye contact with the same officers he usually greeted with enthusiasm. "I'd like to talk to Chief Randolph, please."

Wilma Gaither, busy writing something in a logbook, didn't so much as glance up. "Do you have an appointment, sir?"

When he said *no*, she recognized his voice and looked up. "Oh, Senator. I didn't recognize you." She giggled nervously and checked her hair. He'd had that effect on women all his life, and while he was vain enough to appreciate it most days, today he wanted to get in and out as fast as possible.

"That's fine, Wilma." He kept his voice low and pitched it seductively. No random person walking in off the street would get away with using her first name. She blushed. "I'm sure you can imagine this isn't too much of a social call today. I'd like to speak to the chief, and maybe see my son. I would appreciate if you could call him on the phone rather than broadcasting it on the intercom, if you wouldn't mind." He blinked and put on his most earnest face. Because, after all, privilege counted.

"Of course." She picked up the phone and dialed, smiling through the conversation. She even patted him sympathetically on the hand. "Chief, Senator Sykes is here to see…oh, okay…yes, sir, I'll tell him." She put the handset back on the cradle. "Sir, Chief Randolph will be out to see you in about five minutes. He's going to wrap up a meeting and have Steve brought up to an interrogation room." Her voice trailed off when she said *interrogation.*

"Thank you, dear." Quincy sank into a chair closest to the front desk, but out of the direct view into the station. He shot off a quick text to let his detail know he'd be about fifteen minutes. Martha replied right away to let him know they were parking the car.

At the eight-minute mark, Randolph walked out to greet him, hand extended. Seemed he liked to make an entrance, too. "Senator, what can I do for you?"

Quincy stood, and they shook hands. "Ward, thanks for clearing the deck to meet with me. I've been following the investigation into Officer Lawson's murder—it's not every day an officer in my own neck of the woods is murdered." He let his grin fade and forced sadness into his gaze. "I was…shocked, I think…when Jennifer called last night. I was hoping to see my boy. Make sure he's okay, help get an attorney in place for him."

"You don't seem as angry as I expected you'd be," Randolph admitted as he led Sykes through the door into the back.

Quincy shook his head, trying to achieve humble. "I've seen so much violence in my position. I don't want to believe Steve could do this, but until the investigation is completed, I won't judge him. I stand by my son, for now."

Randolph nodded sagely. "I put him in a room so you two could talk privately."

"I appreciate it. What happened out front? It looks like a war zone."

"Traffic accident. Big one. It tied up the morning commute for hours. Here we are."

There were two interrogation rooms at the new police complex. Both had solid steel doors leading into sound-proof rooms that were rigged for audio and video. The back walls had two-way glass that allowed people to watch the interviews. Randolph led them to Interrogation A and opened the door. Steve sat at the table, with his back to the door and his head leaning forward. When his father stepped into the room, he lifted his head and sat as still as a statue. It made the fine hairs on Quincy's arms stand on end.

"Son." He gasped and laid a hand on Steve's shoulder. He squeezed his fingers and took the seat next to him, trying not to show any other outward reaction. Regardless of how he felt about the younger man, his appearance was distressing. "Are you okay?"

Steve turned his head and glared at his father, hatred burning in his eyes. Quincy reared back, unprepared for such menace coming from the lazy boy. He recovered quickly and took stock, glancing around to make sure nobody had stepped in to witness the reaction. Steve's nose had been broken and reset. He looked shockingly bad, with mottled black and blue bruises beneath both eyes. It looked painful.

He said nothing. Just stared. He might have been ready to write the kid off, but the public would interpret it as America's favorite senator allowing the podunk Apex Police Department to treat *his child* like a common criminal. This was police brutality in action. He didn't give a fuck what happened to Steve, but he did care how it affected his reputation. And he could get behind police reform. His mind swirled with the possibilities of a new platform.

Quincy pushed back from the table, his chair slamming the wall behind him, and roared. “What the hell happened to him?”

Randolph slipped in and closed the door. “There was an accident during booking. These things happen. But you’re all good now, right, Steve?” He cut his eyes to the two-way, and Quincy realized this meeting was being recorded. He needed to ham it up for the cameras.

“Yes, sir.” Steve’s dead eyes cut back to Quincy, which made him squirm. Something was going on.

“Everything’s going to be okay, right?” the chief prompted.

“Yes, sir. Everything’s going to be okay.” Steve’s voice sounded robotic. Whatever Chief Randolph prompted, Steven mimicked. Color rose in the hollows of the boy’s cheeks, making those garish bruises look like Halloween makeup.

Quincy cleared his throat. “Son, I had Joyce Dupree suggest an attorney for you—James Edwards. He should be here any minute.” Steve shook his head *no*, but Quincy ignored him and forged ahead. “I know you and Jennifer don’t have the money for a good attorney, so I’m covering it for you. I don’t want you to worry about a thing. I was all set to be calm today, but seeing you like this? Fuck ’em.”

Chief Randolph raised an eyebrow and held up his hands in a passive gesture. “You’ll get no argument from me, Quincy. That’s your son, and this is what you’re supposed to do.”

He snorted over that ridiculous jab. Randolph had

no idea how much pull he actually had. If he wanted, Quincy could have papers drawn up to put Steve in his custody so the jackass could be spirited away to a country without extradition. *If* he wanted.

For now, he was content to let his son drown in the shitpile he'd created himself. "You're right. If you don't mind, I'd like to talk to my son before his attorney gets here. *Off* the record." He glanced at the mirror, sneering to make it a good show.

"I already have an attorney," Steve said quietly.

"What are you talking about? I haven't seen Edwards." He looked at the chief, who shrugged his shoulders. "Chief, I need you to leave the room so we can talk, please."

"Yeah…no. I'm not leaving just yet, Quincy. We have some questions for you, too, since photographs of you snooping on private property are what caused the events that led to Officer Jason Lawson's murder, and your son's confession."

He whipped his head around to glare at Steve. That wasn't his son. His son wasn't a killer. Hell, it wasn't even his son. If disowning Steve could be done without divulging his own identity, he'd do it in a heartbeat.

"I've been working with a law enforcement liaison." When Steve wiped his nose on his sleeve, Randolph stepped forward to give him a tissue.

Quincy blinked a couple of times. "Come again? You mean, like a public defender? No. That's not gonna happen." The Sykes family didn't do public defenders.

Steve slapped his hand on the desk, rattling his handcuffs against the metal table. The boy had been so maudlin and hunched over, this show of temper was alarming. "You're not listening to me. I *already* confessed, Senator. I'm working with a department liaison. I'm not talking to your mouthpiece."

Rearing back like the little shit had slapped him, Quincy came to his feet to pace in front of the table, waving his arms. "Fine. I came to offer you an olive branch, because you're my son and my son cannot be a cop killer. But you want to talk to a *liaison* and cut your own deal? That makes life a lot easier for me."

The door opened, and Ben walked in, followed by Mike Dixon. They flanked him, stopping him in his tracks. "Sit down, Senator," Ben said.

"Fuck you," Quincy screamed, enraged that the situation was rapidly moving out of his control. He pulled out his phone and unlocked it. Before he could send a text to Ed, Mike grabbed it and held it out of reach.

"That wasn't a request, Quincy," Mike's said in a menacing voice. "Sit. Down."

A bead of sweat dotted his upper lip and along Quincy's hairline. This was not good.

"Give me the phone."

"Sit down and I'll put it on the table between us," Mike said. "You can still see it, but you can't touch it or call for your security detail. Yet."

"I will have your badges for this." Darting a glance at the clock, Quincy saw that he'd been in here more than thirty minutes. Ed and Mark should've come to find him by now. He'd fire them, see if he didn't.

"I don't think so, *Quincy*," Randolph sneered. "Let's see how the next few minutes go before you spout off about badges."

Chief Randolph waited for Ben and Mike to sit

next to Quincy, then took the chair at the head of the table. He patted Steve's hand and smiled.

Ben's voice was calm when he asked, "Why did Jason Lawson have photos of you peeking over the fence at Abby Markham's house?"

Quincy looked around the table. All four men stared at him with matching calm expressions. Though Steve's face was beat to shit, even he had a steady, watchful gaze.

"Oh, for fuck's sake, I've told you several times that I was curious to see *my old house* after she got in touch with my office."

"The morning Officer Lawson died, he passed off a flash drive of photographs which documented you looking over the fence and digging around the perimeter along the lake," Randolph said. "That's not counting the first time Lawson noticed you but didn't record or tell anyone about it."

"It sounds like you have a problem with your process, chief," Quincy said smugly. Steve looked down at his hands. One fat tear rolled to the end of his nose and plopped down on the table. "I didn't know Lawson had photos, and I sure as hell didn't ask Steve to cover it up or kill him. He did that on his own."

Steve jerked like he'd been struck, and more tears fell. Ben gave him a tissue. "Mike and I were curious about the weird coincidence between the time capsule, the photographs…your peeping. Then there was Steve and Jason's ongoing fight, which ultimately ended in an accidental shooting. So, we did a little more investigating while I was in Washington."

Mike laid a folder in the middle of the table. Quincy's heart began to pound. "When you had the outburst in your office," he said calmly, "the one where you *fell*, and your personal attorney Joyce Dupree was there? We were curious about your reaction to the note we received saying Paul Pope wasn't dead."

Mike opened the folder and spread out some papers. One was the letter, written in neat script, clipped to the photo of Pope, in his Army uniform. Another was a photo of Quincy and Pope from just after the war. He flipped to a photo of Quincy, Margaret, and Steve. A photo of Quincy by himself, as a college student. And finally, a photo of Quincy, Margaret, Steve…and Terrence Pearson.

Quincy's breath stuck in his throat, and he forced himself to breathe normally. This was not happening. He tried to grab his phone but Ben jerked it away.

"Since Ben and Mike were so far away," the chief said, "I grabbed my old buddy Teddy Barnes—he's the director of the North Carolina State Bureau of Investigation—and we drove up to Buntner to meet with Terry. I told you guys he was so nice, right?"

Mike said, "You did. It's amazing what the Innocence Project has done with people who've been shut up for decades. Given the opportunity, so many of them could be contributing members of society."

"That's true," Randolph said. "He had so many great stories. He told us he'd been close with Margaret when they were younger. He was also so fond of his young nephew." Steve made a gasping sound, but the chief kept going. "He said that Paul never really liked him. With him being a 'drug-smoking hippie' and Paul being a bona fide Army hero, they mixed like oil and water. But he loved, loved, loved Quincy. And he loved you, too, Steve. By the way, Terry said despite all of this craziness happening right now, he would visit you in prison. He said he would not leave you to rot in the cell alone."

All color drained from Steve's face. It looked like the boy might faint dead away.

"Well, I loved him, too," Quincy said. "But it was his family who put him away. I couldn't deal with him after Maggie's death. I just kind of…forgot about him."

Ben clapped a hand against his knee. "How lucky he didn't forget about you."

Steve cried out with an angry sound that made everything in the room just…stop. He grabbed Quincy's left wrist and jerked him across the table, meeting him nose-to-nose. "You killed my mother. And my father!"

Ben wrestled Steve back from the table and held him in a strong bear hug. It was difficult because Steve fought desperately against the hold, trying to get Quincy again.

"I didn't kill anybody," Quincy screamed. "They died in the fire." Steve stopped struggling for a moment, long enough for Quincy to realize the direness of his situation. He ran his fingers through his hair and said with a shaky voice, "I need to call my attorney. I'm not saying anything else."

Chapter Thirty-Three

Abby was dozing on a lounge chair by the pool when Ben got home. He stood in the sunroom after changing into swim trunks, watching her through the French doors for a moment. In the last two weeks, the stitches had come out of her chin and the plastic surgeon had checked the cuts peppering the left side of her face. Everything had healed nicely, but he would never forget how she looked with blood covering her face, terrified and cowering in the foot of the car.

He walked out and closed the door behind him with a quiet *snick*. The closer he got, the faster his heart beat. The sandwiches he'd picked up were hampering his progress, so he was relieved to set the tray down on the red picnic table under the giant cherry tree. A bright chartreuse green orchid sat in the middle of the table in an elaborate pot filled with river pebbles. Jim had had it delivered yesterday. The pot was a black ceramic design he'd bought from an artist in Oaxaca, and it was stunning. He ran his fingertips along the smooth pottery, warmed by the sun.

"Whatcha got there?" Her voice was drowsy.

"Lunch." He hurried to get to her chair while she was still lying down. He did that most days…hurry to be closer to her. "Sandwiches and beer. They'll wait."

Small beads of sweat pooled in the hollow of her neck and shallow navel, shimmering in the sun like diamonds along the skin not covered by her sexy little bikini. They made his mouth water, and he licked his lips. She held her hand out to shield her eyes from the sun and smiled. "Sounds like we have a few minutes, then." She opened her arms, gesturing for him to join her.

"That's what I was thinking, too." He leaned down and licked her neck, trailing his tongue along her collarbone from one shoulder to the next, capturing those tantalizing beads. She shivered and squirmed on the teak chaise, making him chuckle. Running his hands down her torso, he stopped at the little ties on her bikini bottoms and tugged on the strings. The material parted away from her body, and she moaned. He'd locked the house up when he got home, so he wasn't worried about any unwanted guests.

Shucking his trunks, he wrapped his big hands around her slim thighs and parted them, taking a moment to look his fill at the juicy center of her. His girl was always ready for him, just like he was always ready for her. It was too enticing to ignore, so he leaned in and swiped his tongue through her delicious, creamy folds, swirling it around her clit and sucking it into his mouth. Abby's hands dropped to shoulders and squeezed. "Ben," she said on a sigh.

The damn stitches in his left shoulder still hampered his movements, so he held out his hand and switched positions with her. She grinned, knowing the reduced range of motion and strength were irritating him. In short order she climbed on his lap and took him on the best kind of joy ride.

"Jim called today," he said a while later. Abby laid along the full length of him; her head was tucked under his chin and a layer of sweat glued them together. It was hot as hell out there in the direct sun, but between the humid air and Abby's lax body, it was like laying beneath a giant heating pad. It did wonders for his shoulder. And his heart.

"How's he doing?" She used his chest to scratch her nose. Then her stomach growled against his. If they stayed like that, he was going to have crazy tan lines on the front, and they were going to need a sunscreen reapplication. Instead, he ran his palm down the long, graceful line of her back and down to her left ass cheek. He squeezed and played with it for a moment, running his long fingers through her sweet, juicy bits. Her breath hitched, and he was a goner.

He slapped her soundly on the ass. "Let's eat, woman."

She yelped and jumped up, rubbing her bottom and laughing. Her smile shined as brightly as the sun as she walked over to the picnic table, naked as the day she was born, with a bright red palm print on her tight left cheek. *My cheek.* He rubbed his chest, near the point of impact but farther to the right, over his heart. He'd been paying attention to that spot more and more lately, and he was staring at the culprit.

Two weeks into his month-long recuperation and his muscles were still complaining when he used them. The bullet may have made a clean through-and-through on his left shoulder, but the recovery was a bitch. Between the physical therapy three times a week, daily swims, and making love to Abby as often as fucking possible, he was determined to get it back in perfect working order. For her.

To his delight, she laid a beach towel along the

picnic bench and sat, nude, to eat her lunch. She was unwrapping the turkey and avocado BLTs when he sat down next to her…also nude. He twisted off the tops from the two bottles of beer and kissed her on the shoulder. Her hair had been pinned in a messy bun on top of her head earlier, but their "nap" had done a number on it. She let him dig into the sandwich and wash it down with half the beer before asking him about Jim. Her eyes darted to the orchid, and she smiled around a mouthful of sandwich. "I'd like to thank him for the plant."

He snorted. The *plant* probably cost five hundred dollars. "I told him you'd love it. He's coming for dinner tonight."

Since she'd just taken a big swig of beer, she wiggled her hips and shoulders. "I'll run to the store to grab some stuff. Want to grill salmon for us?"

"That sounds good." He popped the last bite of sandwich in his mouth and washed it down with the last of his beer. "You know we aren't supposed to know any of his undercover stuff, right? He finished the project he'd been called away for, and a couple days ago relocated back to the states. I asked Mike to connect Jim with his FBI team, and I think he's waiting to see how the shift from one government agency to another will work, particularly since he's always worked covertly."

"Is he staying at a hotel? You know I've got space here."

He pulled her closer, so their hips touched, and he could wrap an arm around her waist. "I know, honey, but he's going to stay out at my grandmother's house for as long as he wants. There's a thousand projects he can work on. It'll be a good place to decompress and get some R and R." And maybe claim as his own, he hoped.

"What time will he be here?"

He looked at his watch. "In about two hours."

"What? Ben!" She scrambled off the bench and hustled to the door. "I hate to leave the lunch mess with you, but do you mind cleaning it up for me?"

"Nope. I'll take care of it."

He'd been with her long enough to know she liked order in her house. It was a one-hundred-eighty-degree flip from her studio and work, where the artist in her reigned supreme and things were always in a degree of controlled chaos. So he cleaned up the lunch stuff, put the pool towels in the laundry, and made up a guest room for Jim. Even though his friend was staying at his grandmother's across town, he figured they would all be visiting late into the night.

****

After a delicious dinner, Abby set out a French press with a strong espresso her father sent her once a month from Paris, along with a platter of brownies and cherry-pistachio biscotti. Her ribs ached from laughing so much. These men were out of control, regaling her with wild stories of their days in the Army. Jim was stricken to learn of how heartbroken Ben had been at the news of his "death," though Ben was as upset to learn that his friend had lived such a dangerous life that prevented him from reaching out. They'd lost ten years of time, but their connection was still there.

Best yet, Jim had been invited to participate in a training regimen, of sorts, that would fast-track him into the FBI. He would likely split his time between the local office in Charlotte and Washington DC with Mike, but that would start in the new year. For now, he had four months to decompress and get his new house renovated. When he'd arrived for dinner earlier, he had a cashier's check for Ben.

"I guess I'm homeless," Ben had said cheekily, and she'd kissed the breath right out of him.

"I guess you're not," Jim replied. She could tell he was pleased with his part in her decision to take a leap of faith with Ben.

The cicadas and tree frogs serenaded them with wild abandon. The bright, full moon cast beautiful light across Abby's back yard. The air smelled of lavender and lilacs, both of which had come from her father's gardens in Provence. He and Bob were especially excited to come over for their month-long holiday this year. They wanted to meet Ben, and if everything went as planned, she and Ben would fly back with them for the New Year. If he hadn't proposed to her by then, she was going to propose to him.

"This afternoon's news reported that Sykes has been indicted for identity fraud," Ben said. "His party has asked him to resign; he's decided not to fight it."

Jim snorted. "That's because the tapes I gave Mike have finally made their way to the Senate Subcommittee on Ethics."

"Will he go to jail?" she asked.

"No," Ben said. "He'll cut a deal that will let him disappear quietly."

"Yeah, really the only formal crime he committed was assuming the identity of Quincy Sykes. The initial FBI inquiry looks to point toward Quincy—or, rather, Paul Pope—telling the truth. Quincy and Margaret really died in the fire. Pope saved the baby, but in the immediate days following the fire, things were crazy. He's paid taxes all these years; he was a good soldier, and in the years since has been a ball-buster in the Senate."

"Will he go back to being Paul Pope?" Abby asked and poured herself an espresso and added a splash of coffee liquor. She offered dessert to Ben, and he took two brownies and a biscotti, which made her smile. Jim took three brownies and ate one in a single bite. Bless their hearts, these boys loved chocolate.

"No. He's lived as Quincy Sykes for the last four decades, but he'll never be able to hold public office again. He'll likely retire and live a quiet, private life where nobody sees or hears from him again."

She slapped the table with the flat of one hand. "I can't believe he's going to get away with it. With driving Steve to do what he did."

Ben covered it with his hand, and he stroked his thumb gently over her fingers. "Life isn't always fair."

"He knows where the bodies are buried," Jim said. He poured an espresso for himself. "But don't you worry, so do I. He'll get what's coming for him."

She cut her eyes to Jim, but he was looking at his espresso cup, following the swirl of the spoon as he stirred in cream. Ben squeezed her hand gently, and she didn't ask for more.

Instead, she cleared her throat. "I also heard on the radio that Steve had given testimony in federal court in Raleigh over the weekend, and because of his willingness to testify he would be able to avoid a big trial. Does that mean he's just going to go straight to prison?"

Ben cleared his throat. "Nothing like this has happened in the Senate in recorded history."

"Does that mean it happened before?" she asked.

"Well, not necessarily," Jim said. " 'Recorded history' means that nobody could find any evidence of it occurring before. Chief Randolph was part of the transport team for Steve to DC, and he testified on behalf of Steve. Steve's a dick, but he wasn't a bad cop. The circumstances of his altercation with Lawson weren't premeditated. They were based entirely on the situation created by the man posing as Senator Quincy Sykes…and his father. The court was lenient on his sentence in that regard."

Jim was quiet for a few minutes while he finished dessert. Abby was pensive, lying back on the chaise and watching the stars twinkle. He set his plate on the table and leaned forward, and said, "I'm going to tell you something that you can never say aloud. You can never ask me or Ben about again. Okay?"

She turned to look at him and nodded.

"Steve and his family are going into witness relocation, and they'll likely be shipped off to the west coast, or Canada somewhere where nobody will recognize them."

"What about his kids—" She stopped short at the looks that both Jim and Ben gave her.

"Well," she said, stretching. It was after two a.m., and she was pooped. "We made up the guest room for you. I make a mean French toast if you'll stay for breakfast."

Jim stood and helped her up. He kissed her knuckles in a very gallant, old-world gesture. He was handsome enough that it made her blush, and Ben rolled his eyes. "I believe this is the first time a beautiful woman has invited me to stay for breakfast that I'm going to say yes."

****

"Quincy—it's time to stop wallowing in the bed you made and get up," Joyce Dupree said loudly, calling upstairs from the kitchen on the first floor.

Checking her watch, she huffed out a breath. Martha Scott, that whore, cut tail and ran as soon as Quincy's security detail fought their way into the Apex police station last month. She just stepped out of the car, chartered her own flight back to DC, cleaned out her office, and left the country. Rumor had it she collected Senator Alice Ruffin's boy toy, Jackson no-last-name, on her way out.

Quincy was never one for prompt appointments, but this was ridiculous. She'd been waiting for him long enough to put on a pot of coffee and toast one of the rosemary-olive oil bagels he favored for herself.

"Quin!" she yelled louder. Nothing.

She stormed up the stairs and flung his bedroom door open. It opened with such force that it banged off the wall but she stepped through quickly. As he was still in bed, she stomped over, whipped the covers down toward his feet and…gasped.

A gruesome expression replaced Quincy's Sykes' erstwhile handsome face. Milky eyes bulged; his mouth gaped wide, like he'd been gasping for breath. A bright purple line ringed his throat; droplets of blood stained the pillow beneath his head. Pinned on his pillow, next to his left ear, was a note: "Paul Pope is dead now."

Joyce screamed, then fainted.

A word about the author…

Becky Moore is a lifelong southerner with a penchant for storytelling and a propensity to try anything at least once. As a result, she can make an adventure out of any situation. She loves to read and write contemporary romance and romantic suspense.

In her down time, Becky loves to spend time with her husband and son. They live in the urban wilds of central North Carolina. She's an avid gardener, hiker, kayaker, bicyclist, swimmer, and community volunteer. She spent over a dozen years working as a writer, graphic artist, photographer, and PR whiz in the advertising, hi-tech, performing arts, and HIV/AIDS fields before venturing into her current status of author, freelance writer, and community college adjunct instructor.

Visit Becky at: www.BeckyMoore.net

Thank you for purchasing
this publication of The Wild Rose Press, Inc.

For questions or more information
contact us at
info@thewildrosepress.com.

The Wild Rose Press, Inc.
www.thewildrosepress.com